River of Heaven

River

_of_

Heaven

a novel

Lee Martin

Shaye Areheart Books
NEW YORK

Copyright © 2008 by Lee Martin

All rights reserved.
Published in the United States by Shaye Areheart Books, an imprint of the Crown Publishing Group, a division of Random House, Inc., New York.
www.crownpublishing.com

Shaye Areheart Books with colophon is a registered trademark of Random House, Inc.

Material from chapter one is adapted from a piece that originally appeared in *Glimmer Train*, Summer, 2006.

Library of Congress Cataloging-in-Publication Data

Martin, Lee, 1955–
River of heaven : a novel / Lee Martin.—1st ed.
p.   cm.
1. Secrets—Fiction.   2. Bachelors—Fiction.   I. Title.

PS3563.A724927R58   2007
813'.54—dc22   2007015007

ISBN 978-0-307-38124-8

Printed in the United States of America

Design by Lynne Amft

10 9 8 7 6 5 4 3 2 1

First Edition

To Mildred and Harry Read,
my dear aunt and uncle

Even brothers should keep careful accounts.

— Chinese Proverb

River of Heaven

I

THIS EVENING TOWARD DUSK MY NEIGHBOR, ARTHUR POPE, strides across the driveways that separate our houses, a casserole dish held between his hands. I see him through the kitchen window as I stand at the sink opening a can of Natural Balance duck and potato for my basset hound, Stump. I reach to switch off the light, but, too late, Arthur has spotted me—I can tell by the way he lifts the casserole dish higher, extends it with his oven-mitt-covered hands—and I have no choice but to wave at him and then go out into my side yard and open the gate.

"Ahoy, neighbor." A former Navy man, this is the way he talks. Unlike me, he's kept fit over the years. He still does calisthenics, even keeps a barbell set in his basement—a manly man with chest and shoulders and arms that aren't what they were thirty years ago, but still they're impressive. A thick head of wavy gray hair. A bounce to his step. "Time for mess." He bows his head over the casserole dish and sniffs. "Andouille jambalaya," he says. "Permission requested to come aboard, sir."

It's October, and the leaves have started to fall. Here in

Mt. Gilead, our small town in southern Illinois, we can burn them on Saturdays, air quality and the ozone layer be damned. We rake our leaves to the sides of our streets or onto our backyard gardens, and set them to burn. The air smells of the must and the smoke the way it has this time of year as long as I can recall since I was a kid in Rat Town—that's what we've always called the neighborhood in the lowlands on the south edge of Mt. Gilead, a mess of tumble-down houses. Each spring there, when the Wabash River rises, the floodwaters still come up to the doorsteps. I'm glad to be safe and dry here in Orchard Farms, this modest gathering of ranch homes on streets with names like Apple Blossom and Cherry Blossom and Peach Tree.

Arthur thinks he knows my life—me, Sam Brady, a bachelor all my sixty-five years—and I wish I could believe that he does. He thinks he knows it because his dear wife, Bess, is now six months gone, and he imagines that we share the misery of men living alone. "You and me," he said once not long after she died. He laid his hand on my shoulder. "Jesus, Sammy. We're a pair."

But my life is not his. I'd tell him this if I had the heart. I'd tell him I have no idea what it is to love someone all that time—nearly forty years he and Bess were married—and to lose them one day without warning. An aneurysm in her brain. "Arthur, my head hurts," she said, and then the next instant, she fell to the kitchen floor, already gone. All my adult life I've lived alone, except for the dogs, the latest being Stump, who stands now at the screen door waiting for his duck and potato.

"He gets contentious," I tell Arthur, nodding toward Stump. Nothing could be further from the truth; like all basset hounds, Stump is long on patience, steadfast with his devotion, mild-tempered, and affectionate—a perfect companion. His nose is up against the storm-door glass. His velvety ears hang in loose folds, their ends curling slightly inward. He stares at me with his sad-ass eyes. "Stump," I say to Arthur. "He puts the hurt in me if he doesn't get his grub."

"Don't we all." Arthur lifts the casserole dish toward my nose. "Sailor, don't we all."

What can I do but let him into my house and tell him to set the casserole dish on the range? He tells me exactly how he made it, and I know what's coming next. "I could give you the recipe." He snaps his fingers. "Or you could come on down to the Senior Center—that's the ticket—and, Sammy, you could learn to do for yourself."

It's not the first time he's asked. He's learned to cook by joining a widowers' group—the Seasoned Chefs—and every Wednesday evening he goes downtown to the Senior Center and works up a new dish. But me? "Sorry, Arthur," I tell him. "No can do."

For a moment, I'm tempted—I'll admit that—but then I think of myself trying to make conversation with all those men, widowers who have a genuine right to their loneliness, and I can't imagine it. You see, I'm a man who chooses to be alone, a man who has a secret. I'm a closet auntie, a fag, a queer—you know all the words. Here in Mt. Gilead, even in this day and age when the world is supposed to be more tolerant, more accepting, it's clear that many folks think this is a wrong thing to be. I see the graffiti spray-painted on the sides of garbage dumpsters along alleys, on the bathroom walls at the city park, on the Salvation Army collection bins in the Wal-Mart parking lot. Those words. I hear them on the lips of schoolboys and cocksure young men swaggering around the Town and Country Lanes, where I sometimes bowl a few lines, even from people like Arthur, older men who still believe that naming something they fear puts it in a place where it can't hurt them. I've heard them all my life, these words. I've let them, for better or worse, make me a cautious man, on guard, well aware that danger always waits just around the corner.

The truth is I don't much know how to be around people. I've spent so many years avoiding them for fear that they'd find out the truth. Trust me, this isn't the sort of place where you can make it known that you're the kind of man I am and then expect to live a comfortable life. I read the letters to the editor in the *Daily Mail*, letters from churchgoing folks—maybe even some of the men at the Seasoned Chefs—who write about the abomination of homosexuality, the perversion, the sin. They think they know so much, but they don't know anything about me, and I'm determined to keep it that way. It's easier—at least it has been for me—to lock the truth away and live quietly with my dogs. It may be a stupid way to live—cowardly, even—but such is the truth of the matter. I've given up companionship for fear of losing it. Better to never have it than to watch it disappear.

The past forty-six years, before I retired, I worked for, and finally owned, a custodial service. When I was a young man, the boss would send me out somewhere—Sherman's Department Store, the IGA Foodliner, Loy's Skating Rink—and I'd spend the night hours, after all the customers and the workers had gone, stripping and waxing floors. Later, when I was the owner, I kept that job for myself. I even took jobs out of town—as far away as Paducah, Kentucky, and Cape Girardeau, Missouri—just for the pleasure of all that time on the road, all that quiet and no one else around.

Stump bumps his nose into the back of my leg. I get down on a knee and scratch his ears. I let him sniff my face, give me a lick. I stare into those sad eyes. "I'm about to get busy," I say to Arthur.

"Busy?" He stands with his hands on his hips. He still has on his oven mitts and he looks . . . well, if you want the truth . . . he looks like a man afraid of his own hands. "Sammy," he says, but I cut him off before he can launch into what I know will be another attempt to persuade me not to be so much of a loner.

"Winter's coming," I tell him. "I've got to build Stump a new house."

"What's wrong with the one he's got?"

"Oh, it won't do," I say, still looking into Stump's eyes. "Nope, not at all. Not for a dog like this."

I START WITH A PICTURE IN MY HEAD: A KIDS' PLAYHOUSE I saw once years ago in a backyard in a town I was passing through on my way to somewhere else. I'd never seen anything like it, that house, made in the shape of a sailing ship: hull and deck and mast and crow's nest, something out of *Peter Pan*. What a sight, this ship. All for the sake of a kid, some lucky kid. I had to pull over to the curb, had to sit there and talk myself out of going into that backyard, walking past the playhouse up to the real house, a house of brick and bay windows. I wanted to put my face up to one of those windows, just for the chance to get a glimpse of the miraculous life I imagined going on inside.

Sometimes I take Stump out for a walk at night, and we slip through the dark, past houses all lit up. I see people's lives going on: mothers rocking babies; an old man in an arched doorway, leaning over to kiss his wife; a woman wiping her hands on a dish towel; a teenage girl dancing to music. Sometimes I'll hear someone laughing, a television playing, a voice calling out, *Sweetie, hurry. You've got to see this. My God, what a hoot.*

I spend weeks drawing up the plans for Stump's ship. I while away several pleasant days at the public library studying how to build the curved hull, the castle tower, the stern wheel, the crow's nest. Then I gather my lumber and tools, and I get to work.

"You've got it all wrong," Arthur says to me one afternoon when he comes to watch me in the side yard with my saws and hammer and nails. I've caught him on certain afternoons peeking out his window, and now he's finally come to tell me exactly what he thinks. I'm nailing together the hull, overlapping the planks the way you would a clapboard house. "That's a clinker hull," he says. "Now, sailor, how in the hell are you going to cut cannon ports in a clinker hull? What you want is a carvel hull, the planks all flush and even. Then you'll be in business."

"Cannon ports?" I stop driving nails. The air, after all that *pop, pop, pop*, clears out, and I watch a lone maple leaf come drifting down, twirling and then floating, until it finally settles on Stump, who's sleeping in the sun. "Why would I want cannon ports?"

Arthur narrows his eyes, sets his jaw, tips back his head. "Sailor," he says, "what if Seaman Stump suffers an enemy attack?" Then he gives me a wink, and it almost breaks my heart because I know he's telling me he's lonely. I know he's asking me to please play along. What he wants more than anything now is to help me build this ship, to have my company to help him pass the hours, and I'm willing to grant him that.

Stump is lolled over on his side, the maple leaf stuck to his white belly, but he doesn't know it. His legs are up in the air, and one of them twitches, the only sign that he might have felt that leaf at all, but he keeps snoozing, belly full, warming in the sun.

"Arthur," I say, and I say this in all earnestness, careful not to hurt his feelings. "I've never known Stump to be the fighting kind."

"Sailor," Arthur says, "do you want to be authentic or not?"

"A carvel hull," I say, imagining the two of us working together.

"Let me grab my carpenter's apron," he says, and apparently, I want to be authentic because I don't stop him, and the next thing I know we're pulling off the planks and starting over.

While we work, he tells me stories of the earliest ship-builders—the Egyptians and the Chinese—the ones who knew that to build a sailing vessel was a matter of faith. They could make it watertight—hull and keel and prow—and then set it to launch with no guarantee that it would ever return to port. The gods that ruled the seas might, at any instant, take a whim to dash a ship against an outcropping of rocks, or spin it topsy-turvy with giant waves, or the winds might get fickle and carry it so far from course it would never be able to right itself. So the builders carved eyes into the ships' bows so they might better find their way. The sailors watched the stars. The North Star poked a hole through the top of the sky. The Milky Way was a river running from heaven.

I like to think of the old shipbuilders and their faith. I imagine them fitting the timbers together, raising up the castles and masts. Day after day of this work, their methods tried and true, mastery learned over time.

Now, here we are, Arthur and I, each afraid to admit that we've reached the age where our circumstances—this widower, this secret auntie—sweep us, scared to death, into our last years.

Soon the conversation turns to Bess, as it often does. Arthur stands across from me, marking lengths of plank for the deck. "I always thought Bess was looking out for me." He lays a two-by-four between two sawhorses, measures with his tape, and then draws a mark with his thick, flat carpenter's pencil. "She was my friend. My first mate, I always called her. Sammy, do you remember that?"

I'm at my table saw cutting the planks that he's marked, and just before I bring the blade down, I say, "I do, Arthur. I surely do. You were her Popeye; she was your Olive Oyl."

The saw whines, its blade slicing through wood. Sawdust sifts down to coat the toe of my boot. The scent of freshly cut pine sharpens the air. When I raise the saw blade, and its shrill noise falls back, I see that Arthur has laid down his pencil, and he's bowed his head. His carpenter's apron, its strings tied too loosely, sags from his hips. His hands grip the two-by-four, and it looks as if he can barely hold himself up.

"Arthur?" I say.

He snaps up his head, and what I see in his eyes surprises me. I know that somehow I've hurt him.

"How can you say something like that?" he asks, his voice smaller than I've ever heard it. "Make a joke like that? Popeye and Olive Oyl . . . a cartoon, for Pete's sake. Jesus, Sammy. I'm talking about Bess and me. I'm talking about people who meant something to each other. Forty years together. But, of course, you wouldn't know anything about that, would you?"

All along, I've been wanting to tell him this: when it comes to love and what we've lost, he and I are not the same; he's owned an abundance I'll never know. Now that the moment is here, though, what I feel inside isn't the relief I'd prefer. Instead, I'm miserable because Arthur knows without a doubt that I'm a man who's afraid to get too close to anyone. The greatest gesture of love I can manage is to build this ship, this fancy house for my dog. I can't even tell Arthur I'm sorry, and finally he picks up the two-by-four he's marked and hands it to me. Without a word, we go back to work, and for just that instant I get a sense of what it must have been like for him and Bess—all the times they must have hurt each other, all the compromises they made for the sake of love.

"She took care of me," Arthur says after a while. "Bess."

His voice is so quiet I can choose not to hear it if I prefer. But I do hear it. I hear the way it quivers. I take it inside me, knowing that later, in the night, when Stump has fallen asleep by my chair, and the house is still, I'll remember the way Arthur said her name.

I'll recall, as I do now, how night after night, all summer, I used to hear her laugh coming from their house. "Arthur, you kill me," she said one night as Stump and I passed by, and she said it in a way that told me that whatever Arthur had done, it delighted her. She was sitting in a chair by the living room's picture window. She tossed back her head, threw up her hands as she laughed. I stood in the dark and watched her, this petite woman who tap-danced in the community talent show, who still wore Arthur's high school class ring on a gold chain around her neck, who could look at me—yes, even me—with a smile that made me believe she'd been waiting years for me to come along, and I thought, *My God, she's an angel.*

So we finish Stump's house, Arthur and I. We measure and saw and cut the angles just so while Stump dozes on the grass. How good it is to work in the autumn sun, to feel its warmth on my face, across my back, to coax this ship along, plank by plank, no thought of the time passing, the light shortening as we move toward winter.

We work, for the most part, without talking, falling into a comfortable rhythm of measuring and sawing and nailing. We put a pet door into the hull so Stump can enter, and we design a gang-way so he can waddle up to the top deck—the *promenade*, Arthur insists I call it—with as much dignity as a basset hound can man-age. We cut a hatch into the deck and equip it with another pet door so Stump can move back and forth from the hull to the deck. He can be topside, or he can go below. I catch on to the sailor's lingo. Pretty soon, I'm talking about fore and aft, bow and stern, port and starboard. "Steady as she goes," I say to Arthur as we raise the mast tower, and he says to me, "That's it. Now you're get-ting your legs."

I let him cut the cannon ports in the hull and rig them with hinged shutters that we can prop open or close. Stump, when he's below deck, sticks his face out a cannon port and sniffs the air. "Ahoy," I say to him, and he barks.

Then, one day toward evening, we're finished. For a moment, we stand in the last of daylight, admiring our work, and, pleased that I am, already I miss the way the hours have so pleasantly unfolded with Arthur.

"I've got a surprise," he says. "It's over at the house. I'll be right back."

While he's gone, Stump sniffs around the perimeter of the ship, and I imagine he's trying to make up his mind about such a thing.

Then, Arthur's back, and he has a flag. "The lady who teaches the Seasoned Chefs stitched it for me," he says. He unfolds it, and I see that it's a Jolly Roger of sorts, only instead of a skull, there's Stump's face, and below it the crossbones are Milk Bone dog biscuits.

"Not too authentic," I can't resist saying to Arthur.

"Well," he says, "who's to notice except us old sea dogs?"

He gets up on deck with a stepladder and hangs the flag from the mast tower. Then he comes back to where I'm standing, and we put our hands on our hips and tip back our heads to study that flag furling and popping in the wind.

Stump lifts a leg and pees on the stern.

"Looks like he's christened it," Arthur says with a laugh. "Now all it needs is a name."

I don't even give it a thought. "How about we call her *The Bess*?"

For a long time, Arthur doesn't say a word. He just keeps looking up at that flag. His eyes close for an instant. Then he opens them and says, "If that's what you want."

"It is," I tell him.

This may not seem like much, this story I'm telling, but you have to understand what it is to be me—a man who has always been afraid of himself. You have to know the rest of my story, the part I can't yet bring myself to say. A story of a boy I knew a long time ago and a brother I loved and then lost. I'm sorry, but for now I'm afraid all I can give you is this picture of me moving through the twilight as I fetch a can of red paint from my basement. I hand a brush to Arthur and he takes it, his eyes meeting mine, both of us unashamed of how sentimental this all is. He kneels down along the prow of this ship—the house of Stump—and with great care he paints the first stroke, the bristles of the brush folding back with a slow, steady grace that stirs me on this evening near to winter. I know this is as close as I've come in some time to living by heart, and what shakes me is the understanding that this is as close as I may ever come—this moment already beginning to fade—here on dry land.

2

IT ISN'T LONG BEFORE THE LOCAL NEWSPAPER, THE *DAILY Mail*, gets wind of Stump's ship, and one morning a reporter calls, a young man—at least he sounds young to me on the phone—who says he'd like to do a story about this ship I've built for my dog.

Stump paws at my foot as if to say that should I see fit to hand him the telephone, he'd be glad to tell this reporter how much his new ship suits him. "It sounds awesome, Mr. Brady," the reporter says. "Just the sort of human interest story our readers would enjoy."

"Oh, it's not that interesting," I say, but I can't deny I'm flattered.

"I was hoping I could stop by this afternoon. Snap some photos. Ask you a few questions. We'd like to run something in our *It's Us* section."

"In the newspaper?" I ask, although I know the section he's talking about; every Friday it offers profiles of people with unusual hobbies and whatnot.

"Like I said, Mr. Brady, it's an interesting story. Right up our alley. Shall we say one o'clock?"

I've always taken an interest in those features, looked forward, even, to the Friday paper and what I might find out about someone: the man who built a pioneer village on his farm just outside town, built with his own hands a jail, a saloon, a one-room schoolhouse, a library, and blacksmith, pottery, and candle shops; the woman who runs a foster home for injured or orphaned albino squirrels, our claim to fame in this town we bill as The Home of the White Squirrels (a twenty-five-dollar fine if you run over one with your car, and there's an ordinance the City Council keeps trying to pass that would require all cats—notorious squirrel killers—to wear collars with bells so the squirrels would always have fair warning that they were in danger); the blind man who forty years ago gold-plated a Coca-Cola glass but never could convince the company to patent the idea, so there it was, one of a kind and he couldn't even see it. I went to the auction they held at his house after he died and bought a box of odds and ends—old tins of shoe polish, a hair brush, a collapsible drinking cup—and wouldn't you know it, there it was buried down deep in the box, that gold-plated Coca-Cola glass, tossed there like it was a piece of junk. I keep it in my basement, afraid to leave it out in plain view in case someone might take a notion to make off with it.

"Those photos," I say. "Would you take one of my dog?"

"The two of you together. And that ship. We've got to see that ship."

The notion of a photo of me and Stump and his ship tickles me. I might even clip it from the paper and carry it in my wallet so when we meet someone while we're out on our evening walks, I can take it out and say to this someone, "Look, it's us."

Or maybe I'm just pretending. Maybe I'd never be able to do that at all.

"Better make it two-thirty," I say. "Stump always likes a nap right after his lunch."

INDEED THE REPORTER TURNS OUT TO BE YOUNG, A TALL, lanky boy with arms too long for the sleeves of his corduroy sport coat. His hair is cut short in what we used to call a burr; his scalp shines beneath the bristle and I try to imagine what it would feel like to rub my hand over his head.

"Mr. Brady?" He uses the eraser of his pencil to push his eyeglasses, which have too much play in them, up on the bridge of his nose. "I'm from the paper, sir. We spoke on the phone."

What happened, I wonder, to proper introductions? *Hello, my name is . . .*

"I'm Sam Brady," I say, and I stick out my hand.

The boy tries to meet my offer with his own hand, so we can shake, the way gents do when they first meet, but he fumbles his pencil and it drops to the floor of my porch. We both bend over, reaching for the pencil, and our heads touch—not with a bang, but with a gentle brush of skin on skin, my own skull shiny and bald—and I'm delighted to know that his bristly hair isn't bristly at all, but has the feel of velvet.

"It's two-thirty," he says, as if that will do as an introduction, this reminder of our agreed-upon meeting time.

"And you are?" I say.

I see him grimace. A tightening of the lips, for just a moment, an involuntary frown he hasn't intended for public display. Then he says, "Duncan."

"Duncan how much?" I say the way that men my age do in this part of the country.

Again, the boy momentarily grits his teeth. Then he says it, as much as I can see he hates to. "Hines," he says. "My name is Duncan Hines. There. Now we've got that out in the open. Just like the cake mix. That's me. Go ahead. Take all the time you need to laugh."

It's another bright day, one of the last before we make the final turn to winter. From where I stand on the porch, I can see the prow of Stump's ship, and it excites me to think that folks are about to take notice. The old Duncan Hines slogan comes to me, and I can't stop myself; I blurt it out. "So rich. So moist. So very Duncan Hines." Then I'm embarrassed because what kind of thing is that for a grown man to say to this boy I don't know from Adam?

If he takes offense or thinks it odd, he doesn't show it. "Let's just say, my parents had a sense of humor. Now about this ship you've built for your dog."

I tell him to follow me. We come down the porch steps, and I open the gate into the side yard. Stump is there, and he yaps a couple of times before I tell him to keep the sass to himself. "This young fella's about to make you famous," I tell him, and Duncan Hines gets down on his knees, not giving a snap about his nice khaki-colored slacks and what the grass and the dirt might do to them.

"Well, lookey, here," he says, giving Stump a scratch behind his ears. "You're some dog."

"Sometimes I think he knows it," I say.

"Why, sure he does. You betcha. What I wouldn't give for a dog like you." Duncan Hines gets up from his knees, and he lifts his arm toward Stump's ship. "That's something," he says. "Boy, it sure is."

"That's a carvel hull," I say, trying not to toss the term around too smugly, like I'm a know-it-all.

"A carvel hull," Duncan Hines says, and he writes it down on his notepad.

Then I'm telling him all about how I built the ship, built the hull and the promenade and the mast and the crow's nest. "See those cannon ports?" I say. I glance over and see him write down the words, *cannon ports.* "Won't those come in handy," I say, "if Seaman Stump ever comes under enemy attack?"

"You don't mean to say, there's actually a cannon in the hold of that ship."

For a moment, I consider letting him believe it's true, but I confess that I'm only joking. He rubs his hand over his velvety head and I see a blush come into his face. I imagine I can tell him anything and he'll believe me. That's the sort he is. The perfect sort for the human-interest profiles he writes. A curious, eager boy—he's only nineteen, I find out, a student at the community college who writes the *It's Us* stories for the *Daily Mail*—ready for the world to amaze him.

I tell him I'm thinking of installing a heating system in the hold of the ship so Stump can spend winter days and nights there if he takes a mind to. Duncan Hines writes it all down, what I plan to do, the story of how I got the idea—that kid's playhouse—the way I puzzled out how to build it.

"You did this all by yourself?"

I want to say, yes, yes indeed, I did. But just then Arthur comes out of his house and waves his arm in greeting. "Ahoy," he says, and starts toward us.

"My neighbor," I say. "Arthur. He helped me."

For a good while, I don't have to say a word because Arthur is only too glad to tell Duncan Hines all about the time he spent in the Navy and what he knows about nautical history and how he was glad to contribute his expertise to the building of Stump's ship. I get the feeling that I could disappear, sink right into the ground, and neither Arthur nor Duncan would notice.

Then I realize that Duncan has asked me a question, one that I didn't fully register and I have to say, "I'm sorry. I didn't catch that. Come again?"

"I asked you if you've always lived in Mt. Gilead."

"Sammy grew up in Rat Town," Arthur says. "Didn't you, Sammy?"

"Yes," I say. "That's right. Rat Town, but I've lived here in Orchard Farms a long time. Arthur and I have been neighbors a good number of years."

"My family came from Rat Town," Duncan Hines says. "My mom's side anyway."

"Who were your people?" I ask.

"My grandmother was a Finn. She married a man they called Grinny, but his real name was Norvel. Norvel Hines."

All the while I'm posing with Arthur and Stump for the photo Duncan takes, I'm stunned. I didn't even know there were any Finns left hereabouts. I can't imagine what I look like, standing here on one side of the ship's prow, Arthur on the other side, and Stump on deck at the point between us.

"Perfect," Duncan says, but I don't feel that way at all, recalling the story of Dewey Finn, a boy who lived next door to me in Rat Town, a boy I've done my best to leave behind me for good. I stand here now, the thought of him more than I can bear, wondering exactly what Duncan knows.

3

DEWEY FINN DIED ON A FRIDAY EVENING IN APRIL. THIS WAS in 1955, and now this boy, Duncan, has brought back the feeling of what it was like to get the news.

By the time the word reached Rat Town, the rain that had been falling three days straight had let up, but we knew there was more on the way. The river was rising, and we feared that overnight the floodwaters would spill over the streets and spread across the yards. I was with my father, helping him build a sandbag levee around our house, when the sheriff, Hersey Dawes, pulled his patrol car to the side of our street, opened the door, and came up onto the sidewalk.

My father stuck his shovel into the sand pile and leaned on the handle, one foot resting on the blade. "Someone in trouble?" he called to Hersey, and Hersey came into our yard and told us what he would soon have to tell Snuff and Betty Finn. Dewey was dead. This boy with wild red hair and freckles across his nose. This skinny boy with green eyes and long lashes and a smile that always put me at ease. Dewey Finn.

Hersey was a sturdy man, broad-shouldered and big-chested, and for years it had been his job to deal with the sort of business that would bring most men to their knees. I could see, though, that this was something that shook even him, and he was relieved to have this excuse for putting off for just a while what he would eventually have to carry to the Finns.

"Jesus, Bill," he said to my father, and then he bit his lip and shook his head. He closed his eyes for a second, and I knew he was trying to forget wherever it was he'd just come from and what he'd seen. "Right now, I'd let you have this job for a song."

My father was a good-natured man with black hair that he combed straight back and held in place with Lucky Tiger tonic. He worked in the mill room at the Kex tire plant, and he carried a buck knife in a leather scabbard clipped to his belt. At work, he used that knife to cut slabs of rubber as they came off the mill drum, but on this night he was using it to slice lengths of twine that I tied around the gunny sacks we were filling with sand.

"I wouldn't want it, Hersey," my father said. "Not for a million dollars. I can't even imagine doing what you're going to have to do."

Hersey took a breath and drew back his shoulders, and I understood he was practicing on us before he went on to the Finns.

Just after six, he said, the B & O National Limited passenger train took the curve north of town, and there at the trestle—too late for the engineer to apply the brakes—lay Dewey on the tracks as if he'd stretched out for a nap.

"You wouldn't want to see what a train can do to a body," Hersey said. "I can tell you that."

"No, I don't imagine," my father said, and then we all stood there, not saying a word.

Finally, Hersey looked toward the Finns' house—that square

house with the asphalt-shingle siding and a little peaked roof over the front step. Dusk was coming on, and someone had switched on a light inside. I saw one of Dewey's sisters—Nancy, I thought it was—pass by an open window. A radio was playing. That snappy tune, "Hey, Mr. Banjo," by the Sunnysiders. It was date night, and soon the boys would be coming for the Finn girls.

"I've said too much." Hersey shook his head. "I shouldn't be talking like this. Not in front of Sammy." He turned to me, then. "Do you know any reason why Dewey would go and do something like this? Put himself in the way of that train?"

I told him I didn't.

Then Hersey asked me whether I'd been with Dewey after school. Everyone knew we were friends, he said. Had I been with Dewey? Had I talked to him? Had I picked up on anything that might explain why he'd feel so miserable that he'd put himself across those tracks and wait for that train?

"No, sir," I said. I held a burlap sack open while my father tipped a shovel of sand into it. The sack sagged with the sand's weight, and I felt the strain in my forearms. "I never saw Dewey today," I said. "Just at school. That's all."

The truth was I'd seen him just after supper head off for the B & O railroad tracks that ran behind Rat Town. It was where the two of us often went in the evenings just to get off by ourselves, to be away from our houses where there was always too much going on: Dewey's sisters fighting over who got to play the radio, my mother yapping at my father for drinking too many Falstaffs and never taking her uptown to bingo at the fire hall and later a piece of pie at the Verlene Café.

Some evenings, Dewey and I sat on the railroad trestle and talked about everything we wanted once we got old enough and rich enough to have it. Dewey wanted a Chevy Bel Air with a chopped top, frenched headlights, and lake pipes. Then, he said, he'd get the hell out of Rat Town. Never look back. "I swear, Sammy. Just go. That's what I'll do. Just go wherever I take a mind to."

I wanted to be a singer. It makes me laugh to remember that now, but then I thought it would be swell to be a singer in a white dinner jacket and a bowtie, my hair, like my father's, shiny with Lucky Tiger. Dewey and I sang together those nights on the trestle, even though neither of us had a voice. We sang songs we'd heard on *Your Hit Parade:* "Sincerely," "Moments to Remember," "The Shifting, Whispering Sands." We were miserable at it, but we didn't care. Who could hear? It was just the two of us, legs swinging back and forth as they dangled over the trestle. Across the fields, we could see the houses we'd eventually have to go back to, but for the time being we felt far away from them, and we lifted up our voices and sang.

"This is the place I feel the best," he told me once. "Right here with you."

I got this funny feeling in my stomach, then—funny in a good way, the way it was when I was riding in Cal's '49 Ford Coupe, and he took a hill too fast and we came down the other side with a dip that made me say, *Oh, doctor*—and I told Dewey, "Me, too."

The evening he died, my father and I watched Hersey Dawes go into the Finns' house, and we listened as the radio went dead. Such an eerie quiet, and I knew Hersey was filling it with his news. Soon he came out of the house and drove away in his car.

My father and I finished building the sandbag levee. Then he took me next door to the Finns, to pay our respects.

The oldest sister, Marge, let us in. Mrs. Finn was sitting on the couch between the other two girls, Jo Ann and Nancy. They were all huddled up, sort of slumped into a heap, and they were crying.

I could smell the perfumes on the sisters. I could smell the sprays they'd been using on their hairdos when word about Dewey had come. By this time, the boys who'd come to escort the Finn girls to the Arcadia Theater had been turned back with the news. I knew they were uptown at the Verlene or sitting in their cars around the lake at the state park, smoking Lucky Strikes or Chesterfields or Pall Malls and telling the story of what had happened.

Snuff Finn was in the doorway leading into the kitchen. He was leaning against the jamb, his arms crossed over his chest. I'd always been a little bit afraid of him because the rumor was he sometimes beat men who didn't pay their gambling debts. To make a little extra money, he worked for the mobs that ran the juke joints along the river, the bootleg gangs that had reported to Al Capone during Prohibition and now had illegal gambling operations in all the dance halls and supper clubs.

"I don't know a word to say." My father's voice, though he kept it low, seemed too loud a noise for the quiet house. "I guess there's not words made for this. You need any help around here, you let me know. River's up. I've got sand and gunny sacks and twine."

Snuff nodded. Then he looked up, and his eyes found me. "How come you and Dewey weren't together?" His voice was hoarse as if he hadn't had water in a long time, or maybe he'd shouted himself dumb. "You two were always like that." He raised a hand and crossed his fingers. "Something went on between you, I reckon. Else wise, you'd been with him. You were always with him. Something went on, only I don't know what."

"I was helping my dad," I said.

"That's right, Snuff. The boy was helping me with the sand."

"Nah," Snuff said, "it's not as simple as that. You weren't with him for a while now. Something went on between the two of you, but Dewey, he wouldn't say what it was, only that the two of you were on the outs."

"Sammy?" my father said.

I didn't know what to say on that night in the Finns' house where sorrow had come any more than I know how to say it now.

"We just got to knowing we were different," I said. "I guess that explains it as best I can."

My father and I left the Finns' house and went back to our own. My mother was on our front porch, watering the tomato seedlings she'd just set out to harden before planting them in our garden. The lights were on in our front room. Big drops of rain were coming down, drops the size of half-dollars. They slapped the broad leaves of our maple tree, punched the sandbags my father and I had stacked, clanged against the watering can my mother set down on our steps.

"More rain." My mother shook her head. She'd taken care to keep the tender tomato seedlings back on the porch, away from any downpours that would drown them. "Can we stand it? Will we be all right?"

I looked out over our yard. "We've got more sand," my father said, "more gunny sacks. Don't worry. I'll take care of things."

He walked to the edge of the porch, looped his arm around a post, and leaned out into the rain, turning his head in the direction of the Finns' house, where Nancy had come out into the yard and was sitting on the muddy ground—just sitting there in the rain—her arms crossed over her stomach while she rocked back and forth. The other girls came out into the yard and took her up by her arms and led her back into the house.

"What was it like over there?" my mother asked.

"Just what you'd think." My father ducked back under the porch roof and wiped the rain from his face with his red bandana handkerchief. He blew his nose, and then folded the bandana up and stuffed it back into his hip pocket. "You can imagine, can't you? To lose a boy like that? Jesus, what a thing."

"I'm baking a cake," my mother said, and I could smell it, that smell of sweetness coming from inside our house. "I'll take it over to Betty Finn tomorrow. That's all I can think to do."

She came to me, then, and she wrapped her arms around me. She was a flesh-starved woman, just an itty-bit of a thing, but she squeezed me so hard I felt an ache in my chest and back. "Sammy," she said, and she went into the house to see to her cake.

I remember that the dark fell all of a sudden, the way it can when you're thinking the twilight will last a little longer. I looked up at the sky and saw a skein of clouds pass over the moon.

The rain came in earnest. My father and I stood on the porch and watched it slant down.

"Different," he said in a low voice. "The two of you were different. What did you mean when you told Snuff Finn that?"

"Just what I said."

The wind was up now. Rain scattered across the front part of the porch, and my father and I moved out of its way, retreating toward the house.

"So you knew it was true about Dewey?" my father asked. "All the talk about him being queer? You knew it to be a fact?"

"It was true," I said.

"And you didn't want no truck with it?"

"No, sir."

"So you stopped being friends."

"He was . . ." My voice shrank inside the noise of the wind and the rain, and I couldn't find the words that wanted to come next.

"You couldn't say what he was to Snuff." My father went on. "That's nothing a man would want to hear about his boy."

"I couldn't tell the truth."

"That's right," my father said, as if we were coming to an agreement never to speak of this again. "Some things you just can't say."

4

ON WEDNESDAY EVENING, ARTHUR AGAIN ASKS ME TO COME
with him to the Senior Center for his Seasoned Chefs cooking lesson. I'm so grateful for the help he gave me with Stump's ship, I
don't see how I can refuse him. I take a deep breath. Then I tell
him I'll be glad to accept his invitation.

He claps his hands together. "Sammy, you won't regret it. I
promise."

At the Senior Center, the Seasoned Chefs wear cooks' aprons,
the kind that tie around the neck and at the small of the back, only
these aprons aren't white. They're egg-yolk orange with black script
letters that say, REAL MEN DO IT IN THE KITCHEN.

These real men are milling around, helping one another tie
their aprons, chatting about the new coffee house uptown where
you can buy espressos and cappuccinos and herbal teas, even
cucumber-infused water if that's your pleasure. "Cucumber water,"
a man says, and shakes his head, amazed.

It's easy to pretend that our town is a different place than it
was years and years ago, more progressive and enlightened. We
have that coffee house, and the Arcadia Theater, where I used to

watch Rock Hudson pictures from the balcony, now has three
screens. In those days, everyone knew that Rock had family
here—his real name was Roy Scherer—and from time to time
he'd come to visit. His aunt and uncle had a farm not far from
town, and, when he was a teenager, he spent his summers there.
Once—this was much later when he was a star—I saw him drinking a root beer float at Tresslers' lunch counter. Imagine that.
Anyway, as I was saying, the Arcadia has those three screens, and
at Christmas there's a spectacular light display at the city park,
and cooking classes like this one for men who suddenly find themselves on their own. When you get down to it, though, nothing
much has changed about the way people feel about men like me.
It could very well be that some of the men in this room would shy
away from me if they knew the truth, but still I can't help but
envy the Seasoned Chefs and the easy way they move among one
another, knotting aprons, patting backs. Ask anyone who lives
alone. Ask them what it's like to go days, months, sometimes years
and have no one to touch them, not even a finger grazing a wrist,
a hand brushing across a shoulder. A hug? Some people would
pay money for that. Trust me, there are these people in the world,
more than you probably want to know.

The teacher, a woman with rouged cheeks and bright red lip-
stick, is setting out mixing bowls and saucepans and measuring
cups, laying out whisks and ladles and spatulas and stirring
spoons. She's maybe a few years younger than the youngest of the
Seasoned Chefs, a trim woman with blonde hair—dyed, if I'm any
judge—wearing dark slacks and a white turtleneck sweater. A
woman who seems vaguely familiar to me.

"That's Vera." Arthur slips an apron over my head and helps
me tie it. "She's got that household hints program on the radio.
Very Vera. You ever catch it? If you need to know anything—how

to get barbecue sauce out of a good shirt, how to make refrigerator pickles—you can just call her up and ask."

"Have you ever done those things?" I ask him.

"Not yet. But I could if I ever wanted to." He leans close to me and whispers. "Sometimes, I phone up her show and ask her a question just to hear her talk—you know, right to me."

Vera claps her hands together and tells us it's time to learn her special recipe for chili con carne. She does a little flamenco stomp, the stylish heels of her black boots clicking smartly on the floor. She snaps her fingers over her head, and the Seasoned Chefs—"Ready, boys?" she asks—gather around her.

I work with Arthur. "Stick with me, Sammy," he says, "and everything will be shipshape."

We listen to Vera as she shows us how to brown the ground beef. "Stir it over a low flame," she says. "Don't let it stick to the pan."

"That's a snap," Arthur tells me, and we get to work.

It's easy, this cooking. I stir the beef while Arthur opens a can of tomato juice. We're getting everything ready: beef and juice and kidney beans. We gather the seasonings: cayenne pepper, chili powder, salt, and then Vera's secret ingredient—just a squeeze of lime juice. "Oh, that's zesty," I hear a man say, and the other Seasoned Chefs agree. *Yes, that's zesty. A little squeeze. That's very Vera.*

I don't mind saying that I'm caught up in it all: the satisfying aroma of beef sizzling and browning, the men's high spirits, Vera's heels tapping over the tile floor and her bright voice cheering us on: "Follow the recipe so you won't make a mess-of-me."

Once, she even stops and pats my back. "That's lovely," she says. "That's wonderful. Arthur, you've brought us a ringer."

For some reason, I get a picture of Stump in the side yard, carrying around that rubber horseshoe he likes to gnaw on. He's probably dropped it on the step, the way he often does when I'm out of the house. I find it there when I come home, and old Stump, sitting beside it, waiting for me to open the door and let him in.

I wish I could trust this feeling I have, this thing rising up in me I can only call joy. I want Vera's hand to linger on my back because at this moment, when she's telling me that what I'm doing is lovely, she's touching me in a way I haven't felt for years, her hand rubbing slow, gentle circles.

"This is my neighbor," Arthur says. "Sam Brady."

"Sammy?" Vera takes me by the shoulders and turns me so we're face to face. "My goodness," she says. "You must not remember me. I'm Vera Moon. I was a friend of your brother's."

It comes to me, then, exactly who she is, and I nod and say hello. "Of course," I say. "Vera."

She and Cal weren't just friends. They were sweethearts. In fact, he'd told me that out of all the girls he had a fancy for she might just be the one who could keep him. "I really mean it, Sammy," he said. "She doesn't know it yet, but I believe she's got me on a string." Then he went away, and, as far as I know, that was the end of things between him and Vera. He came back to visit from time to time, but he never stayed long enough for anything between them to stick, and he never took her with him, and now all these years have passed and here she is on the end of a life she lived without him, without even knowing, maybe, how close she came to having a completely different one.

"Whatever happened to Cal?" she asks me.

I'm too ashamed to tell her I don't know, and I'm thankful that one of the Seasoned Chefs calls her name, and she excuses herself, and I don't have to tell her that seeing her makes me wonder what all our lives would have been like if Cal hadn't gone away from us. He went to Germany, the Korean conflict winding down by then. He worked in a dental clinic on the Army base in Frankfurt, and when he came back to the States, he learned a carpenter's trade and moved around the country—North Carolina, Kansas, California—before finally settling in Alaska, where he made good money helping build the oil pipeline. He came back to visit only on occasion, and then as the years went on he didn't come back at all, and now it's been more years than I can count, so many years it seems most of the time like I never had a brother at all. We don't speak on the phone. We don't exchange letters. Truth be told, I don't even know for certain that he's still alive. The last thing he said to me—I remember this very distinctly— was, "I guess we all have to live the lives we've made, but I don't think I can live mine here, not now."

I'm glad I don't have to tell Vera that it was in some measure my fault that Cal left town. I've spent all these years mourning that fact, wishing he'd walk through my front door sometime and say, "Hello, Sammy. It's me."

At the end of the evening I thank her, as I do the other Seasoned Chefs before I leave—*Thank you for letting me join you. Thank you for your conversation*—and Arthur when he drops me off at home—*Thank you for inviting me.*

"Sammy," he says. "Forget about it. We're neighbors."

He insists I take our leftover chili con carne, freshly sealed in one of Bess's Tupperware bowls he knew to bring.

This politeness, I think, as I step through my gate. Yes, the rubber horseshoe is on the step, and yes, Stump is waiting. This courtesy, I tell myself as I unlock the door and hold it open so Stump can waddle into the house. This is as much as I can hope for; this is what I have.

•   •   •

ON FRIDAY, WHEN THE PAPER COMES, I CAN BARELY BRING myself to look, but, of course, eventually I do. That's the way we are, isn't it? Too curious for our own good.

Here I am on the front page. In the photo, Arthur's chest is puffed out, and there's a grin on his face, as if he's got everything right where he wants it. Stump seems equally at home, sitting there at the bow, his muzzle tilted to the sky, the dignified captain of his ship.

And then there's me—little, old, bald-headed man, his face tipped down, eyes just up enough so you can see them but not enough, like Arthur, to stare you full in the mug. Here I am, looking just about as scared as a man can be. Now what kind of face is that to show to your neighbors? Right now, in homes across our town, folks must be calling out to someone, *Hey, c'mere and take a look at this. Saddest damn thing.*

That's the sad-assed truth of me. Old bachelor man, so much time on his hands he can build a fancy house—*a ship, for mercy's sake* (oh, I can hear the neighbors talking now), all for his dog. *Says here he's got plans to put in a heating system. Geez-a-loo. I thought I'd heard it all.*

I fold the paper so the picture doesn't show, and I stuff it down in my trash can. Then the phone rings, and it's Arthur calling up to ask me whether I've seen the paper, and, of course, I have to say that I have.

"A heating system?" he says.

"Just an idea. Something I'm noodling around with."

I can hear newspaper rustling over the telephone, and I know he's looking at the article as he talks to me.

"Jesus," he says.

Then there's a long silence.

"What?" I ask him.

"Nothing," he says, and I know he's taken note of the way I look in that photo, an odd man who can barely stand to look at the camera.

I'm afraid I'm disappointing him. I'm not the confident sort—not a sailor full of swagger—that he'd wish for a friend. Still, ever since we built Stump's ship, we've fallen into the habit of keeping each other company at night, usually at my place since he's always looking for any reason he can find to escape his own house where he spent so many years with Bess. "I see her everywhere," he told me once. "Just for a second, and then she's gone."

So I've let him into my home. We've played dominoes. I've brewed coffee. We've watched old movies on television, pictures we remember from when we were younger men: *Tie a Yellow Ribbon*, or Arthur's favorite, *In Harm's Way*. Some evenings, we doze off in our chairs, and we sleep until Stump licks my hand and wakes me. For a few minutes, then, I watch Arthur sleep, and it pleases me that I can offer this place of ease and rest. Then Stump barks, or a cannon explodes in the picture on TV, and Arthur comes to and says, "I was sleeping good, Sammy. I was lost to the world." He gathers up his coat and hat. "Another night," he says. Then he goes back to his own house where he's left the light burning above the steps to his side door—a watch light, he calls it—so he'll be able to see his way in.

A man can make a life like this—dominoes and coffee, and old movies and a nap, and now a photograph in the paper for everyone to see.

THEY START TO COME. PEOPLE I DON'T EVEN KNOW. ALL through November and into December, they come. They drive slowly past my house, stop on occasion and sit in their cars, pointing at Stump's ship. If he happens to be on board, someone might come to the fence and baby-talk him. Somebody else might start in with the sailing lingo.

"Aye, Captain," I hear a boy say this evening.

The sun is setting, dipping down below the power lines and maple trees, their bare branches dark against what's left of the light. I remember what the old-timers used to say when the sun set red: *Red sky at night, sailor's delight.* I'm in the garage checking the antifreeze in my Jeep Cherokee and through the six small glass panes that stretch across the top of the garage door, I can see the sun break apart as it sinks below the trees. Orange streaks the sky, which is a darker shade of blue now, a blue close to purple this near to dark.

The boy is maybe ten or so, a boy I've seen in the neighborhood, but no one I know to call by name. He wears a sock hat— not a tight-fitting watch cap like sailors wear, but a loose one with a tail that hangs down his neck, a white yarn ball at the end resting between his shoulders. He snaps off a salute to Stump, who is unimpressed. Stump slowly tips back his head to watch a white squirrel skittering along a power line, his glorious tail curving out behind him. Another dog would set up a howl and tear across the yard to tell that squirrel to vacate the premises immediately. But not Stump. He calmly watches the world go by. Even this boy, yakking at him from the fence, is nothing he can't tolerate.

"A pirate walks into a bar." The boy is telling Stump a joke now, not caring whether someone might come by and hear him. I imagine this is a joke the boy has taken a fancy to and now he simply wants to hear the sound of it coming from his mouth. "A pirate walks into a bar," he says, "with a steering wheel down his pants."

Okay, I'm hooked—charmed, you might say, by the ridiculous

premise. I'm eavesdropping, and I don't feel guilty because after all this is my dog the boy has decided to entertain.

He acts it all out, thrusting his narrow pelvis forward as if he's got that steering wheel right where the pirate does. "Bartender says, 'Buddy, you've got a steering wheel down your pants.'" The boy scrunches up his face into what he must feel a wizened old pirate with a steering wheel in his cargo bay would look like. "'Arrgh,' the pirate says, 'and it's driving me nuts.'"

I can't help myself. I laugh. I laugh over the silly joke and the boy's joyful telling. I laugh with more gusto than I have in years, and the boy hears me. He looks toward the garage where he must see my face pressed close to the glass, and all I can think to do is to wave. He waves back. Then he turns and runs down the street, the tail of his sock hat trailing behind him.

THIS MORNING, I LOOK OUT MY KITCHEN WINDOW AND SEE a girl—a teenager I'd guess—on the deck of Stump's ship. It's Saturday, a week until Christmas Eve, and I'm listening to *Very Vera* on the radio. She's telling her listeners how to wrap Christmas packages like a pro.

"You want clean, crisp lines when you fold and tape the edges of the wrapping paper," she says. "So the trick is to use double-sided tape—you can pick some up at Wal-Mart in the crafts section. This tape is sticky on both sides so you can give gifts that look like they were wrapped at the stores. Clean lines with no ugly pieces of tape showing. Even you men can pull this one off, and it's sure to impress that special someone."

Stump, never one to appreciate the fine points of gift wrapping, dozes on the braided rug, his chin on his paws.

I turn off the radio and go to the back door to get a better look at the girl. She's resting her back against the mast as she smokes a cigarette. Her shins are bare. That's the first thought I have—not, *Who is she?* not, *Please get off my dog's house I built like a ship with my own hands*—but instead, *Her pants are too short.* The day is cold, too cold for her to have her legs uncovered above her high-top black sneakers.

I open the back door, but not the storm door, and I feel the cold on the glass. Stump wakes up and waddles over to nose around my leg, sniffing the winter air that carries with it this morning the damp smell of a gray sky. Clouds are banking in the west, knuckling up like fists. By afternoon, I figure, we'll have snow. So there's that smell of wet laundry in the air, and the tang of wood smoke from Arthur's Franklin stove, and the tobacco, burning sharp and sweet, as the girl puffs on her cigarette. All of these scents delivered, so Stump believes, for his inspection and delight.

He bumps his nose against the storm door, and the girl must hear that because she turns her head toward my house. She tosses her cigarette butt out into my yard, and she puts a hand on the deck of Stump's ship as if she's ready to press against it and push herself to her feet.

But she doesn't get up. She's just there, ready. I can feel my own calf muscles tense, the way hers must, and I don't mind saying it's a pleasant feeling, this quiver of flesh, this pulse that tells me here's something I hadn't planned on, this girl on Stump's ship, looking as if she's just as surprised to see me as I am to see her.

Who is she anyway, and why should I be moving now, stepping out into the cold without as much as a sweater, to say, *Hello, hello, my name is Sam.*

Stump goes on ahead of me, barking once at this girl he didn't intend to find on the deck of his ship. He enters below deck and sets out to investigate.

The girl is on her knees now, her hands laid flat on the tops of her thighs.

"It's all right," I tell her. "I'm just coming out to say hello."

Stump noses his way through the hatch and comes up on deck. He sniffs the soles of the girl's black sneakers. He moves along her leg and sniffs her knee. He presses his nose into her sweater sleeve.

"That tickles." She giggles and tries to squirm away from Stump. "You old hound dog." She takes his muzzle in her hands and backs him out of her sweater sleeve. She scratches around his ears, tips back his head, and pulls her face down close to his, inviting the inevitable. Stump licks her cheek. "Kissey-kiss," she says. "You handsome boy, you. You old heartbreaker. Good boy. What a good boy."

"That's Stump," I tell her. "Looks plain to me that he likes you."

"At least someone does," she says.

The wind is up now—that west wind pushing those knuckled snow clouds closer. The flag atop Stump's mast snaps and pops. The sharp air cuts through the thin gabardine of my trousers, and, again, I think of the girl's bare shins. She doesn't even have a coat on—I realize that now—just that cable-knit sweater.

"Do you mind me asking what it is that causes you to be out here?" I rest my hand on the ship's stern and lean toward the girl. "To come into my yard on a day like this—feel that snap in the air?— snow coming, and you with your legs bare and not even a coat."

"It's him," she says.

"Him?"

Next door, Arthur steps out into his yard. He holds a black electrical cord in his fist, a cord that's been cut. The plug dangles from one end, and the other end, the one that should be connecting to something, is stripped back, frayed copper wiring showing.

"Madeline." He shakes his fist, and the cord ends snake and jounce. "Damn it all to hell," he says.

"Him," says the girl. "My gramps, or should I say, the Pope." She points her thumb back over her shoulder, and, when she lowers her arm, a butcher knife slips from her sweater sleeve, landing with its blade point stuck into the deck, just a whisker from Stump's paw. "Sorry," she says. Then she yanks the knife from the deck. "Sorry," she says again. Then she climbs down from Stump's ship and lets herself out of my yard, forgetting to close the gate behind her.

"The gate," I say, but it's too late. She's tromping over the frozen ground to where Arthur waits. She storms past him into the house. She slams the door behind her. Arthur gives me a shrug of his shoulders as if to say, what's a guy to do.

"That's my son's kid," he says. "Maddie. She's going to be on board awhile."

He goes into his house, and I go to my gate and close it, trying my best not to pay attention to the voices I hear rising behind Arthur's walls.

"You can't prove I did that," Maddie says.

IT WAS THE RADIO, ARTHUR TELLS ME, THAT OLD PHILCO Transitone he keeps on his breakfast table. He restored it himself: AM/FM, eight-tube receiver. "Maddie didn't care for *Very Vera*," he says after lunch when he asks me to accompany him to buy Maddie a Christmas gift. "You can help me, Sammy," he says. "An old dog like me? I don't know what kids want."

"You think I know anything different?"

"You're my first mate now. Maybe together we can figure something out."

His first mate. That's what he used to call Bess. The thought that I've become that important to him warms me, and when he asks me if I'd like to ride out to Wal-Mart with him, I say I will.

So, it was the radio; that's how the argument started. Arthur tells me this as we drive down Route 130. The snow is coming down now, big wet flakes starting to stick to the grass at the city park where the Christmas light display has been up and running since Thanksgiving. It's one of those pretty snows, the kind I generally like to watch from inside my house as it weighs down the branches of evergreen trees and piles up on roofs and sidewalks. But today I'm out in it with Arthur because he asked me, and as he tells me the story of Maddie, I keep my eye on the snow and the folks moving through it outside the Dairy Queen and Dave's Party Pack Liquor Store and the strip mall where the Wal-Mart used to be before it became a Supercenter and had to have a bigger building a mile north. I'm listening to Arthur, but at the same time I'm thinking about the snow and how the first one of the year always makes me feel like a boy again with a day off from school.

Then Arthur says, "I was just listening to Vera on the radio after I had my breakfast. She was giving some hints on gift-wrapping—hey, don't let me forget to pick up some double-sided tape—when all of a sudden Maddie says, 'I don't like this woman. I don't ever want to hear her again.' Later I find the radio cord pulled out from the wall and hacked up with a knife. Now what would make Maddie go and do that way? Can you tell me that?"

Of course, I can't tell him. I don't know anything about his granddaughter, only that she was nice to Stump and he seemed to take to her, and, although it surprised me to find her in my side yard, it wasn't at all an unsettling surprise; it was, if anything, a little wrinkle I didn't mind. A little zest, Vera would say. A little shazam to give the blah-blah-blah a kick.

The truth is I don't know anything about teenage girls, and all I can say to Arthur is, "I'm sorry. No. I couldn't begin to guess. I didn't even know you had a granddaughter."

He slows for the stoplight on 130 where the road turns into the Wal-Mart parking lot. "She's had some upset in her life of late. Sure, there's that, but is that any call to hack up my radio cord? I'm trying to help her out. I know Bess would have wanted us to do that."

"Upset?"

"Her mother." The light turns from red to green, and Arthur turns his Chrysler into the parking lot. "Well, she's another story."

Maddie's mother, Arthur's daughter-in-law, lives up I-57 in Champaign-Urbana. "If you can call it living," he says. The leather of his bomber jacket squeaks a little against the Chrysler's seat as he turns down an aisle of the parking lot. "She's messed up with that junk, that methamphetamine. She can't make a home for Maddie. Hell, she can barely remind herself to eat and sleep, and my boy Nelson . . . well, the truth is we don't know where he is. He took off for Mexico a few years back and we haven't heard from him since. There's no one on the mother's side, not the grandparents or any aunts or uncles, who want anything to do with Maddie. So, it's up to me, savvy? I'm the only one she can count on."

He finds a parking spot at the end of the aisle, and we get out of the car and hunch our shoulders against the cold and the wind.

"Ready, sailor?" he says.

"Aye," I say, and we start the walk to the store.

A Santa Claus is ringing a bell at the Salvation Army kettle by the front door, and I stop long enough to fish my coin purse out of my pocket and drop three quarters into the kettle.

"How come you carry that old thing?" Arthur asks me.

It's one of those oval purses made from vinyl and slit down the middle, so all you have to do when you want change is squeeze it in your palm. My father brought it home from the tire plant where they were giving them away as a promotion. It's black with white lettering that used to say KEX TIRE REPAIRS, but years of use have worn away some of the letters so now it says, EX PAIRS.

"Sentimental, I guess." I close my hand around the purse and shove it back in my pocket. "I got it when I was a kid."

Once we're in the store, we get to work trying to figure out exactly what a butcher-knife-wielding, radio-cord-hacking, Very-Vera-hating, sixteen-year-old girl might want. We reject the gifts even has-beens like us know someone like Maddie would hate: the baby 14-karat-gold pink cubic zirconia earrings ("too girlie," Arthur says), the Winnie-the-Pooh houseshoes ("too 'I've forgotten how old you are,'" I suggest), the black silk bra and panty set ("too old for how old you are," says Arthur).

"Maybe a gift card," I say. "Then Maddie could get what she wants."

"A gift card's no good." I know the voice belongs to Vera an instant before I feel her hand on my back, and smell her perfume—that scent that makes me see vases of peonies and crisp linen curtains lifting from windows on breezy spring days. Then she's there, between Arthur and me, her jingle-bell earrings chiming as she shakes her head. "A gift card says, 'I didn't care enough to pick out something special for you.' Please excuse me for overhearing. Now, boys, who's the lucky girl you're shopping for today?"

"My granddaughter," Arthur says.

"Age?"

"Sixteen."

Vera snaps her fingers. "Gents," she says. "Follow me."

We leave electronics for girls' fashions. Vera stops at a rack full of skirts and blouses. The sign above the rack has a picture of two girls, blonde and tan, each of them wearing the same clothes Vera is pointing out to us now. MARY KATE AND ASHLEY SPORTS WEAR, the sign says. REAL FASHIONS FOR REAL GIRLS.

I've seen this Mary Kate and Ashley on television. They were on a sitcom when they were just itty-bitty girls, but now they're all grown up.

"For Maddie?" Arthur says. "Gee, Vera. I don't know."

Vera whisks a hanger off the rack and holds up a skirt that to me looks no bigger than a dish towel. "Here's a cute skirt." With the other hand she takes another hanger from the rack. "Oh, and look at this halter top. Now what teenage girl wouldn't like this outfit?"

"It's sort of skimpy, isn't it?" Arthur says.

"Oh, come on," says Vera. "Get with it, sailor."

Arthur takes the clothes from her. He holds the hangers away from him as he gives the skirt and top a once-over. "Sammy?" he says to me.

"Vera's the expert," I say.

"Trust me, Arthur." She lays her hand against his cheek. "Real fashions."

"For real girls," he says.

She pats his cheek. "Now you've got it."

WHEN ARTHUR AND I GET BACK FROM WAL-MART, WE PARK on the street because once the snow stops he'll want to clear his driveway. We're at the tail end of the storm, just a few specks slanting down, and here in the late afternoon, the light is blue with the coming dusk. By five o'clock, the last of the sun will slip below the horizon, and there we'll be, in the dark. Arthur will get out his snowblower, and he'll do his driveway and the sidewalk, and then he'll come over, as he always does, and do mine. I've insisted it's unnecessary, this favor. I have a snow shovel. I may be sixty-five, but I'm in good health. I'm capable. "Sammy," he's told me. "It takes so little."

We linger in his car, neither of us, it seems, anxious to step out into the cold. Lights are on in his house, and we can see Maddie at the picture window. She parts the sheers with the back of her hand—a motion so elegant I can almost believe that the skirt and top Vera talked Arthur into buying will be exactly what Maddie wants. She looks so ladylike, half-hidden behind the sheers, and I wonder if, like me, Arthur is thinking about Bess and how many times she may have stood in exactly this way, made exactly this sweep of her hand to part the sheers so she could look for his car coming down the street. Maddie waits at the window—I'm not sure whether she's spotted us—and I think she must feel alone in Arthur's house. All the rooms blaze with light. Here she is, far from her own home, which, as he's explained, hasn't been much of a home at all, and now she seems anxious for another voice in the house, even if that voice belongs to her grandfather whose radio cord she cut with a butcher knife.

She must see us, then, and she must be embarrassed to be found watching because she lets the sheers fall closed and she moves away from the window.

"It's not easy," Arthur says. "This time with Maddie."

Then he tells me about the night her mother locked her out of her house.

"It was snowing," he says, "and the kid was barefoot. Barefoot, Sammy. Jesus." He curls his fingers around the steering wheel, and I can feel the rage in his grip. "Her mother, Treasure—honest to God, Sammy, I'm not making this up. Treasure—I guess you'd say she never grew to fit her name—she throws Maddie out because she won't go to Wal-Mart and buy Sudafed. That cold medicine. That's what they use to make that junk, that crystal meth. I tell you, Sammy, when they're messed up with that junk, they don't care about anything else. Her own kid, barefoot and the snow coming down and her mother not giving a rat's ass that she's out like that. Maddie had to spend the night in the shed just to get out of the cold. She tied rags around her feet. Jesus, it breaks my heart."

As it does mine. "It's good she's with you now," I say to Arthur.

He relaxes his grip on the steering wheel. "Here's hoping I can convince her that's true," he says. Then he opens his door, and the cold comes in around my legs, and I can't move, seized as I am with the image of Maddie barefoot in the snow.

"You'll freeze in there," Arthur says, lingering, his hand on the open door.

"I'm thinking about that story you just told me." I shake my head. "Maddie and her mother."

"You can't reason what makes people do the things they do. I figure we're all lucky if we've got at least one person to stick by us." He turns and stares at the lighted windows of his house. "That's what I aim to do for Maddie. Love her. Whether she wants me to or not."

5

THIS MORNING, MONDAY, I'M WATCHING TELEVISION BY MY-self. Arthur is home with Maddie, and now it's just Stump and me, and I have to admit I miss Arthur's company. I think about giving him a call, just to gab, but I don't. He has his own life to live, this new life with Maddie, and who am I to try to butt into that?

Stump dozes on the rug by my chair, and I'm about to nod off, too. I've got the television on CNN, the volume down low, and the voices of the newscasters are lulling me to sleep. Then I hear one of them say a name, "Calvin Brady," and suddenly I'm wide awake.

I punch up the volume and scramble to catch up with the story, a hostage situation at a feed supply and grain elevator in Edon, Ohio. A gunman holding three employees hostage. One of them is seventy-year-old Calvin Brady. I watch the footage of the scene, most of it shot from a helicopter hovering above the site. I see the flat-roofed sheds and the office building where a red and white checkerboard Purina sign is tacked to the wall. I see rail-road tracks, the rail bed dusted with snow, and the cement silos of the grain elevator reaching up into the gray sky. The camera from the helicopter looks down on the police barricades, the officers in

45

SWAT gear, rifles drawn. Fields stretch out behind the elevator. Canada geese feed on shelled corn left in the stubble. Specks of snow stir in the wind.

Then the photographs go up on the screen: the hostages being held by the yet unidentified gunman. One of them is a woman, forty-three-year-old Mora Grove. She's a gaunt-faced woman, and in her picture, her hair is back in a ponytail, and her lips are pressed together as if she knows this day is coming and she can't stop it to save her life. The owner of the grain elevator is fifty-one-year-old Herbert Zwilling, a beefy man with a flattop haircut and a big, toothy grin. Then there's my brother—I'm certain as soon as I see him—my brother, Cal. I can hardly begin to say what comes over me as soon I look at his face, slack now with age, a face so much like my own. My chest fills with the knowledge that he's alive, but held hostage now by some lunatic with a gun.

Then my phone rings, and it's Arthur calling. "Are you watching CNN?" he asks.

I tell him I am.

"Your brother," he says.

"Yes," I say. "It's him."

I keep the television on throughout the day, waiting for more news, and while I wait, I talk to Stump. I tell him about Cal and how, when we were kids, I thought he hung the moon. Back then I thought he was like someone I'd see in a movie, one of those rockabilly cats, all slicked up and ready to bop. He was a real tomcat, my father said. Cal, who wore gabardine slacks with red flames stitched on the hip pockets, and two-tone shoes just right for dancing to Carl Perkins or Jerry Lee Lewis or Lefty Frizzell at the juke joints. Some evenings, I'd see Cal all jazzed up in one of his shiny rayon shirts, sleeves rolled up on his biceps. He'd be uptown, sitting on the hood of his coupe, just waiting for the world to come to him, and I'd think, *there he is, there's my brother.*

One night, Grinny Hines came out of the Verlene Café and said, "Buddy, that shiny shirt makes you look like a queer." Cal got off his coupe, stood face to face with him, this man who made his money from running gambling operations for the mob that operated out of places like St. Louis and Chicago and Detroit. He was a dangerous man, this Grinny Hines, but Cal didn't care. He punched him between the eyes and put him down. That was Cal, quick to act when he needed to, unwilling to take any guff, which worries me to death now that I know he's at that feed supply with that gunman.

I tell Stump how the two of us, when we were boys, slept in the same bedroom in our shotgun house in Rat Town. Two bedrooms in that house: one for my mother and father, and one for Cal and me. Sometimes, when I was a small boy, I'd wake up afraid of the dark—maybe I heard a noise outside, or maybe I thought I saw some sort of shape in the shadows—and I'd lie there trying my best not to call out to him, not to admit I was scared to death.

One night, he must have known that I was frightened because he said to me, "Sammy, are you asleep?"

"No," I said, "are you?"

I ask Stump how I was supposed to know how stupid that was. I was just a kid.

Stump's on the floor by my chair and I'm rubbing my finger over his head. "I'm talking to you, ain't I, dope?" Cal said, and the next morning he told the story to our parents and it quickly became our family joke. One of us would make a blunder—drop a dish, stub a toe, knock over a glass of milk—and someone would say, "Hey, you asleep?"

When I think about the times when everything was good in our house, I think of that good-natured teasing, and I wish our life together could have always been like that. But there was Dewey Finn, and, because of him, everything between Cal and me would change forever.

ARTHUR COMES OVER IN THE AFTERNOON, AND HE SAYS, "Gee, Sammy. Shouldn't you maybe go out there? Shouldn't you be there for your brother?"

How do I admit that more than likely Cal doesn't want anything to do with me? How do I tell Arthur that once Cal found out that I walked the wrong side of the street when it came to the baby-oh-baby, it was the beginning of the end of what it meant to be brothers?

"I'm going to wait it out," I say, and I keep the television on, hoping for more news.

It comes in bits and pieces. The gunman is a man named Leonard Mink. CNN has a picture of him now, and I lean forward in my chair studying it: a lean man with a long nose and not much of a chin. His cheeks are all caved in, and his hair is combed up in spikes and held in place with styling gel the way young men do these days. To me, he looks like an ostrich, a very pissed-off ostrich, and it's easy for me to imagine him in that grain elevator office holding a gun on Mora Grove and Herbert Zwilling and my brother.

The standoff continues, and eventually CNN cuts away to report the other news of the day: the recovery of New Orleans in the aftermath of Hurricane Katrina, the war in Iraq. Dusk comes on, and soon I hear the whack of the evening paper against my front door and then the delivery boy's bicycle, chain rattling against its guard, as he heads on down the sidewalk.

Stump wakes up when he hears the noise, and he yawns and sniffs at the air. I move through my house, switching on lights, and when I open the front door, I find Arthur's granddaughter, Maddie, standing on the porch, the rolled tube of my newspaper in her hand.

Without a word, she steps inside. Again, she doesn't have on a coat, just a T-shirt, her slender arms bare, and a pair of blue jeans that hang from her hips, gathering in folds around her tennis shoes. She lays the newspaper on the library table by the picture window. Then she turns to face me. "If you'd like company," she says, and her eyes go down to the floor. She folds her hands in front of her. "That is, if you wouldn't mind," she says, "I'd like to sit with you awhile."

I glance over at Arthur's house, where I see a light on in the kitchen. I can even see him at the sink, washing dishes, and I realize I've let the time go by all day without a thought of eating anything.

"Does your grandfather know where you are?" I ask.

"He told me it was all right."

I never would have guessed that I'd be eager for this company, but here she is, this girl, and it pleases me to know that she and Arthur have talked about me today, that more than likely he went home, after being here to watch the television with me, and he said to her how sad it was for me to know about Cal held hostage out there in Ohio, and how a man hadn't ought to be alone at a time like this. Now here she is to keep me company, and the gesture overwhelms me as if somehow the three of us are family.

"Okay, then," I say, and I close the door.

"Have you had supper?" she asks, and it's like she knows I haven't, knows I wouldn't even have given it a thought. "It's all right to be worried," she says. "I don't have any brothers or sisters, but I know what it's like when people go away from you. People you love. I can imagine what it's like for you now."

I remember what Arthur told me about his son, Maddie's father, and how he took off for Mexico and hasn't surfaced since. I suspect she can imagine what it would be like if she were to turn on the television one day and see a photo of him flashed on the screen, the same way it's been for me seeing Cal. It's like a door opened and the dead just walked right in.

"You must have better things to do than to spend time with me," I say.

Stump is sniffing around her feet, and she gets down on her knees and scratches his head. "Who says I came to see you?" She looks up at me and smiles. How lucky I am to have this girl I'm just starting to know, who's willing to offer her smile, her gentle teasing, as a way of saying she's here with me, here because she knows there's no one besides her and Arthur to ease my way. "Stump," she says. "What say we get something to eat?"

So we do. I open a can of duck and potato for Stump while Maddie warms a can of chicken noodle soup on the stove. She makes herself at home in my kitchen, finding a pan in the cupboard, opening the pantry for the Saltine crackers. "You can set the table," she tells me, and I'm happy to have that chore, to find the soup bowls—I even use the Currier and Ives china bowls that my mother always saved for holidays—and the spoons, and the cloth napkins I keep folded in a drawer. Just like that, we set up shop, moving about the kitchen, bumping into each other once or twice and sharing a chuckle over what klutzes we are.

Maddie drops a spoon, and without thinking I say, "Hey, you asleep?" She picks up the spoon and looks at me. "It's what my brother and I used to say to each other," I tell her, and she comes to me then and puts her hand on my back. I think of the way Vera touched me at the Seasoned Chefs.

"He's going to be all right," Maddie says. "Just wait. You'll see."

Then, as if she's conjured it, Cal's name is coming from the television, and we hurry into the living room to see what's happening.

He's on the screen, not just his photograph, but him, in the flesh. It's dark in Ohio, and he's outside the feed supply, his face lit up by the news stations' lights. There are microphones in his face, and reporters are shouting questions at him: *What happened in there? Who fired the shot? Is Mink alive?* Two police officers are trying to escort him through the crowd. It's snowing hard now, and the snow is gathering on the bill of his cap. He keeps his face down, and then he's gone, the police officers parting the crowd of reporters, and I see them easing him into the back of a squad car. My last image of him is through the window of the car, as it drives away. He still has his head bowed, but at least I know that he's safe.

The camera focuses on a CNN reporter, a handsome man with blond hair. He says the story isn't yet certain, but earlier in the evening, the woman, Mora Grove, walked out of the feed supply. She said it was Cal who convinced Leonard Mink to let her go. Cal just kept talking to him, kept telling him she had nothing to do with what had brought him into that feed supply with his gun, a hunting rifle. Then it was just Cal and Herbert Zwilling and Mink still inside. Nearly an hour went by. Then a single shot was heard inside the feed supply. From this point on, the facts still needed sorting out. All anyone knew for certain was that Leonard Mink was dead, and the hostages were all alive. "From every indication," the reporter says, "there are at least two families tonight who have Calvin Brady to thank for the fact that their loved ones are coming home to them safe and sound."

Again, Maddie lays her hand on my back. "You see?" she says. "I told you he'd be all right."

I don't know what to say. I stand here in my house, thankful that my brother's alive. I'm thinking about how the years of silence between us have been stones on my heart, and I'm trembling from the relief I now feel and the shame, too, because he's a hero, and I know I could never be that, not in a million years.

When I'm alone (Arthur has come to collect Maddie, and the three of us have lingered awhile, hoping for more news from Ohio, but nothing has come), I call Directory Assistance and get Cal's telephone number. I've looked up Edon in my atlas, a town in northwest Ohio, population 898, two miles from Indiana. I dial the numbers and listen to the phone ring in whatever home Cal has in this small town. No one answers. Not now, nor when I try again an hour later, nor any of the times I try on Tuesday morning, and finally I give up, and it seems like things are the way they've always been, not a word for my brother and I to say to each other.

Then later in the afternoon, when I'm out in the yard with Stump, a car parks across the street, one of those sport utility vehicles—a black Ford Explorer with a wheel cover missing on its front driver's-side tire and mud flecked up on the hind fender. What kind of dope, I wonder, is the man behind the steering wheel who doesn't take better care of a jazzy set of wheels like this?

I shade my eyes with my hand to get a better look, and the power window on the Explorer goes down, and I see that the man at the wheel is Cal.

He has a cap on his head that says WISH YOU WERE HAIR. The cap is too big for his head. It sags down over his ears. He lifts his hand, puts two fingers to the brim of that sloppy cap, and gives me a shy salute.

I take a few steps across the yard, meaning to go out to the street and talk to my brother, but before I reach the gate the window on the Explorer goes up and Cal drives away.

The rest of the day, it seems that it's all been a dream, and for a while I even find myself doubting that it was really Cal I saw in that Explorer. When evening comes, I settle down in my chair with the *Daily Mail*. Stump flops down on the rug. It's quiet for a good while, just the sound of Stump grunting as he burrows into sleep, the rustling of the newspaper as I turn the pages, the ticking of the cuckoo clock on the wall.

To my surprise, I find an Associated Press item about the hostage crisis averted in Edon, Ohio. I'm just starting to read it, when Stump stirs. He tips up his muzzle and barks. Then the knock comes on the front door, and I get up to see who it is.

It's Cal. He still has on that cap, and standing the way he is on the dark porch, it's hard for me to see his face beneath the shadow of its bill.

"Sammy," he says. "It's me. It's your brother."

"I saw you this afternoon," I say.

He nods. "I didn't know what to say to you, then. I couldn't even get out of the truck." He looks down at his feet. "It took me a while to work up the nerve to come back and try again." He takes off his cap. He twists it around in his hands. Finally, he lifts his head and looks at me. "Sammy," he says, "it's been a long time."

I tell him it surely has. Then I open the door wider so he can come into my house.

It's strange at first, having him here. I ask him whether he'd like something to eat, or some coffee, or a bottle of pop. "Maybe you'd like a Pepsi-Cola," I say, and he says, no, nothing. "Sammy," he says, "I just want to sit down for a while. I'm give out."

So we do. We sit in the living room, Cal on the couch where a quilt is still bunched up from when I took a nap, and I in my reclining chair.

Stump starts to waddle over to investigate, but I grab his collar to keep him near me, not knowing how Cal might take to him.

"It's all right," Cal says, so I let Stump go. Cal holds out his hand, and Stump gives it a sniff and a lick. "Now he's got my scent," Cal says. "Now we're friends."

I wish it could be so easy for Cal and me, but we have all those years of silence between us, and we have to take it slow.

"Winter's here," I say.

He nods, grateful, I'm sure, for this harmless chitchat about the weather. "There was frost this morning." He has a copper bracelet on his left wrist, the sort folks wear to ward off arthritis, and he keeps fiddling with it. "I had to scrape off my car windows."

"The woolly worms are more black than brown this year. That means we're in for a rough winter."

"Dad used to talk about signs like that. You remember?"

"Yes, I remember," I say. "Woolly worms and walking sticks, thick hulls on walnuts, dark breastbone on a goose."

"Frost this morning," Cal says, even though he's already made mention of it. "A hard frost," he says. "We've already had snow in Ohio."

Of course, eventually we have to get around to it, the question of why he's here. "Cal, all this time," I say.

He's scratching Stump behind his ear, and Stump, shameless as he is, just keeps leaning in for more.

"I know. Sammy, believe me. I know."

"And now here you are."

"I saw that piece in the *Daily Mail* about that fancy dog house you built, and I thought it was about time we tried to patch things up."

"You take the *Daily Mail?*"

"Always have, wherever I've lived." His voice breaks. "Jesus, Sammy, you think I've ever forgotten you, forgotten home?"

I let a few moments go by, just so I can marvel over the fact that this is my brother. I want to go to him. I want to put my arms around him and tell him how good it is to see him. I want all those years without any word to melt away and leave us like we were, two boys who loved each other before we came unraveled and our lives scattered, willy-nilly. But I can't bring myself to tell him how much I've missed having him in my life, can't let him know how much the distance between us has hurt me.

"I saw you on television," I say. Then I ask him the question I've wanted to ask him ever since he came into my house. "Cal, what in the world happened at that grain elevator?"

He bows his head as if he can barely stand to think of it. "You walk away from something like that, and you start to take stock of your life—I can tell you that for sure. You start to tally up all the things you've done wrong, all the mistakes you wish you could put right." He raises his head to look at me. "Sammy, I've spent a long time trying to forget what went on here with Dewey Finn, and now this mess in Ohio has brought it all back."

"That was a long time ago," I say. "We were different people."

"I'm a hero," Cal says. "At least, that's what people back in Ohio think, but the truth is I'm in a mess—trouble I can't even tell you about—and I need a place to be." He lifts his hands from his lap, and for a moment I think he'll reach them out for me to take. Then he presses his palms together and touches his fingers to his lips as if he's praying. "Sometimes your heart tells you what you ought to do, and, if you're smart you listen. I know you don't owe it to me, Sammy, but still I'm hoping we can remember what it means to be brothers. Years don't change what runs between us.

We know each other better than anyone on account of what went on with Dewey. Folks back in Ohio think they know who I am, but, Sammy, they don't know the truth."

HIS STORY STARTS WITH A PENNY, JUST A LITTLE THING LIKE that the way the stories that matter often do. "A penny," Cal says. "Right outside the door at McDonald's. I walked past it at first. Then I thought, well, a cent's a cent. If I don't pick it up, some other Jake will. So I went back." He gives me a helpless look and shrugs his shoulders. "All I wanted was that penny. I had no idea what was coming down the pike."

He bent over to pick up the penny—"It was heads up, Sammy. Now, you know they say that's good luck."—and the door to McDonald's opened. "That was the first time I saw him," Cal says. "That was the first time I met Leonard Mink."

Only he wasn't Leonard Mink, then. Not when Cal met him outside that McDonald's in Bryan, Ohio. He was Ansel King. That's the alias he was using. "It was just before Thanksgiving," Cal says. "The corn harvest was done, and the days had turned cold and rainy."

Ansel King because he, Leonard Mink, was up to no good. He was a member of the Michigan Militia, a survivalist group, a few of whom had decided to make some noise this country would by-God notice. Mink needed fertilizer—ammonium nitrate—and a lot of it. That and nitromethane, an explosive often used in drag-racing fuel, and he'd have what he needed to make a truck bomb hefty enough to bring down the Sears Tower in Chicago. Make what Timothy McVeigh did in Oklahoma City look like a popcorn fart.

But that day outside the McDonald's in Bryan, Cal didn't know any of this. Mink was, to Cal's way of thinking, just this man, sort of bony and lanky, just this thirtysomething-year-old man with that long nose and that spiky haircut. "Just a kid it seemed to me," Cal says. "You know. Just like you'd see in any small town. No one you'd ever think was up to no good. He said, 'Excuse me, sir.' Then he saw what I was after—that penny—and he said, 'Looks like it's your lucky day.' Like I said, that was the first time I saw him."

"The Sears Tower," I say, remembering going up in it once when I made a trip to Chicago to see the sights. One hundred and ten stories high, 1,450 feet in the air. From the Skydeck that day— a clear day in early May before the hot days of summer when the heat and the humidity hold in the smog—I could see four states: Illinois, Indiana, Wisconsin, and Michigan. I think about the federal building in Oklahoma City and how it exploded that day in 1995. "Mercy," I say, and I hope that's all I need to say to let Cal know I understand exactly what it would have been if Leonard Mink had been successful with his plan. Another Oklahoma City. Another World Trade Center. This is the world we live in now.

"Mercy is right," Cal says. "That's why I had to stop it."

The cuckoo clock on the wall behind me marks the hour— eight o'clock—and Stump lifts his head to watch the bird slide out of the chalet house and set to calling. Stump waddles over and puts his front paws up on my legs, wanting, I know, for me to pull him up onto my lap so he can get closer to that cockamamie bird. I hoist him up, and he watches until the bird has gone back into his house and the quiet settles over the room.

"Stop it?" I put Stump down and nudge him away with my leg, intent now on what Cal has just said. "How were you going to stop it? How did you even find out what this Mink was up to?"

For a good while, Cal doesn't answer. He just looks down at his hands. Then he nods, and when he finally speaks, his voice is small and as distant as the years that stretch between us. "Let's just say I found out," he says. "Now I know too much, and there are people who aren't happy about that. Please, Sammy, don't ask me to tell you anything more than that."

I'm thinking he could be anyone, this man who sits now in my house. He could be someone I've never known, a stranger come to say the thing he's never been able to say to anyone else. Or he could be who he is, my brother, Calvin Brady, who has lived his life away from me and has chosen me now to hear his confession.

"Were you?" I say, and then I stop myself.

"Was I a part of it?" He narrows his eyes. "Sammy, do you really think I'd be involved in something like that?"

I'm ashamed that such a thought even flickered in my head for an instant. "I'm just glad you're all right," I tell him, and for now I let that be enough. "Cal, I'm glad you're here."

I MAKE UP THE BED FOR HIM IN THE ROOM ACROSS FROM mine, the spare room I've always kept in order the way folks do who expect overnight guests from time to time. The bed is the bed I slept in when I was a boy in Rat Town: rails, the head and foot pieces all made from cast iron. The night table beside it has the same lamp on it that I had then. Amazing how long something can last when you set it aside and rarely use it. A lamp with a shade that has a world map drawn on it, thin lines—the explorers' routes—crossing the oceans, curving around the contours of the continents and the islands. I used to trace my finger over those routes, feeling the nub of the shade's fabric, the heat of the bulb. I liked to fall asleep imagining the explorers—Columbus, Magellan, Da Gama—on the dark oceans, nothing but the stars overhead to help them chart their way.

"My God," Cal says when I turn on the lamp. "How old is that thing?"

"Old," I say. "Like us."

Cal nods. "As old as that."

I find a set of new sheets in the bureau, and we get to work putting down the fitted sheet and tugging it tight at the corners of the mattress. Cal gives me a hand. Together, he on one side of the bed and I on the other, we shake out the top sheet and let it billow up above the bed and then sink down. We smooth it with our hands, working like that, folding hospital corners, just the way our mother taught us when we were boys.

"Have you made those corners all your life?" I ask. "Those hospital corners like Mom showed us?"

"All my life," he says. "Some things you don't forget."

The thought comforts me. I imagine the two of us, all these years when I had no idea in the world where he might be, rising each morning and making our beds the same way, the folding of sheets into those hospital corners a small, simple thing we carried from home. The way fingers fold the corner of a sheet into a triangle and tuck it beneath a mattress—a little thing like that to remind us that we're brothers.

"Sammy," he says, and his voice cracks as if these are words he's been trying to work up from his throat a long, long time. "Sammy," he says again, "you and me . . . well . . . goddamn it." And I know he's trying to tell me he's sorry that he's stayed away all these years.

"We've got time," I say. "We've got lots of time." I lay out blankets. We slip the pillows into their cases. We work in silence, and when we're done, we stand on opposite sides of the bed, looking at each other. "You should get some sleep, Cal. You've come a long way."

"I left my truck on the street, Sammy, on account I didn't know if you'd let me stay."

"You can put your truck in my garage," I tell him, and I realize I'm agreeing to provide harbor from whatever trouble bears down on him from Ohio.

He nods. "I've got a duffle bag."

"I'll give you a hand," I say, and together we go outside.

We're in the phase of the new moon, and without its light, the stars are brilliant overhead. *Star light, star bright,* I think, recalling that old kids' rhyme Cal and I used to say those summer evenings when we sat on the porch with our mother and father and kept our eyes out for the first star. Tonight, I see the North Star at the tip of the Big Dipper, and I make my wish: that this can be the start of something for Cal and me.

He opens the door to his Explorer, and the dome light comes on. I see the litter that covers the passenger seat and spills down to the floorboard: wrappers torn from Hershey bars, paper coffee cups from 7-Eleven, a pair of black socks rolled into a ball, a *USA Today* newspaper, a pocket-size Gideon's Bible, a Phillips head screwdriver, a Wal-Mart road atlas, a compact disc of the Three Tenors in concert (Carreras, Domingo, and Pavarotti—imagine that), all this belonging to my brother. It's the CD that fascinates me most; something about the idea of Cal driving down the road, singing along to *Core 'ngrato,* weeping perhaps to *Il lamento di Federico,* amazes me. My brother, a fan of opera. My brother who somehow walked away from that feed supply and grain elevator in Edon, Ohio, a hero, and now can't live with it for reasons I suspect he'll tell me in due time. The things we don't know and wouldn't guess in a million years.

The things I never could have imagined, I think, as Cal and I turn in for the night. We go to our bedrooms, and we fall asleep, the way we did so many nights when we were boys and we had no idea what was coming at us from the world we'd already made, the one we wouldn't know until we found ourselves smack dab in the middle of it, shaking our heads, bewildered by how all of this had ever come to be, wondering how our lives had turned into stories we never could have dreamed.

6

IN THE MORNING, CAL IS UP BEFORE I AM. I WAKE TO THE
smell of coffee percolating and sausage frying on the stove. In the
kitchen, Stump is already going at his duck and potato.

"Hey, sleepyhead," Cal says to me. "Mister Sandman pay a
long visit, did he?" It's only 7:30, but from the looks of things,
Cal's been up and at it awhile. "I couldn't let Stump starve, so I
poked around and found his food. Then I thought I'd rustle us up
some breakfast."

"Thank you," I say. I sit down at my kitchen table, feeling
somewhat a stranger in my own home.

Then I hear Arthur's usual knock at my back door. *Shave and
a haircut.* I always answer it by knocking on the inside of the
door. Two distinct raps. *Two bits.*

"It's my neighbor," I say. "Arthur Pope."

"Arthur Pope," Cal says, and I know he's recalling him.

I get up to open the door. From the step, Arthur points behind
him. "You got another truck in your garage. What gives, sailor?"

"I've got company," I say. "My brother." I step back, and Arthur
pokes his head around the door frame. "Do you remember Cal?"

Arthur comes into the kitchen. "Cal Brady," he says. He stands with his hands on his hips. "You got yourself in the middle of a mess, didn't you. I saw it all on TV. Up until then, I hadn't heard your name in ages. I would have sworn you were dead."

"No," says Cal. "I've just been away for a while."

"Come for a visit, have you?"

"That's right. Me and Sammy. We've been catching up."

"How long's it been?"

Cal and I glance at each other and then look away. Neither of us wants to be the one to say it. Finally, the silence gets to be too much, and I say, "It's been a lot of years, Arthur. You know how time goes."

"It goes fast," he says. "I'll tell you that. It goes fast and then you're dead."

"Or you feel like you might as well be," says Cal.

"Sailor, that's the truth," says Arthur, and he tells the story of how Bess died and left him alone, and then he and I built that ship for Stump. He's yakking away. The Seasoned Chefs and *Very Vera*. Yakkity, yakkity, yak. "And I said to Sammy." He pulls a chair out from the table, swings it around so it's facing him and straddles the seat. " 'Sammy,' I said." He slaps his hands on the top of the chair back like he's doing a drum roll—rap-a-rap-rap. " 'I never thought I'd make it after I lost Bess, but now I've got this other life, and sometimes I'm amazed there's all these things that I love to do.' " He points a finger my way. "Isn't that what I said to you, Sammy?"

If he did, I don't recall it, but I say, yes, yes, isn't it the truth. "Life's full of surprises," I say, "no matter how old we get."

I look at Cal as I say it. I want him to know that already I've forgiven him for the years of silence between us, all those years when I didn't know where he was. It can happen that fast. The hurt can become something else, some old love the heart remembers.

That's what Arthur's saying. You can walk through a door into a life you thought wasn't yours anymore. Here's my brother, Cal. Who'd have thought it?

"That's how you must feel," Arthur says to him, "seeing what you've just been through. What was the story with that man anyway? That Leonard Mink."

"He was a crazy man." Cal pours pancake batter into a skillet. "I just got in his way."

"Hey." Arthur snaps his fingers. "You look like you know a thing or two about cooking. You ought to come with Sammy and me to the Seasoned Chefs tonight."

I've forgotten that tonight's the night for another cooking lesson from Vera. I can't imagine what it might be like for Cal to see her again after all the time that's passed. "It's Vera Moon," I say to Cal. "That's who teaches the cooking class." I watch Cal's face for a sign of what this fact means to him, but he doesn't react at all. "Gee, Arthur," I say. "You're going to have to give me a rain check tonight. Cal and I have a lot of catching up to do."

This disappoints Arthur. I have no doubt of that. "Sammy," he says, "it's our regular date."

"I'm sorry," I say.

"No problem," says Cal. "I don't mind tagging along."

SO WE GO. WE RIDE IN ARTHUR'S CHRYSLER, ME IN THE FRONT seat and Cal in the back. He's slapped on some cologne, one of those spiky scents I sometimes smell on young men when I pass by them in a store or a restaurant, and I think for a minute what it would be like to be young again, just starting out and all my life ahead of me. I wonder whether it's what Cal feels tonight, like he's stepped back fifty years and he's on his way uptown to see his girl.

Arthur sniffs the air. He glances up at his rearview mirror. "Cal, you've got a good stink going there."

Cal pats his cheeks and smells his hands. "Too much?" he asks.

"Nah." Arthur gives me a wink. "Just right."

I love my brother for that cologne and the fact that he put on too much, anxious to make a good impression tonight. I can tell he's nervous—he keeps swirling that copper bracelet around on his wrist—and a little shy, and that makes me love him even more. He's left his cap at home, that one that says WISH YOU WERE HAIR, and he's put on a fresh shirt, a white corduroy shirt that looks like it's never been worn; I can see the fold marks creasing the front of it, and the collar is still crisp. He's wearing a pair of blue jeans—how many of us can do that at this age and not look like idiots?—and he's got these slippers on, the kind with no backs—clogs, I guess you'd call them—and he looks like a man who's got a little mileage on his motor but who still knows how to step out on the town. Which he always did when he was a young man, hanging out in the juke joints on the weekends, dancing up a storm. Now he's going to a cooking lesson with the Seasoned Chefs, going to see Vera Moon.

"Relax, Cal." Who'd have thought I'd ever be the one saying this to my brother. "It's a nice bunch of folks."

At the Senior Center, Vera takes his hand between both of hers, and it warms me to see the two of them together. "Cal Brady," she says. "It's been forever and a day. My goodness, just look at you."

"Vera," he says, and he brings one of her hands up to his lips and kisses it. "The years have treated you well. Of course, you were always a looker."

A blush comes into her face. "And you were always a smooth talker." She draws her hand back. Then she touches him lightly on his shirtsleeve, takes that corduroy between her fingers and pets it. "Looks like neither one of us has changed a bit," she says, and though I've never been one to play this sort of game, it's easy to see the old spark kindle up between them. "Welcome home, Cal Brady. Welcome to the Seasoned Chefs."

Arthur draws me aside. "Nervous," he says in a low voice so Cal can't hear. "Yeah, right."

We put on our aprons. I help Cal tie his. "Was I too forward, Sammy?" He glances around the room, looking for Vera. "I don't mean to offend anyone. I have the feeling Arthur thought I was out of line."

"Don't worry about him," I say. "He's got a little crush. That's all."

"Him and Vera?"

"On his part, to be sure. Her? I really couldn't say."

Cal nods. "So that's how it is. All right, then. I don't feel so bad."

The door opens and I'm surprised to see Duncan Hines walk in. The tips of his ears are red from the cold, and he has a notepad and pen in his hands, a camera hanging from a strap around his neck. The warm air inside the room hits the cold surface of his eyeglasses and they fog over. He has to take them off, and he stands there, just inside the door, squinting.

Vera's voice calls out. "Mr. Hines," she says, and she sweeps through the crowd of Seasoned Chefs to greet him. "So good of you to come."

"Hey, there's that newspaper reporter," Arthur says to me, the sight of Duncan making him forget the earlier wound of Cal kissing Vera's hand. "Think maybe we'll be in the paper again, Sammy? More PR? Boy, I feel like a celebrity."

Vera claps her hands together, and the Seasoned Chefs, who have been all abuzz since Duncan's arrival, dummy up so they can listen to her. She stands in the middle of the room, looking, as she always does, regal and composed.

"Gentlemen, it's a special night," she says. "Not only are we getting close to Christmas, we have Mr. Hines with us to do a feature for the newspaper." The Seasoned Chefs applaud. A few of them take out pocket combs and give their hair a once-over. One man uses his finger to groom his mustache. "And, on top of all that," Vera says with a smile, "we welcome a newcomer to the group." With a flourish of her hand, the way the pretty girls on game shows do when they gesture toward a prize, she directs our attention to Cal. "Cal Brady," she says. "Sam's brother. I'm sure you'll make him feel at home."

Tonight, we're learning how to make divinity candy. A delicate operation, to be sure, Vera tells us, stressing how important it is to cook the corn syrup to just the right temperature. "That's why you'll need your candy thermometers." She holds one up for us to see, and I notice that there are others waiting at each of our stations, next to saucepans and the ingredients: the Karo syrup, the eggs, the granulated sugar, the salt and vanilla. "Your recipes are all laid out for you," she says. "Combine the proper measures of sugar, syrup, water, and salt, and heat it until it reaches 260 degrees, the hard ball stage."

"Very scientific," says Arthur.

"Cook it too long and it'll reach the hard crack stage," Vera says. "Then, gents, you'll have trouble." She tells us we'll have to beat the egg whites while we're cooking the syrup and that perhaps we should work in pairs so we won't forget to keep an eye on the thermometer. "And don't let it touch the bottom of the pan because you'll get an inaccurate reading, and eventually the thermometer could explode. Nothing like a little broken glass to ruin a good piece of candy."

"Hmm, crunchy," Arthur says, and the Seasoned Chefs laugh.

When we're ready to get down to business, I tell Cal he can buddy up with Arthur and me.

"No need," says Cal. "Three's a crowd. I'll just go it alone."

Arthur pretends he's mortified, but I can tell he's secretly pleased. "Alone? Are you crazy, sailor? We're talking the dangers of hard crack here. Hard crack and explosion."

Cal unbuttons his cuffs and rolls back the sleeves of his corduroy shirt. "Sailor," he says to Arthur. "I think I can handle it."

And he does. Much better than any of us. While the rest of the Seasoned Chefs look like cartoon characters—they squint through their bifocals and try to read their candy thermometers, they end up with balls that are too soft ("Story of my life," one man says with a shake of his head), or else they cook the syrup too long and it burns—Cal works expertly and efficiently, beating his egg whites while also keeping his eye on his candy thermometer. It doesn't take long for the word to go around, and soon the Seasoned Chefs have given up their own efforts and are watching him go to town. He pours the syrup over the stiff egg whites, and he keeps beating—one arm pouring and the other beating—and it's a thing of beauty really, the way he seems to be two people at once, and finally he's stirring in the vanilla and some chopped walnuts and just a smidge of red food coloring to give it a delicate pink tinge before he starts spooning it out in airy puffs on the wax paper.

He seems to be unaware that we're watching; to him this is nothing extraordinary at all, but to us—and even to Vera, who stands with one arm across her stomach and the other propped on it, her hand to her cheek, her mouth slightly open, as if she's seeing the most wonderful thing—such flare and grace in the kitchen is miraculous.

"I'll be damned," Arthur says, and then we begin to clap.

Cal is embarrassed by the show of appreciation. "What?" he says, and Vera tells him he's an inspiration. "A divine inspiration," she says, and she rubs her hand over his back, the way she did mine the first night I came to the Seasoned Chefs.

So I know what Cal is feeling as he turns to her; at least I have a good guess. He's traveled a long way. He's lived through what he did in Ohio, and now here's this woman, this *Very Vera*. He walked away from her once, but here he is and her touch is the most wonderful thing in the world. I wish I could say I didn't feel jealous, but that wouldn't be the truth.

"Bravo, Cal," she says. "You certainly made sweet work of that."

"I've lived on my own quite a while," he says in a shy voice, and I'm sorry that he has to admit this. "I guess I picked up a few things."

Then Duncan Hines sweeps in, and he tells Cal he'd like to ask him a few questions. "Golly, you'll make a great story."

"For the paper?" Cal asks.

"The *It's Us* section," Arthur says. "Comes out every Friday. Sammy and I were in there back in the fall. Weren't we, Sammy?"

Cal reaches behind him and unties his apron. "You don't want to talk to me," he says to Duncan. "I'm just a visitor here. All these other men, they're the regulars. They're the ones your readers would be interested in."

"Oh, just a few questions," Vera says.

He has the apron over his head now, and he leaves it in a wad on the counter, lets it drop right on top of the divinity candy he's just made. "I'm no one," he says, and he tries to move away, hoping, I imagine, to lose himself in a corner somewhere, maybe even step outside for a while.

But Arthur grabs him by the arm. "Turn to, sailor. You heard the lady." Vera is carefully lifting the apron from the divinity. "Now, give this boy what he wants," Arthur says. "Hell's bells, you're no stranger. You grew up in Rat Town."

"My grandmother grew up there," Duncan says. "Nancy Finn. Maybe you knew her?"

Cal looks at me and then bows his head. Arthur lets go of his arm.

"Yes, I knew her," Cal finally says without looking up.

"How about a picture, then?" Duncan says. "A picture of you and Vera."

Vera holds the apron out to Cal, inviting him to slip back into what was such a festive mood only a few moments earlier. But it's too late; whatever delight we managed has cracked and come apart now.

"Sorry," Cal says.

Duncan lifts his camera and sights through the viewfinder. "Just a quick one," he says.

But before he can snap the shot, Cal reaches out and closes his hand around the camera's lens. "I said no pictures." He pulls the camera down from Duncan's face. "No pictures," he says again, and this time his voice is hushed, a quiet plea. "I'm sorry," he says to Vera. "I don't mean to be rude. It's just . . ."

He stops, unable to find the words to explain why the idea of an interview or a photograph for the paper pains him so. I want to tell him I understand. I remember what I felt when I saw my own picture in *It's Us*, like I'd put my secret life out there for everyone to see. Whatever it is that Cal lived through during his time with Leonard Mink, I can tell it's left him stunned and afraid of what he might show to the world.

"What I mean is . . ." He tries again, but still the words won't come.

"We all reach a certain age," I say, "where we can barely stand to look at ourselves in the mirror, let alone think that thousands of people are looking at us in the newspaper. You understand what my brother's trying to say, don't you, Vera?"

She pulls the apron back to her and folds it, taking great care to keep it tidy. Surely she knows. I can't imagine that anyone our age hasn't been tromped on enough to know sometimes all this living is too much and all we want to do is hide ourselves away. Even Vera, who is so very, very zesty. Even she must know this.

"I'll let you off the hook this one time." She scolds Cal by wagging her finger at him. "But, really, Cal, you must know the truth. You're a very handsome man. Isn't he handsome, Arthur?"

The question catches Arthur off guard. He bites his lip, draws back his head, takes a breath. How to answer this without seeming stingy but also without diminishing what he hopes is his significant stature with Vera. "I don't really study the way men look," he finally says, "but I'll tell you this. He sure does smell pretty."

"Aftershave," Cal says, again embarrassed.

Vera stands closer to him. She leans in toward his neck. "No, that's cologne," she says. "It has a seductive Oriental scent. I'd say green mandarin leaf and crisp yuzu zest layered with the embrace of nutmeg and anise."

Arthur tries to make a joke. "Hell's bells, do you wear it or eat it?"

But no one laughs. It's like Vera and Cal are in their own world.

"Just a hint of sandalwood," he says.

She nods. "Leather and warm tobacco. Very masculine. Very aromatic. Very, very Vera."

7

TOWARD THE END OF THE EVENING, WHEN NEARLY ALL THE Seasoned Chefs are gone, Duncan finds me near the door, where I'm waiting for Arthur to finish helping Vera turn off the lights and make sure the Senior Center is secure. Cal has already stepped outside and is pacing the sidewalk, eager for the night to be done. I know, when he agreed to come along, he never planned on being the star of the evening and drawing so much attention to himself, nor did he ever dream that he'd run into an ancestor of Dewey Finn.

"Granny Nancy says you were friends with her brother," Duncan says to me. He's got that same friendly smile that he always wears as if he's just waiting for the next thing in the world to amaze him. "Dewey," he says. "She had a brother named Dewey. Do you remember him?"

I search Duncan's face, trying to make out if he knows more than he's letting on. "Your grandmother told you about me and Dewey?"

"Just that you were friends, and he died when he was young. Do you remember how it happened?"

"Yes, it's true. We were friends."

"Mr. Brady." Duncan takes a step toward me. His smile is gone now, and his voice is low and tight. I can see that he's quite aware that I'm deliberately evading his question about the circumstances of Dewey's death, and he's not happy with that fact. "I was down at the police station annex the other day. You know, that building on Whittle that used to be the jail. Mr. Brady, I found something I'd like you to see."

"Something about Dewey?"

"That's right. Could you meet me at the *Daily Mail* office in the morning?"

I'm thankful, then, that Vera and Arthur interrupt us.

"Ready, Sammy?" Arthur says.

"Good night, Mr. Hines," says Vera. "Good night, Sam." She peers out through the picture window. "Oh, and there's Cal. I must say good night to him."

We all step outside, then, and Duncan's request threatens to slip away into the cold air.

I start walking toward Arthur's Chrysler. Then Duncan calls after me. "Ten o'clock?" he says.

Arthur, thinking he's asking for the time, checks his wristwatch. He turns around and says to Duncan, "No, it's nine fifteen."

"Mr. Brady?" Duncan says, and I give him a wave of my hand.

"WHAT DID HE WANT WITH YOU?" CAL ASKS WHEN WE'RE finally alone in my house. "That Duncan Hines?"

"He wanted to talk about Dewey."

"Good Christ. What did you tell him?"

"Nothing. Honest, Cal. I didn't tell him a thing." I try to keep my voice steady, but I'm certain Cal can hear how much Duncan has me on edge. "But it's going to come out."

"Not if we don't tell it."

"Maybe we should tell it. Tell the whole thing. Don't you think Nancy Finn has a right to know?"

"Don't talk like that. Keep talking like that and I'll get in my truck and leave."

"Leave me alone to face it, just like you did all those years ago?" I make my voice go hard, trying to cover the desperation I feel now that I'm convinced Duncan is on to something. "You owe it to me to stay this time. You know that, don't you? Surely you won't leave me again. Please, Cal. I don't know how much longer I can keep everything to myself." I stop talking, hoping that he'll say the next thing and give me the assurance I want. When he doesn't, I go on. "What I'm saying is I need you here with me the same way I needed you then. The only difference now is, like you made plain, you need to be here."

He bites his lip and looks away from me. "Has there been anyone for you, Sammy? You know what I'm asking. Have you had anyone who mattered to you?"

It pains me to admit how alone I've been all these years. "No, not really," I say. "No, no one to speak of."

He takes a deep breath and lets it out before squaring his shoulders and giving me a nod. "I'll take it on," he says. "You understand what I'm saying? I'll be the one to stand up to the truth if the time comes when we need to. Until then, you keep your mouth shut. Got it?"

I tell myself that in exchange for this I won't ask Cal anything else about what went on in Ohio. It's clear to me that he understands this, and we have a bargain. I'll offer him this place to hide, and in exchange he'll keep me away from trouble.

"All right," I say.

He looks me in the eye for what seems like a very long time.

Then he says, "Sometimes I think that night with Dewey made my whole life."

"Mine, too."

"Made it something I didn't want it to be. Sent me out on a road that ended up in Ohio."

"Now you're home. Now it's you and me."

"Good Christ, Sammy." He lets loose a ragged sigh, and I know the weight of his living as well as I know my own.

It warms me to know that he's willing to stand beside me in the face of whatever's coming. Tonight, having him in my house means the world to me. Christmas will soon be here, and for the first time in years I'll spend it with my brother. I remember the way Christmas was in Rat Town, the way it was before Dewey died, before Cal left. I remember snow falling and the smell of coal smoke from people's chimneys, and the tangerines my father brought home in paper sacks from the Little Farm Market. My mother taped Christmas cards to the door frame that led from our front room to our kitchen, and she baked cookies and divinity and fudge. Each year, my father and I went off into the woods behind the railroad trestle, and we cut a cedar tree and brought it home and set it up by our front window. I remember coming down the street at night—maybe I'd been to a basketball game at school or to the Verlene to see what new records might be on the jukebox— and I'd see the lights on our tree, and I'd hurry, anxious to be home, out of the cold, where my father had the radio on—Burl Ives might be singing "Frosty the Snowman," or Gene Autry might be doing "Rudolph the Red-Nosed Reindeer"—and my mother was wrapping packages. "Don't peek," she'd say as I came through the door, and make a big show of covering over whatever she happened to have on the drop-leaf table. I remember all that, such a feeling of being in the right place with the right people. I remember what it was to have a family.

"Looks like it's a night for ghosts," Cal says, as he finishes a glass of milk in the kitchen. "First Vera Moon and then Dewey. There was a time when I thought I'd make a life with her." He rinses out his glass and sets it in the sink. He looks at me, and I see the heat in his eyes, and I know he's holding me to blame for the way his life turned out.

"Look at us now," I say. "Maybe we've got a chance to make things right."

Cal shakes his head. "After what went on in Ohio, it's going to be a long time before anything's right with me. I keep thinking, if I hadn't stopped to pick up that penny that day outside McDonald's. Maybe if I hadn't done that."

He rubs his hand over his mouth, and I keep quiet, realizing that he wants to tell me more of this story, that he's been itching to get it off his chest, and once he starts he won't be able to stop until he's said it all.

"IT WAS LIKE THIS, SAMMY." HE CALLS UP THE SCENE, AND A spooky thing happens. He does his own voice, and he does Leonard Mink's, and it's like that dead man has come into the room with us. To be more exact, it's like I'm not even here anymore, like it's Cal and Mink the way it was back in April in Bryan, Ohio.

Cal picked up that penny, and Mink said, "You wouldn't know where a fella could get a car pretty cheap, would you?" He pointed across the lot to a blue station wagon, an old Pontiac. "I think I've blown the head gasket on that old warrior, and I suspect it's going to cost more to fix than the car's worth."

"I might could set you up with something," Cal said. He knew Herbert Zwilling over at the grain elevator in Edon often had a used car or two to sell. "You think that wagon could make it fourteen miles?"

"I'm willing to give it a shot," Mink said, "if you'll lead the way and keep me in your mirror in case I break down."

"How about we get some breakfast first?" Cal flipped the penny up in the air. I close my eyes and see it twirling. Then Cal says to me, "I know what it's like when a fella's down on his luck. Sometimes all he needs is a hot meal. 'My treat,' I said, and then Mink reached out and snatched the penny out of the air."

"Sir, I'd be obliged." He pressed the penny into Cal's hand, and then he closed his own hand around Cal's, and for a moment they held that penny between them. Then Mink pulled his hand away, and the penny was gone. It wasn't in his hand. It wasn't in Cal's. Mink winked. Then he reached up to Cal's ear—that old sleight of hand—and there it was, that penny. "I'm pleased to meet you," Mink said. "I'm Ansel King."

So he was King to Cal, Ansel King, and there they were in that McDonald's, Cal and this man he would later know was Leonard Mink, and Mink was wolfing down hotcakes and sausage and a milk shake. "I could see he was hungry," Cal tells me. "It was like he was starved to death."

"I've been moving around some since I got out of the Army," Mink said. "You know, going where the work is, trying to find a steady job."

Cal held his hands around a cup of coffee. "Were you in that mess over in Iraq?" he asked.

Mink nodded. "I was in the first one, Desert Storm. I was a gunner on an M2 Bradley."

"Infantry," Cal said.

"That's right. I shot the twenty-five-millimeter cannon."

"Could you make it mean business?"

"Sir, I won the Bronze Star Medal."

"I know what that means," Cal said. "I was in the Army myself."

Like I said, that's where he went after he left Rat Town.

"The last I knew of you," I say, "you were in Fairbanks, Alaska."

Cal nods. "I made some good money working on that pipeline after I got out of the Army. Then I decided to do some traveling. That's how I ended up in Ohio. You know, just seeing the country. I never married, Sammy. Never had anything to keep me in one place."

He knew what it was like to want to get something that would last, to land somewhere he could call home. Truth was he felt sorry for Mink, this young buck, skinny and looking caved in. "Where you bunking?" he asked him, and Mink told him he'd just hit town and hadn't found a place. "Try the Paradise Inn, over at Edon," Cal said. "Thirty-four bucks a night, but the owner, I bet she'd go down some if you ask her right."

Again, Mink was obliged. If he could get another car cheap, he said, he could get out and hustle for work. "I'm a good worker," he said. "Once I get a job, I stick with it until I get it done."

Cal laughed. "I can tell that by the way you eat. Good lord, boy. You really go to town."

Something about Mink stuck with him. There was that hard-luck story, yes, and the fact that he was a Bronze Star decorated war veteran, but it was more than all that. It was something in his eyes—some steel in those blue eyes that made it look like he was mad as hell or scared to death, like he lived right between those two extremes exactly the way Cal had once he'd left Rat Town, not

knowing what was waiting for him elsewhere and not sure he gave
a good goddamn.

"So about my car," Mink said. He took a last swallow from
his milk shake, slurping at it through the straw.

"You ready?" Cal said, and Mink told him he was.

It could have been like that, Cal says to me. It could have
been this one kind turn done a man down on his luck, nothing
anyone would really take count of and nothing to come of it except whatever lies on the other side of goodness.

"So I took him over to Edon and introduced him to Herbert
Zwilling," Cal says. "I let Mink follow me over to Edon, and sure
enough he had a blown gasket, and he was right; it was going to
cost more to fix than the car was worth. Herbert Zwilling had this
Plymouth Volare. An old 1979 model, faded maroon, the paint
gone down to the primer in spots. Duct tape holding the uphol-
stery together. A red steering wheel cover. I remember everything
about it, Sammy. Mink let Herbert have his Pontiac for junk and
threw in two hundred fifty bucks in cash for the Volare. I found
out later that was going to be his getaway car; that was the car he
was going to drive out of Chicago after bombing the Sears Tower."

Cal stops here. He takes in a long breath and then lets it out.
I suspect he's reliving it all, wondering, as he must have again and
again, how things might have been different if he hadn't stopped
to pick up that penny, if he hadn't paused just long enough for his
life to bump up against Leonard Mink's. Here we are still sitting in
my living room. I think for a moment how funny time can be, how
it can wash over you in a second and then a fistful of years and all
the people in them can turn to air and leave you gasping for
breath, dazzled at the far end of what you swore to be your solid
purchase on this planet spinning beneath your feet.

"I wasn't in on it," Cal finally says. "I've already told you that. Mink and I became drinking buddies, and he finally told me he meant to bring down the Sears Tower, and then before I knew it there we were in that feed supply—me and him and Herbert Zwilling and Mora Grove—and Mink had that rifle."

He wanted ammonium nitrate, and he wanted Herbert Zwilling to sell it to him, but Zwilling was holding out for more money than Mink was willing to pay. "I believe he was going to do whatever it took to get it," Cal says. "Only Mora Grove—she was Herbert's bookkeeper—she was back in her office, and she saw Mink walk in with that rifle, and right away she called 911. That's how we came to be holed up there, Mink threatening to kill us all."

"Why were you there the second time, Cal?"

"Like I said, I knew what Mink was up to. I was there to warn Herbert Zwilling."

Cal knew trouble was coming because the night before he'd been at the VFW with Leonard Mink. Cal had a place out in the country, and sometimes it got pretty lonely, and he went into the VFW to have some company for a while. "It was just me and the wind and the coyotes all mournful in the night," he says. "I didn't have anyone to do for. No family at all."

I can't help myself. I say, "You had me, Cal. You had a brother."

For a good while, it's so quiet in my house, I can hear the gears working in the clock on the wall and Stump's little grunts as he settles into sleep on the floor beside my chair.

"You're right, Sammy." When Cal finally speaks, his voice is small. "I'm no kind of brother. What else can I say?"

"Say what you've come to say," I tell him, and then I wait.

He was feeling the old misery inside him that night. "It's just that time of my life, Sammy. You know what I mean, don't you? That time when you can see more of it behind you than you can ahead? I was taking stock, you see, mulling over the things I'd done, all the ways I'd come up short and let down the people who'd meant the most to me. I was thinking about the way it used to be here in Rat Town. There was you and me and Mom and Dad. I wasn't even here when he died. That's how long it's been. I just read about it in the paper."

"You could have come back when you saw about Dad. It could have been that easy, Cal. Anytime, you could have come home."

"It wouldn't have been that easy, Sammy. Trust me."

So this misery, the gloom that comes from knowing most of your living is done, and what's worse, a good portion of it has been made up of things you regret. And nothing to do but carry it with you through the rest of your days. So it is with me and my brother.

Cal knew about Mink and the Michigan Militia and the plot to bring down the Sears Tower because that night at the VFW, they were drinking shots of Wild Turkey, and Mink started in on how the government had blood on its hands, started talking about Ruby Ridge and the federal marshals that came down on Randy Weaver. "You remember this story?" Cal asks, and I tell him I do. I remember Weaver, one of those survivalists with a stockpile of weapons and ammunition, and how the feds surrounded his cabin there in the woods of northern Idaho, and ended up killing his wife and son. Mink was pissed off about that, and then there was the Branch Davidian compound outside Waco. The feds set fire to it, Mink said, and killed everyone, killed women and children. "You'd think this country would have learned something from what McVeigh did in Oklahoma City," Mink said. "But, no, people won't learn a goddamn thing until we do it again, do it as many times as it takes. You know what I mean?"

Cal's head was lit up with Wild Turkey, and he said, well hell yes he knew what he meant, and that's when Mink started talking about the Sears Tower and that ammonium nitrate and just exactly how much he'd need. "I can tell you're a man who knows how to stand up for himself," he said to Cal, and it was the most perfect thing he could have said, considering what he wanted, to get Cal to agree to grease the wheels with Herbert Zwilling. The most perfect thing because somewhere deep inside him Cal was still the boy sitting on the hood of that coupe, listening to Grinny Hines tell him his snappy rayon shirt made him look like a queer. He was still the boy who was by-God ready for action. "You are that kind of man, aren't you?" Mink asked, and Cal said, "Damn straight."

This was the night before Mink walked into the feed supply with that rifle just like Cal had a feeling he might. "You see, Sammy," Cal says. "I woke up the next morning scared to death on account of what I'd said I'd do."

In the midst of the Wild Turkey and the hair-on-your-chest, cock-in-your-hand, fuck-yeah-let's-get-'em, Cal had said he'd take care of everything. Shit, yeah, he'd tell Herbert Zwilling what was what. "You just leave it to me," he told Mink, and they kept on drinking.

The morning, though, cleared Cal's head, and he could hardly stand to look at himself in the mirror.

Whenever he got down in the mouth, he went driving. Just got in his truck and hit the road. He'd listen to music—something mournful from George Jones, something jazzed up and sharp as a razor from Johnny Cash, and even opera, no matter he couldn't make heads or tails out of the words, he could still feel all that sorrow, and sorrow was what he felt, just out driving the morning after he'd told Leonard Mink he'd make sure he got that ammonium nitrate.

"Sammy, it's like this. Sometimes the dark gets inside me, and, when that happens, I can't predict what I might do."

He had a revolver, a Ruger Single Six with walnut grips, and when he went out driving the country roads, he took a shot now and then at a road sign or a mailbox just to let off some steam. "Oh, it was a stupid thing," he says, "but that's what I am sometimes—a stupid man." He'd done jail time in the past. Mostly public drunkenness, on occasion an assault charge. Somebody would say something he didn't like, and look out. "I can be a mean SOB. I know you might not think it to look at me. Good God, Sammy. I'm old and gone to shit."

So he was driving that morning, and he found himself going by the Paradise Inn. The Volare was there, backed into a spot in front of room number one. "I pulled in, and I got out and knocked on that door."

Mink let him in. He shut the door, and he took Cal by the arm, squeezed his bicep so hard it hurt. "You got it all planned out?" He gave Cal a rough shake. "Do you? You going to get me that fertilizer?"

Cal looked around the room. The bed was made up, the comforter tucked up around the pillows and smoothed out across the mattress. One boot was on the floor at the foot of the bed, a camouflage Army boot, like Mink would have worn in Desert Storm. The mate was on his right foot, the laces untied, the tongue hanging out. The heater was on in the room, and the air was close and it held in Mink's smells: the steamy, wet towel scent from his shower; the pleasant menthol of his shaving cream; the rich, metallic odor Cal recognized as the one that came from oil, the kind someone would use to clean a gun.

That's when he saw the rifle broken down and laid out on newspaper spread across the dresser.

"Last night," Cal said. "That was just talk, right? All that stuff about the Sears Tower? That was just bullshit between drinking buddies, right?"

Mink shook Cal again. "I don't bullshit, friend. When I say something I mean it."

"We were drunk," Cal said.

Mink pushed him over toward the dresser. "You see that rifle?" He waited, squeezed Cal's arm harder until Cal said, yes, he saw it. "You think I don't know what to do with it? Now either you make sense to your friend, Zwilling, or I'll have to see how persuasive I can be."

Mink shoved him, and Cal stumbled up against the dresser. Mink went to shove him again, and that's when Cal pulled that Ruger Single Six from his coat pocket. He let his arm swing up and the barrel of the Ruger came up under Mink's chin, and Cal kept pulling it higher, lifting Mink onto his tiptoes. Cal tightened his grip, and he could tell Mink sensed what might happen. His head went back, and Cal followed it, the Ruger's barrel still beneath his chin. He watched with delight as the heat went out of Mink's eyes, and he knew he was in trouble.

"I could have killed him, Sammy." Cal's voice goes flat now in my kitchen as if he's merely stating the fact he's turned over in his head time and time again until he's assured himself it's true. "I was mad enough to pull the trigger. I was this close to doing it, and I could tell Mink knew it. I won't lie. I took pleasure from that fact. Then, strange as it was, I heard your voice, Sammy, and it was the way it used to be when we were kids. I heard it as clear as day: *Hey, you asleep?* And I backed away. I let my arm drop, that Single Six stone heavy."

Mink took a step toward him, but Cal managed to raise that Single Six again, and he stopped. He let Cal back his way out of that room, get in his truck, stow that Single Six in the glove box and drive away.

Cal went to the grain elevator, and he told Herbert Zwilling he was afraid this Ansel King—this man he would soon know to be Leonard Mink—was on his way over there, and Cal wouldn't be surprised if someone ended up getting killed.

In the time it took him to finish telling Herbert Zwilling the whole story, Mink was there, and he had that rifle, the rifle that had taken him only a flash to reassemble, and Mora Grove made that call to 911, and in a snap the police were there and then the SWAT team, and Mink said, "Well, folks, it looks like we've got us a little situation."

Cal stops his story there. He stands in my kitchen and lets the minutes go by.

Finally, I can't stand the silence, and I say, "Did you kill him? Is that how Mink ended up dead?"

"You know the rest, don't you?"

"No," I say, "I only know that Mink ended up dead and everyone else walked away."

"The Sears Tower, Sammy. He would have found a way to get the job done. Mink. That's what people like him do. They find a way. I talked him into letting Mora Grove go, and then it was time to see whether Herbert Zwilling and I were going to make it out or not. I said to Mink, 'Well, what's it going to be? I'm tired of waiting, and I'm curious how you intend to get out of this mess. See that SWAT team out there? They're waiting, too. I think it's time to play your hand.' He said maybe I'd like to walk out there with him and tell the police everything there was to tell."

I take a breath and hold it, trying to decide whether to ask for the rest of the story, the one I might not want to know. Then I say it. "What did you know, Cal?"

He comes over to me, gets up close to my face the way I imagine he did in that motel room when he held that Single Six under Mink's chin. "You want to talk about Dewey Finn?"

"No," I say.

He backs away. "Okay then. And I didn't want to tell the police what I knew. Still don't. So there we were, me and Herbert Zwilling and Mink, and Mink asked me if I still had that revolver. I told him no, I'd left it in the glove box of my truck. That was the truth, Sammy. I'd been in such a hurry to warn Herbert Zwilling, I hadn't given a thought to having it with me when I walked into that grain elevator. 'I'll have to see for myself,' Mink said, and he told me to put my hands against the wall so he could pat me down. That's when I saw my chance. He was holding that rifle in his left hand while he used his right one to search me, and I swung around." Here, Cal demonstrates how he turned with his elbow high. "I caught him in the face, and I heard the cartilage snap in his nose. His hands flew up, and he dropped the rifle. I got to it first, and that's when I put an end to things. That's what I did, Sammy. I by-God made sure that Leonard Mink never got the chance to do what I'm sure he would have—killed Herbert Zwilling and me. I put the barrel of that rifle to Mink's head, and I pulled the trigger."

That's it, the end of the story, and it leaves me trembling with the thought of how everything could have gone another way if Cal had been a different sort of man, the kind who would have waited for the world to do whatever it had in mind for him. He would have ended up dead, and I would have been left to mourn that fact and to face the truth of Dewey Finn alone. But that isn't the way it went. Cal's in my house. The cuckoo clock in the living room sounds ten. Cal reaches up and gives my cheek a pat. "We had a good time tonight, didn't we, Sammy?"

"We did," I tell him.

Then he bids me good night and goes down the hall into his bedroom.

I stand in the kitchen, Stump nosing around on the floor where Cal has walked, recalling his scent. I'm shaken by the story he's told me, but relieved, too, because what happened in that feed supply has brought him back to me. I warm to the thought that now, after all this time, I might know the feeling of family again, even though I'm not exactly sure anymore what that word means. Cal's brought me this chance along with the sadness and the mystery of everything he's carrying with him, everything that eventually—I know this in my heart of hearts—will bump up against the story of Dewey Finn. It's what binds us now, my brother and me: the secrets we each have, these things that haunt us. Soon we'll know what they'll come to mean to the way we live the rest of our lives, and whatever that turns out to be, at least I know Cal and I will be together, brothers from here on.

I hear him singing now, his baritone voice still off-key. He's singing one of those old songs I remember him playing on the phonograph when we were boys and he still lived at home, Lefty Frizzell's "Travelin' Blues."

Stump waddles to the archway that separates the kitchen from the front room and the hallway leading back to the bedrooms. His ears perk up. He sniffs the air. Then he turns back and looks at me.

"You better get used to it," I tell him. "We've got company."

8

AS MUCH AS I WANT HIM HERE, IT'S ODD HAVING CAL IN MY house. The fact is I'm a man accustomed to living alone. I've become good at it. Ask Stump. He knows our routine. Up each morning around sunrise, coffee and toast for breakfast, the *Today* program on the television. I let him out to have a look around the side yard. If it's cold, he's back in a whipstitch, and while I wash the morning dishes he gnaws on his rubber horseshoe. Winter mornings, I let the television play on into the talk shows. I watch the programs where ordinary people show up to tell the whole blamed country about their sins and wounds and deformities. Stump lies on the floor by my chair, and from time to time I ask him if he's ever seen anything like it, the way folks go on. Then there's lunch to see to, and a nap in the afternoon, and before we know it, the boy delivers the evening paper and it's time for supper and a walk. This is the way my life has gone for years, and the past few weeks I've had Arthur's company of the evening to make things more pleasant. I've been getting used to the give and take of that friendship, and now here's Cal. I'm glad to have him with me, truth be told, particularly now when I'm afraid of what Duncan wants me to see at the police annex.

Cal is, as he made clear at the Seasoned Chefs, a whiz around the kitchen, and now he says he's glad to do all the cooking in return for his room.

"Sammy, relax," he says when I protest that I should be the one cooking for him. "I enjoy this," he says. "It's what I do, and I'm good at it."

He ducks his head and gives me a shy, aw-shucks grin. It's this sweetness in him that I remember so well from when we were boys, a sweetness under the temper and tough-guy cool he liked to show the world. At his age now, he's lost the edge of that temper, but then, without warning, it bristles up. This morning he prepares a shopping list, and I tell him I'll go to Wal-Mart after lunch and get everything he needs.

"Can't you do it this morning?" he says, and his jaw tightens. "I want to get to work on a roast for supper. It looks like you could help me out, for Pete's sake. After all, I'm cooking your meals for you." He closes his hands into fists and then relaxes them. His fingers open, and he gives me a strained smile, a forced chuckle, and like that he tries to make a joke of this little moment of heat between us. "I guess I'm still on Eastern Standard time. The day seems a little later than what it really is."

"I can't go this morning," I say, and before I know it I've let his brief show of anger prod me toward something I didn't plan to do: meet Duncan Hines at the *Daily Mail* office. "I have an appointment uptown," I tell Cal. "Ten o'clock. Duncan Hines has something he wants me to see."

"Something to do with Dewey?"

"I expect so."

"You should stay here. You'll give something away."

I shake my head. "It'll look funny if I don't go, like I've got something to hide."

For a moment, I'm tempted. Then I have to admit to myself that I'm curious, not only to know what Duncan's found but also to see what it'll mean to me. I tell myself that maybe what I see won't matter at all, that I'll be able to look at it the way I would if it were something from one of Duncan's *It's Us* stories—something about someone else—and I'll walk out of that annex finally free from that part of my life.

The phone rings, and it's Arthur calling up to say he's going over to the state park to have lunch at the Lakeview Inn and he wants to know if I'd like to come along. I tell him, no, not this time. I tell him my brother's still here, and I wouldn't be a very good host, would I, if I left him here all alone?

"Hell's bells, Sammy," Arthur says. "Bring him along. Three old sailors on shore leave. No one to answer to. We'll have a ball."

I tell Arthur, maybe next time, and I'm surprised by the twinge of regret I feel. Imagine—me, the old stay-at-home, just a wee bit sad to miss a chance to chum around with Arthur. Why shouldn't I say yes? I have Cal's shopping to do at Wal-Mart, and I'm afraid that if I take the time for lunch with Arthur and then come back to town to do that shopping, Cal will get fed up with me, and I'll come home and find him gone (if it happened once, it can happen again), and I can't bear the thought of that. Once, when the only picture I had of him in my head was the way he looked when he was a young buck, all jazzed up and full of himself, it was easy enough to think, wherever he was, he was doing well. But now that I've seen him as an old man—now that I've felt the sadness he carries with him—I can't bear to think of him alone, getting rotten and wheezy inside his skin.

"You know, Sammy," Arthur says. "Folks have been asking about you."

It cheers me to hear this, to know I've become the sort of person people would miss. "Folks?" I say.

"Some of the boys from the Seasoned Chefs. No one in particular."

And just like that I feel unremarkable. "Then why mention it?" I say, my voice sharper than I intend.

"Jeez, you don't have to be a sourpuss. Did you ever think maybe I miss having you around?"

"Do you?"

"Aw, jeez, Sammy, are you going to make me say it?" There's a long silence, and I refuse to fill it. I simply wait. Finally, Arthur says, "Okay, I'm hanging up now. I mean it, Sammy. I'm not going to say it. You can wait all you want, but I'm not saying another word. Honest to God. Not one more word. Sammy? Sammy, are you still there?"

"I'm here," I say.

"Good. That's good," he says, and then he hangs up the phone.

AFTER BREAKFAST, PEOPLE START COMING TO SEE STUMP'S house. Ever since the *It's Us* story ran in the *Daily Mail*, this happens from time to time. Some folks even come to my front door and leave Christmas presents for Stump: chew toys, dog biscuits, things like that. He graciously accepts them with a sniff and a lick.

"Looks like you're making out all right," I tell him.

We stand just inside the front door, and I bend over to scratch around his ears. He whimpers with delight.

"Lots of traffic around here," Cal says. Then he goes back into his bedroom and shuts the door.

I don't tell him how much it thrills me to see the people come, to have them chat a while.

It's one of those bright winter days with lots of sun, and I let Stump out in the yard. He climbs the gangway to the deck of his ship. I go out to chat with the folks who keep stopping by, to accept gifts if they've brought any, so they won't come to my door and cause Cal concern.

Finally, it's close to ten, and I tell Cal I'm going to meet Duncan, and, when I'm done, I'll do the shopping at Wal-Mart.

"It'll be too late for a roast," he says, and I just let him say it, and then leave him to stir in his own juices.

Uptown, the pine tinsel is wrapped around the streetlight poles; overhead the giant tinsel stars and candles sparkle in the sunlight. The time and temperature sign at the First National Bank reads 10:06, 32 degrees. Exhaust steams out of the tailpipes of cars idling in parking spaces by the *Daily Mail* office, and a woman in black slacks and a bright red sweater hurries into the post office. I take my coin purse from my pocket and fish out a quarter for the parking meter. It cheers me to think of myself as a law-abiding citizen with change for the meter and a careful attention to time. If not for everything swirling around me—Cal's story, and now this summons from Duncan—I'd be tempted to fall in love with this glorious day.

Duncan is waiting by the front counter, where a woman wearing white squirrel earrings types away at a computer. Then the phone rings, and she answers it. "Merry Christmas."

Duncan looks at his watch. "Mr. Brady," he says. He has his coat on, a quilted blue jacket, and a sock hat, black and orange striped. He's ready to go, and I know he's been thinking I wouldn't come. "It's almost ten after," he says.

"And I'm here," I tell him.

"So you are. All right, then. Let's go."

We walk across Whittle, around the south side of the court-house and then at Kitchell we turn to the south and walk the half block to the police annex, an old stone-block building, bars still on the windows. All the way, we don't say a word. Then here at the door to the annex, Duncan turns to me and says, "I was stunned when I came across this. I'm working on a story about the annex and the officer who catalogs the things they keep in the basement. I had no idea what I was about to find."

We go into an office on the first floor, and a woman with glasses on a chain around her neck says to Duncan, "Back to look around some more?" She doesn't wait for him to answer. She opens a drawer at her desk and hands him a key.

In the basement, he unlocks the door to a small room, snaps on an overhead light, an old fluorescent ring, and we step inside. Shelves line the walls, and they're stacked with cardboard cartons. Duncan finds the one he's after and sets it on a wooden table in the middle of the room. He takes off the lid.

"Go on," he says. "Look."

I stand over the box and look inside. The room smells of the stone walls—the damp and the must—and the stink of mildew comes from the box itself and what lies inside: even though they're tattered and torn, I know I'm looking at a pair of dungarees; a T-shirt with blue and yellow stripes; a pair of black high-top Keds sneakers, the white rubber toes scuffed and worn; a brown leather belt studded with silver-plated conchos the size of nickels; and a locking buckle, a treasure chest that has to be undone with a key before the buckle will open. I know that's the case because this belt was the most prized possession that Dewey Finn ever had. The underside of the belt is zippered, like a money belt, and he kept the key in a leather pouch right beside the buckle.

"They're his," I say, and my voice breaks. I recognize too late to do anything about it that Duncan has taken note of how shaken I am to be here looking at these clothes, the shirt and dungarees ripped and stained with what I know is Dewey's dried blood.

"That's right," says Duncan. "Dewey's. The clothes he was wearing that day at the tracks."

"So you know how it happened?"

"I've read the newspaper report."

I remember the story on the front page of the *Daily Mail* and the banner headline, LOCAL BOY KILLED AT B & O TRESTLE. A photographer had taken a picture of the train, the National Limited, after it finally came to a stop that evening. Readers of the paper could look at the engine head-on, the way Dewey would have, if indeed he turned his head and saw the train take the curve and bear down on the trestle. He was lying across the tracks, the article said. Dewey Finn, age fifteen, of Rat Town.

For a good while, I can't say anything. It's like I've traveled back fifty years, and I don't have any more idea what to say now than I did when Hersey Dawes came to tell the story of Dewey lying down on the tracks.

"I've got no idea why he did it," I finally say.

"That's not why I asked you to come here." Duncan is nearly whispering, and I remember the way people, not knowing what in the world to make of such a thing, spoke in low, halting tones at Dewey's funeral. "I thought you'd want to see this because Granny Nancy told me you and Dewey were close. Closer than just friends."

I ignore the insinuation. "He lived next door."

Duncan reaches into the box and lifts out the concho belt. He holds it across his palms and away from his body as if it's a snake. "This is quite a belt," he says. "I wonder why someone cut it. Something to do with the accident, I suppose." I see now that the belt has indeed been severed. The tongue still fits into the buckle, which is locked, and the other end of the belt is ragged from whatever blade cut it away. "What I'm trying to figure out," Duncan says, "is how this buckle opened in the first place."

"There was a key," I say, remembering Dewey thrilling to how mysterious this all was. I show Duncan the underside of the belt, where the leather is split, its seam barely noticeable. I part it, and find the hidden zipper. "This pouch," I say. "That's where Dewey kept the key."

Duncan puts his finger into the pouch and wiggles it around. "It's not there."

"It was just a little key," I say. "A little gold key."

"Who knows where it might have ended up?" Duncan lays the belt back in the box. "Imagine my surprise when the police chief told me there were still items stored over here, you know, things from past cases, and I found this box clearly labeled with Dewey's name and the date he died."

He shows me the lid, labeled with black marker, and I have to ask the next question. "Why would these things be here? Why didn't Dewey's parents take them, or why weren't they kept at the funeral home? Why the police?"

Duncan puts the lid down on the carton. "I guess they were looking into it at one time. There's a coroner's inquest, you know."

I remember that indeed there had been an inquest. "That's regular procedure when there's a suicide."

"Or when there's foul play."

Just a few hours ago, I convinced myself I could come here and look at whatever Duncan had to show me and feel distant from it as if it didn't mean anything to me at all, but now I see it was all bluff on my part. It takes me a while before I can find a voice steady enough to speak.

"The inquest ruled it was suicide. I remember that distinctly. He lay down on those tracks."

"Right," says Duncan. "The inquest. I've read it, you know. I've studied the attending physician's report about the wounds to the body, and something doesn't add up, Mr. Brady. The wounds ran vertically down Dewey's body—skull to chest to pelvis. To my way of thinking, that shows he was lying parallel to one rail and not horizontally across the ties the way someone would if he wanted to kill himself." He stops there and looks at me for a long time, waiting, I'm sure, for me to agree with him. When I don't say anything, he says, "These things were probably being stored until the inquest was finished. Then, for whatever reason—maybe the family just couldn't bear to have them back—they got put away here, and then all those years went by, and here we are, aren't we, Mr. Brady?"

I look him straight in the eye. "I don't know anything about the condition of Dewey's body or what it might mean. It was a horrible accident, one that never should have happened, and that's all I know about it. Now, if you'll excuse me, I have to be going. I told my brother I'd do some shopping for him. He wants to make a pot roast."

"All right, then," Duncan says. "I hope you didn't mind me showing you these things. I hope it didn't upset you too much."

"I'm fine," I tell him. Then I turn to go.

Before I reach the door, Duncan says, "I bet Dewey got a kick out of that belt buckle. I doubt there's many others like it."

"One of a kind," I say. Then I tell him good-bye.

IT TAKES A LONG TIME BEFORE I CAN BRING MYSELF TO start my Jeep and go on with my day because now that I've seen those clothes and that belt, all I can think of is the evening Dewey and I were walking down the alley that ran behind our houses, and he took my hand. That was all. He took my hand and held it while we walked. "Sammy," he said, "you're a pal." We were fifteen. We thought we'd be friends forever. But he took my hand. Then, at my back door, he leaned over and kissed me on the lips, and I let him. "Sammy, sweetheart," he said, and then he slipped off into the dark.

Sometimes, I close my eyes and dream myself back to that night. I feel the heat of his skin. I can still call to mind the way that alley in Rat Town seemed all at once a frightening and wonderful place. I had no words for it, the way I felt. All I could do was go on into my house and sit there alone in the dark and try to tell myself I wasn't the boy Dewey thought I was, wasn't like him, wasn't his sweetheart.

I was scared to death because he knew the inside of me, knew it before I did. It was a wrong thing to be, a boy who liked other boys the way he was supposed to like girls. I knew that, growing up in Rat Town where men like my father and my brother ragged anyone they thought didn't have enough lead in his pencil, called him a pantywaist or worse, called him a fairy or a queer, asked him who he was cornholing. You have to understand that I would have done anything not to be the boy Dewey somehow knew I was.

Then Cal told me that he saw us. That night in the alley. He saw Dewey take my hand. He saw that kiss.

He came into my bedroom one evening shortly after, and he said, "What's the story?"

"Story?" I said, not knowing yet that he'd seen what he had.

"You and your girlfriend."

"I don't have a girlfriend."

"Looked that way to me out there in the alley." I was sitting on the side of my bed. Cal put his hands on my knees and leaned in close to my face. He puckered his lips and kissed the air between us. "Sure looked like love," he said. "Sure did, Sammy sweetheart." Then he slapped my cheek, not just a pat the way he did sometimes when he wanted to get my attention, but a smack hard enough to make my eyes sting. "Hey," he said, "you asleep?"

FINALLY, I START MY JEEP, AND I DRIVE OUT TO WAL-MART, where I take my time. I let my slow parade up and down the aisles, the shy nods to the folks around me, bring me back to the world of the living. I find the things on Cal's list—the boneless chuck, the carrots and celery and potatoes, the olive oil and garlic cloves and oregano—and I let the time passing take me farther and farther away from that room in the police annex and those things of Dewey's that, though I didn't let Duncan know this, cut me to the bone.

When I come home, the sun is almost gone, and I know it's too late for Cal to make that roast for our supper.

When I open the kitchen door and step inside, I hear his voice coming from the living room. At first I think he must be talking to Stump, but, no, Stump is waiting by the refrigerator, eager for his duck and potato.

"Zwilling?" Cal says, and hearing the name of the man from that grain elevator in Ohio draws me up short and gives me the whim-whams. Is Cal saying it to me? Is he expecting Herbert Zwilling, or is that man—I remember his beefy face from the picture on the television—standing in my living room right now? "Zwilling, you still there?" Cal says. "I thought I lost you. No, it's this damn phone. The battery's going down."

I understand then that he's talking on his cell phone.

"Don't threaten me," he says, his voice rising. "Just let me take care of things."

I'm not sure what I've heard. I want to say it's nothing, only an ordinary conversation, but I fear that Cal hasn't told me the whole story about him and Leonard Mink and that plot to blow up the Sears Tower, and now here's Cal talking to Herbert Zwilling, talking to him with heat in his voice, and the promise to take care of things. I can't get it out of my head or ignore the way this all makes me feel, as if I've stepped into the middle of something I'm not meant to know.

Stump, tired of waiting for his duck and potato, barks. I slam the door closed, stomp my feet on the rug, make a big show of coming home. Then I call out, "It's me."

Cal doesn't answer right away, and the silence spooks me as if he's using it to gather himself, wondering how much of his conversation I've heard. I'm afraid to move. This conversation I've overheard—it's changed everything between Cal and me for reasons I don't even know.

"I'm in here, Sammy," he finally says, and what else can I do but walk into the living room where he sits on the couch, a handgun—the Ruger Single Six, I suppose—resting in his lap.

9

BEFORE I CAN SAY A WORD TO HIM ABOUT WHAT DUNCAN
showed me at the police annex and the things he said about the
coroner's inquest, Cal snaps the cylinder of the Single Six shut.
"They've been coming," he says. Spread out on the coffee table is a
section of newspaper and on it he has what he's needed to clean the
Single Six: swabs and solvent and brush and small patches of white
cloth and 3-in-One oil. "Coming all the while you've been gone."

I stand in the archway that separates the kitchen from the living room, afraid to move, afraid to take my eyes off that gun.

He tightens his hand around the grip.

"Who?" I ask him. "Who's been coming?"

"People." He raises the gun and uses the barrel to scratch his
chin. "They've been knocking on the door, coming around the
house, putting their faces up to the windows. I don't know who
they were. I just know they were nosing around." He gets up and
comes over to where I'm standing. He has the Single Six in his
hand. He taps the barrel against my chest as if he holds nothing
more than a pencil. "I didn't know what to make of all those people," he says. "I just knew I wasn't opening that door."

I keep my voice calm. I try to understand what's happening here, if indeed it's anything at all. "Cal," I say. "Your gun."

He looks down at his hand as if he's forgotten what it holds. "Jesus, I'm sorry, Sammy. It's just these people. They've got me on edge."

"They're nothing that concerns you." I whistle for Stump, and he comes to me. "It's all about Stump, folks just coming to get a look at his ship."

"That ship," Cal says with just a hint of disgust.

I can't stop myself. I tell him this is my home, and if I want to build a doghouse in the shape of a sailing ship I can. And I can have people stop by to see it, can invite them into my house even, offer them coffee and a place to rest awhile. I'm on a roll and I keep going.

"You were talking to Herbert Zwilling," I say. "I heard you when I came in the door. You said you'd take care of things. I don't know what that's all about, but I don't like the sound of it." I rub my hand over my head. "See? You've got me all worked up."

"You've worked yourself up. Looks like you and Arthur have been watching too many detective shows." He puts his hand on my back. "Jesus, Sammy. Let's sit down. Let's relax."

We sit on the couch, and he tells me Herbert Zwilling, in addition to owning the grain elevator and feed supply in Edon, is a collector, a man who scours the country for one-of-a-kind items. Cal was a finder for him. He went out and found the things Herbert Zwilling had an eye for. Their arrangement started when he learned that Cal was from Mt. Gilead. Zwilling had heard about a man there, a blind man who made a gold-plated Coca-Cola glass. Only one like it in the world.

"That's what I'm supposed to take care of," Cal says. "Zwilling wants me to see if I can hunt down that glass while I'm here, or at least find out something about where it might be."

It spooks me, hearing Cal talk about that gold-plated Coca-Cola glass, the one I found in the box of junk I bought at that blind man's auction. It's such a coincidence I hardly know whether to believe what Cal is telling me. I sit on the couch, aware that I'm in my own house, but it's as if I'm watching from a long way back, further even than the day of that auction and even farther back than the day I first read about that glass in the *Daily Mail*. That piece in *It's Us*, that glass, that auction. How in the world do they all add up to this moment now with Cal? Who would have ever thought that one contained the other? I can't find the words to say it, this feeling I have that if there's a God he's somehow alive in the world, somehow all around us and threaded through the smallest things, the little pieces of time we don't give a second thought until a moment like this—a moment when I have the oddest feeling that what's about to happen between Cal and me was written somewhere a long way back and has been waiting patiently for us to step inside it.

"That glass," I say. "That Coca-Cola glass. It's in my basement."

As soon as I say it, I feel time speed up. I'm aware that Cal is speaking, yammering on and on about what a coincidence this is and won't Herbert Zwilling be pleased, and who would have thought it in a million years, and I know we're getting up from the couch and moving through the kitchen to the basement door and on down the stairs, Stump galumping along behind us, but I'm really not aware of my body, of the steps I take, until I move toward a shelf in the basement and I find the cardboard box I'm looking for.

I've wrapped the Coca-Cola glass in butcher paper and hidden it away in this box. It seems a silly thing to do now that I'm un-wrapping the glass and showing it to Cal. Think about it. A blind man makes this one-of-a-kind, and then he dies and there's no one to give a hoot about that glass so it ends up in a box of this-and-that at his auction where a man who lives alone and doesn't know if he still has a brother alive on this earth buys it, brings it home, wraps it up, and hides it in his basement in this box. What sense does it make? This beautiful glass. I hold it out to Cal. The gold plating sparkles in the light. The slim pedestal widens toward the top, and across the glass in red letters are the words COCA-COLA, in flowing script. "Here it is," I say, and just like that, without a sec-ond thought, I hand it over.

"Well, that's something," Cal says. "That's just what the doc-tor ordered." He asks me how I've come to own it, and I tell him about the auction. "Imagine that," he says. "A glass like this just tossed away. It's a good thing you found it, Sammy." He winks at me. "Zwilling's sure going to be surprised." He holds up the glass as if he's toasting his friend. "He'll pay you a pretty dollar for this."

"What makes you think I'll sell it?"

Cal looks at me as if he's never considered the chance that I won't. He looks at me like a man who's not used to people saying no to him.

"You just had it stuffed away in this box," he says.

I take the glass back from him. "That's no sign it doesn't mean something to me."

"Sammy, don't be a knucklehead. What good is it to you?"

I wrap the butcher paper around the glass, and as I do, I think of the blind man scheming inside his head, figuring out exactly how to do it, gold-plate this glass. I think of the first time he held it in his hand, how he must have run his fingers over it, maybe even lifted it to his nose and breathed in the scent of that gold, pressed it to his cheek, felt the coolness and the raised edges of those etched letters. Surely, he traced them over and over, writing the words again and again with his finger, and surely he was happy. "You tell your friend if he wants to do business, he'll have to talk to me. Call him up right now if you want. Let me see what he has to say."

"Zwilling? No, you don't call Zwilling. When Herbert Zwilling wants to talk, he gets in touch with you."

Cal makes it clear that there's nothing more to say on the subject, and it feels strange to come out of this fantastic story about the Coca-Cola glass. I don't know what to say. I remember, then, that I haven't told Cal about what happened at the police annex. "You're not going to believe this, Cal, but they've still got the clothes that Dewey was wearing that night at the tracks. You remember that concho belt?"

"I remember," Cal says. "Just like it was yesterday. How could I ever forget?"

"And Duncan's read the coroner's inquest."

"The inquest said it was a suicide, didn't it?"

"Yes, but Duncan's starting to think otherwise."

"Tell him about Arthur, Sammy. Arthur and that night. Give him something else to think about."

"Leave Arthur out of this," I say. "He's had enough trouble. I don't care if I ever see that boy again if you want to know the truth. I hope he's done with me."

"I wouldn't count on it," Cal says. "Sounds like he's got his teeth sunk into a bone and he doesn't aim to stop gnawing until he bites it in two."

ZWILLING DOESN'T CALL. FRIDAY GOES BY, AND BY THE END of the day it starts to feel like Cal and I never had that conversation about him. We never went down in the basement and found that Coca-Cola glass, and the next thing I know it's Saturday, Christmas Eve.

My mail has an envelope addressed in what might possibly be the most beautiful handwriting I've ever seen. *Mr. Samuel Brady.* The envelope is red, and the ink is gold. The return address is written across the envelope's flap: *1515 N. Silver,* an address I don't recognize.

My first thought is, a Christmas card, but who do I know who would send me such a card? Not Cal, who would have no reason to put a card in the mail when he could just hand it to me. Not Arthur, who would do the same.

Cal says I shouldn't open the envelope. It could have anthrax inside.

"Anthrax?" I say, stupefied with the thought. "Who in the world would do a thing like that?"

"You never know, Sammy." He drinks the last of his morning coffee. "You just never know."

I put Cal's silly talk out of my head and study the envelope again. A woman's handwriting like that of the girls in school who wrote what the teachers always called "a pretty hand." I envied those girls who could make the act of forming letters seem like love. Even when they wrote with chalk on the board, they could do it. They could make me feel a squiggle in my heart. Each stroke and dip and loop and tail enchanted me. At night, those days after Dewey died, I tried to imitate the graceful movement of those girls' hands, but I could never get it right. Every word I tried—even my own name—looked ugly to me.

"Throw it in the trash," says Cal. "That's what I'd do. Or better yet, take it out back and bury it."

I can feel the gold ink on the envelope; my name has never

sparkled like this, never seemed so pure and wonderful, so . . . well, forgive me . . . so golden. I work my finger up under the flap. "Anthrax?" I say. "Cal, really."

"It could happen like that," he says. "Sammy, please."

But I open the envelope before he can stop me. Inside is an invitation to a special holiday gathering of the Seasoned Chefs at the Cabbage Rose Bed and Breakfast, hosted by Miss Vera Moon. *Regrets Only, 395-2845.*

A New Year's Eve Murder Mystery Dinner, one of those party games where the guests assume identities and become suspects and sleuths. This particular evening will have a gangster motif: *The Case of John Dillinger's Disappeared Doily.* The invitation explains that someone has made off with the doily from Dillinger's favorite chair, a doily he crocheted with his own hands. I've been summoned to *Very Vera's Vice and Vamp Valhalla* to get to the bottom of this despicable crime. *Happy Mickey Finn:* that's the character I'm supposed to play. *A speakeasy piano player known for slipping knockout drops in people's drinks.*

It's the name, of course, that spooks me. *Finn,* and that *Happy* doesn't help either. I hear in it more than a dab of irony, convinced, as I am, that Vera must surely understand that I'm not happy at all.

For an instant, it feels like she's speaking to me in code. *I know, I know,* she seems to be saying. *I know everything about you.* Then I decide this is just the world playing its devilish trick with coincidence. The sort of thing you wouldn't believe if you read it in a book.

"It's an invitation." I hold the card open so Cal can see. "An invitation to a party," I tell him. "No anthrax."

"Not this time," he says. Then he goes down the hall to his bedroom, and he closes the door.

I phone Vera right away, and I tell her it won't do. It won't do at all for me to attend this party. "I'm afraid I'm a stick in the mud," I tell her.

"Oh, don't be silly," she says. "It's just a holiday party, a gathering of friends, a little make-believe to spice up the night. For kicks, for laughs, for a hoot. You know, a whodunit."

This, you see, is the problem. So much of my life I've had this dread that somewhere, sometime, a finger will point in my direction, a voice will say, "Aha!"

Never would it happen that way. At least that's what I used to think before Duncan took me into that police annex. Now I have this feeling inside, this old worry. On Thursday when I was doing the most ordinary things—shopping for shoelaces at Wal-Mart, paying for gasoline at the Amoco, depositing my Social Security check at the Trust Bank—in an instant I could see myself for what I really am, a fraud. Someone would hold a door open for me, smile and say good morning, and I'd hear myself answer with a good morning of my own, and I'd swear the voice didn't come from me, a phony, who had no right to be moving among those kind and friendly folks. I saw a man in Wal-Mart do a trick for a child he didn't know, that one where it looks like he pulls a quarter out of her ear—even Leonard Mink knew that one—just so the girl might stop fussing and her mother could get on with her shopping. I heard a woman say to the bank teller, "Now those are pretty earrings." And I wondered what it would be like to be so in love with your life that you could reach out to strangers that way.

"Ducky, you really can't decline," Vera says. Stump has somehow pulled an empty can of duck and potato from the trash and is nosing the can across the kitchen floor. I watch him, admiring his persistence, while at the same time trying to pay attention to what

Vera is saying. "You're a crucial ingredient to the mystery. Without you, ducky, who will be our Happy Mickey Finn?"

"I daresay you've miscast me. Unless you're thinking in terms of knockout drops. I'm afraid I'm a bit of a snooze when it comes to parties."

Stump has shoved the can into a corner by the pantry, and there he settles down to his sniffing and licking, his rump up in the air, his tail wagging.

"You're shy," Vera says. "What a sweet boy. I could see that the first night you came to our cooking class. Maybe this is just what you need, a chance to be someone new."

"Oh, but don't you see?" I ask her. "I'm an old dog. It's too late for new tricks. Anyway you try to cook it, I'm the same old me."

"You just need a little zest. A little Very Vera."

I can see what Arthur means about her voice and how on the radio it must seem like she's talking right to him. *Ducky*, she says. *Sweet boy*. Her voice is like the pretty hand the girls wrote in school. Her words are all dips and glides and loops and tails. It's clear why once upon a time Cal fell in love with her, and why even now he might be wondering whether it's too late for something to happen for the two of them. "Sam," she says. "Sam, trust me. This is Vera talking. I know what's best."

"You're right," I say, though I intended to keep this conversation short, just my polite thanks for the invitation and my regrets on not being able to accept. "I'm a little shy," I tell her. "I wouldn't know how to act like someone else."

"It's all style. Ducky, it's all pizzazz. It starts with a costume. What will we need? A bowler hat, some sleeve garters, a pair of spats? I'll help with that. Are you free today? I'll come by after lunch."

Stump has given up on the can. He sits at my feet now, a look of expectation in his eyes. "I'm sorry," I say to Vera. "I just can't. My brother is still visiting."

Her voice gets even brighter. "Cal? Why, I guess you'll just have to bring that boy along. The more the merrier, right?"

"I can't."

"But you must," she says. "You're right here on my list. Arthur has already accepted for you."

I turn to my kitchen window and see Arthur and Maddie in his driveway. He's holding a snake of Christmas tree tinsel, twisted and bundled up in a knot. She's waving a fistful of icicles, those silvery strands some people like to drape on their trees. His breath comes out in a white puff of vapor when he speaks. She stamps her foot, throws the fistful of icicles at him, and then stomps off down the street.

"He had no right to do that," I say to Vera. "No right to speak for me."

"He's just trying to be a friend, Sam. If you don't like it, I guess you'll have to take that up with him."

Which I do.

I find him still in his driveway, a single Christmas tree icicle snagged on his ear. "Icicles," he says, with disgust. He swats at his ear with the hand that still holds the tinsel bundle. "Why in hell's bells would anyone want icicles *and* tinsel?" Finally, he throws the tinsel to the ground. "She just wants to fight, Sammy. She's always boiling for a fight, and over the dumbest things. I can barely say her name. 'Maddie,' I say, and she snaps at me. 'Leave me alone,' she says. 'Just leave me alone.' I ought to toss her in the brig."

"Maybe she's got reason." I pick up the tinsel bundle and start untangling it, hating myself as I do, because I've marched out here for the purpose of telling Arthur to mind his own business, only to find myself now offering him this favor. "Your mother throws you out in the snow, and you're barefoot? I imagine you carry that with you a while. How would you react to someone always trying to call the shots? She'll be hurting a long time from something you can't ever really know. Did you ever think about that? Ease up, Arthur. You're not at sea. She's not one of your sailors."

He yanks the tinsel out of my hand. "Are you trying to tell me how to handle my own granddaughter? What could you possibly know about what it is to have a family?"

Here it is, as glaring as the sunshine on the snow: exactly what Arthur thinks of me, an old bachelor who has no way of knowing how to love someone. Snow melt drips from Arthur's roof into his gutters; I hear a puny trickle drip down the drainpipe.

"I'm trying to tell you." My throat closes off, and my words choke in my throat. "Damn it, Arthur." I start again, this time with more force. "I'm trying to say I don't like it that you told Vera I'd come to her party. I'm a grown man. I can make my own decisions."

"Piss poor ones," he says. "Look at you." He jerks his arm toward my house, and the tinsel furls out and hits me in the face. "You and your dog," he says, "and a brother you haven't seen for God knows how long."

That's the worst thing he could say to me, to make it plain that for years the only living thing I've had in this world to care about and to care about me is a stump-legged basset hound.

"Looks to me like you don't have any room to talk about family," I say. "When's the last time you spoke to your son?"

Arthur's bluster retreats. He wads the tinsel up into his fist. "I didn't mean to hit you like that." He gets shy, and I stop myself from going on, storming at him like Maddie. I could tell him he's an old poop who's too full of himself, tell him he's so lonely without Bess all he can do is try to force himself into other people's lives. I could tell him to leave me alone, but I don't have the heart, and when he says, "I'm sorry," I've already turned away from him, already started back to my house. "A party," he calls after me. "A murder mystery. We'll have some laughs. Come on, Sammy. It'll be fun."

CAL DOESN'T COME OUT OF HIS BEDROOM FOR LUNCH. TWELVE o'clock goes by and then twelve-thirty, and, even though I'm hungry, I don't make a move to put any food on the table. I realize this has become what I expect from him, his cooking. I keep waiting for him to come into the kitchen to put together a soup or a sandwich and then the two of us will sit at the table and eat as if we've had this ease all our lives.

Finally, I tap on his bedroom door.

"Cal," I say. "It's almost one o'clock."

There's a long silence. Then he says, "I'm not hungry today, Sammy. I'm afraid I'm down in the mouth."

What it is that's thrown him into this snit I really can't say, and I don't have time to dwell on it because soon I hear someone knocking on the front door, and I remember that Vera said she'd be coming after lunch.

"It's Vera," I explain to Cal. "We're supposed to go shopping. Do you want to ride along?"

"Vera?" he says, a little lift to his voice, and I know he's considering it. "Sammy," he finally says. "I'm no good for anything today. I wouldn't want her to see me like this."

The knock comes again on the front door, and I go to answer it.

"Ducky." The scent of Vera's cologne comes in with the cold air as she steps into my house. She stamps snow from her boots— a pair of cream-colored boots, their tops so high that they disappear beneath the hem of her black wool coat. She steps inside and looks around my living room. "Sam," she says. "So this is where you live."

Suddenly I'm ashamed of my house. What do I have? A few knickknacks sitting around on the coffee table, the old console television set, the library table by the picture window. Mostly things I took from my parents' house after they were both dead: a paperweight from the Brulatour Courtyard in New Orleans; another from the 1954 National Plowing Contest held just up the road in Dundas, Illinois, which at that time was the population center of the country, an equal number of people living to its east and west; a flower vase that looks like an ear of corn; a doo-dad that's half of a chamber pot, a souvenir from Biloxi, Mississippi, that says, FOR ALL MY HALF-ASSED FRIENDS.

"It's not much," I tell her. I'm thinking of how out-of-date my home is: the orange shag carpet here in the living room, the dark wood paneling, the cracked Formica countertops in the kitchen, the dingy linoleum on the floor.

"Don't be silly," she says. "It's fine."

But it's not, really. I can see that now that she's here and I have to imagine my house from her perspective. The things I've grown accustomed to—the doily on my chair, discolored from where I've rested my head all these years; the old brown blanket on the couch, covered with dog hair; the cracked plaster above the archway that leads into the kitchen; the pull-down window shades torn and split—say this is the home of a man who has lost faith and has decided that the world can go on without him.

"Let me grab my coat and hat," I say. "Then we can go."

"What about Cal?" She tilts her head to the side and looks around me down the hallway. "I was hoping he'd do us the honor of his company."

"He's napping," I say. "Perhaps another time."

We drive uptown in Vera's car, a new-model Cadillac. A snow-ball made from white yarn dangles from her rearview mirror. The snowball has a goofy face: black button eyes, a carrot nose, and a cockeyed grin. A red and white striped sock hat sits atop the snow-ball and trails down to a red pom-pom. This snowball face bounces merrily as Vera turns onto Christy and heads uptown.

It's not much of an uptown these days, now that the Wal-Mart Supercenter is open on the highway. Gone is the Tresslers' Five and Dime where I once saw Rock Hudson drinking a root beer float at the lunch counter. Gone is Mike's Ice Cream Parlor and the Janet Shop and the Ball Rexall and Beal's Newsstand. No more Town Talk Restaurant or Turnipseeds or Gaffner's Jewelry or True Value Hardware. What we have now are empty storefronts or buildings turned into meeting places for church congregations and political parties and social service organizations. Even the Brad-ford pear trees, which were always so pretty each spring with their white blossoms, have been cut down so the blackbirds won't have places to roost. That's our uptown now, a place not even the trash birds care to visit.

A few shops have hung on. One of them is a vintage clothing and costume shop called *Déjà New*. It's been here as long as I can recall, passed down through three generations of the family who owns it. They've built a clientele from across the Tri-State. People come from as far away as Champaign and Terre Haute and Evans-ville. Not even the Wal-Mart Supercenter has been able to change that fact. Step into *Déjà New* and you can forget for a while that it's today. It can be any time you want it to be. Choose a rack—zoot suits, antebellum gowns, poodle skirts, flapper dresses, leisure suits, hammertail coats, top hats, derby hats, doublets, snoods—and you can pretend that years have melted away, that you're not even the person you see in the mirror but someone else you're thrilled to meet.

As Vera drives, I find myself, without planning to, telling her about the people who keep coming to look at Stump's ship. I'm telling her how, of course, it's silly, but still it amazes me, the fact that suddenly I, who never seemed to matter much at all to anyone, am now drawing all these people to me. "I know it's wrong to feel this way," I tell her, "but I can't help but be happy for their company. I never thought I'd be anyone who'd matter a whit to folks."

She pulls the Cadillac into a parking space and turns off the motor. I open my door and start to swing out my legs, but she reaches over and closes her hand around my arm and I have no choice but to turn back to her.

"Sam," she says. Then she looks away from me, as if she's suddenly reconsidering. I wonder if somehow I've already disappointed her. She tugs at the fingers of her black, leather gloves and pulls them from her hands. I've never really noticed her hands before, not the way I do at this moment, as she lets them rest in her lap and I see the wrinkled flesh and the age spots and the wedding ring, its band cutting into her skin. If someone were to show me those hands, I'd never guess they belong to Vera Moon. Vera of the bright voice on the radio, the confident voice at the Seasoned Chefs cooking classes, the gracious Vera, the perky Vera, the Vera who always seems undaunted by time's march. "My husband died a long time ago." She traces a finger over the stone in the wedding ring. "So long ago, you'd think it would start to feel like it wasn't anything that ever happened in my life. But that's not the truth of it, is it, Sam? The real things—the ones that matter—they stick with you."

I can't help but feel close to her at this moment when we're both being honest and blunt about our lives and how they often leave us dumb and staggering. "Yes, that's the way it is, Vera. That's it exactly."

"I feel so sorry for Arthur," she says. "He lost his dear Bess. All those men in the Seasoned Chefs. I shouldn't say this, Sam, but you're all so dear to me. You all know what I know. Misery loves company, yes? But they say it's a sin to wish our sorrows on someone else." Her face tightens and I can tell she's trying hard to fight back the tears. "After my husband died, I went back to my maiden name. I know I should be ashamed, but it was just too hard to be the woman I really was. It was too hard to be that widow. Somehow going back to being Vera Moon made me feel better. Maybe it's like that for the people who come to see your dog and his ship. Who's to say what it takes to make our days a little easier?"

I find myself nodding. Yes, I tell her. Yes, that's right.

Then she does the most amazing thing. She reaches over and plucks a loose thread from my coat. "You're coming unraveled," she says with a smile, and it's like we've spent years and years together and can do a thing like this, just like a husband and his wife.

WHEN I GET HOME, I SEE THAT THE DOOR TO CAL'S BED-room is still closed. I try to be quiet as I move about the house, hanging my costume for Vera's party in my closet (a pinstripe shirt that requires a celluloid collar, a bowtie, a pair of dark trousers with a pleated front, spats, red sleeve garters, braces, a derby hat). Then I hear footsteps on the porch and, when I open the door, a folded piece of paper flutters down to my feet.

The UPS man picks it up and hands it to me. "Looks like someone left you a note." Then he gives me a package and wishes me a Merry Christmas before bounding down the steps and going back to his truck.

I let Stump sniff the package. "It's your Christmas present," I whisper to him, "but you have to be a good boy and wait."

I put the package on my dresser. Then I unfold the note, and I bite my lip when I see it's from Duncan. *Mr. Brady*, it says. *I need to talk to you. Please call me. 395-3281.* I tear the paper into strips and drop them in my trashcan.

In the hall, I stand at Cal's door, listening for some sound of him moving about. I start to feel guilty about going off with Vera when I knew he was feeling blue. I decide I'll do something nice for him. I'll drive out to Wal-Mart and buy him a Christmas present— maybe a CD for him to listen to, maybe a cap or a pair of socks.

I go out to my driveway, where my Jeep sits, and as I pass the side door of the garage, I see through the glass that Cal's Explorer is gone. I open the door and step inside. There's the faintest scent of exhaust, a sign that I'm not dreaming, that indeed my brother was here, and now—surely it was happening while Vera was driving me home—he started up his Explorer, and, just like he did long ago, he drove away, leaving me alone to face whatever, thanks to Duncan, might be bearing down on me.

Then I see a piece of paper on the garage floor, a piece of note-book paper folded in half, the crease so worn, it's started to come apart. Written just above the crease, in a cramped handwriting I recognize as Cal's, is a street address, *5214 Larkspur Lane.* I un-fold the paper, taking care not to tear the crease any more than it's already torn, and light shines through in the center.

It takes me a while to understand what I'm looking at, but finally I see that it's a map, hand-drawn: a grid of streets, and a series of rectangles and squares, some of them labeled with the names of the buildings they represent and some of them with question marks inside them. The streets running from the top of the page to the bottom are labeled—Jefferson, Clinton, Canal, Wacker, Franklin, Wells, and La Salle—and the streets running left to right in the center, where the crease is tearing, are designated as Jackson and Adams. The printing is small and cramped with a slight backward slant. I know that the map could have only ended up in my garage because it fell from Cal's Explorer, slid from the stack of loose papers and trash in his front seat, or was lifted up and blown with the breeze of him slamming his door shut on this day he's driven away from me.

I squint to better read the small printing. Inside one square are the words CITY CENTER. In another, BANK. One rectangle is identified as AMTRAK, another as GARAGE. But it's the one in the center of the page that makes my heart pound. I squeeze my eyes shut and open them, taking a closer look, wanting to make sure I'm reading the printing correctly. There it is, exactly what I thought it said: ST. I know I'm looking at a map of downtown Chicago. I know I'm looking at the Sears Tower. A dotted line leads away from it, heading west on Adams, toward what I know now is Union Station and the parking lots around it. There's an arrow at the end of the dotted line and then the words, TO CAR.

10

IN THE HOUSE, I OPEN THE DOOR TO CAL'S BEDROOM, AND I
see that his duffel bag is still in the closet. His shirts and blue
jeans hang from the clothes rod. His socks and T-shirts and boxer
shorts are folded neatly in the bureau drawer. A bottle of cologne
sits on top of the bureau. I open it and breathe in its scent. Then I
go out into my kitchen to wait.

All evening, I sit near the window, hoping that any minute I'll
see Cal pulling into my drive. When he does, I'll ask him straight
out. I'll slap that map down on the table, that getaway map, and
I'll say, "Cal, what gives?"

Night comes, and I open a can of tomato soup and heat it on
the stove. I eat it with Saltines.

Stump keeps going down the hall to nose around in Cal's
room. I let him, even though I know there's nothing there but Cal's
scent, detected only by Stump, who comes from a long line of
hunting dogs. Basset hounds keep tracking, curious about everything they smell. I know, if I were to let Stump out, he'd follow
Cal's trail. He'd go and go. He pads back out to the kitchen and
looks at me, and I swear I can see the disappointment in his eyes.

He paws at the door and whines to be let out into the yard. I make sure the gate is closed, and then I let him out. I watch him as he makes his way to the garage, nose to the ground. He sniffs around the small side door. He sits there and barks, baying at the smell that he knows continues on the other side of that door.

I go outside and open the door so he can go into the garage and have a look-see. He smells the floor where the Explorer was parked. He goes to the wide, automatic door and looks back at me as if he expects me to put it up so he can get out there on the trail and find out once and for all where Cal has gone.

"It's just the two of us," I say. I get down on my knees and take his muzzle in my hands. I tip up his face so he'll look at me. "Just us," I say, and he shakes his head free from my grip. He snorts as if to say he finds the situation completely unacceptable.

IN HOPES THAT IT WILL CHEER HIM UP—ALL RIGHT, WHO AM I kidding, in order to keep from thinking about that map and what it might mean—I decide to give Stump his present. It's a French sailor's costume I ordered from one of those companies that make clothes for dogs. Normally, I'm opposed to this ghastly practice. What's more miserable than the sight of a Chihuahua wearing a tutu or, worse yet, a majestic German Shepherd in a wedding gown? But I ordered the costume back in the autumn after Arthur and I built the ship for Stump. I saw the French sailor's suit in the catalog, and I thought, won't Arthur get a kick out of this. He was taking me to the Seasoned Chefs, and like I've said, we had our domino games and our old movies and our coffee. I'd come to think of him as a companion, and I thought the sight of Stump in a French sailor's outfit would give him a chuckle.

I slip the collar over Stump's head. The collar is blue with white trim, a red bow at his throat and a ribbon trailing down his chest. I set the flat blue hat on his head and, good dog that he is, he looks up at me so I can easily stretch the elastic band over his muzzle and settle it at his throat. He barks once, and the red pom-pom on top of the hat does a merry jounce.

It's the pom-pom that does me in, brings back what Arthur said to me earlier: *Look at you. You and your dog.* Yes, look at me: a sixty-five-year-old gay man, dressing his basset hound in a prissy French sailor's costume. Shame on you for thinking I had no sense of humor about myself. For a moment, I'm tempted to take the costume off Stump and throw it in the trash. What a sad, ridiculous picture we make.

Then he hurries, at least as much as a basset hound will, to the back door. He barks again, letting me know that he's ready for his Christmas Eve walk. He's ready to parade down the street, a jaunty French sailor on shore leave. It's the night of make-believe and magic—soon, the radio disc jockeys and the newscasters on television will be saying radar has picked up Santa and his sleigh—so why can't I dress my dog up in a silly costume and show him off to the world just for the sheer joy of it?

We step out into the cold night air, and everything is so still I can hear Christmas music playing over the loudspeakers in the city park. It's that kind of night—calm—and though I'm five blocks away I can hear the same notes of "Joy to the World" that the people in their cars are hearing as they take their time driving through the park.

All along our street, the homes are decorated with lights. Lights around the windows. Lights hanging from gutters. Lights outlining the roof peaks. Lights in the evergreen bushes. Lights in the pine trees, the cedar, the spruce. White lights, red lights, green lights. It's enough to make me wish that Stump and I might meet someone on our walk, someone who might take note of the sailor's costume and make a joke. *What a handsome little Frenchman. Are you out looking for a poodle? Hoping to meet a Fifi or perhaps a Pierre?*

Maybe that someone could be a man, a man like me. Perhaps you thought I was beyond hoping for romance. Cal asked me if I ever had boyfriends, and I told him no, which wasn't the whole truth. I know you won't believe this, but remember when I saw Rock Hudson one summer having an ice cream float at Tressler's lunch counter? Let's just say we struck up a conversation. Let's just say we became friendly and leave it at that.

And there was a man once who caught my eye in the IGA. I was in my forties at the time, young enough to feel desire and yet old enough to know it came from loneliness. "Old enough to know better," my father used to say when someone wished him a happy birthday and then asked his age, "but too young to resist." Anyway, this man in the IGA caught my eye. There we were, each of us pushing a shopping cart, and I didn't know him from Adam. He was just this man—I'd never seen him around town—just this tall man with a neatly trimmed mustache and the cuffs of his shirt folded back from his wrists. A man my age, his hair starting to gray, this full head of hair combed back from his forehead and held in place with tonic. I smelled it as we passed in the aisle. He smiled at me, and it was a nice smile, one that made me imagine what it would be like to come home to that man every night of my life. At the end of the aisle, I turned around and there he was looking at me. He hadn't moved an inch from where he'd been when I'd passed by him. He stepped away from his cart. I remember he only had three items in it: a loaf of Wonder Bread and a package of lunchmeat—sandwiches for a man who didn't cook—and a small box of cookies, the kind the store asked too much for, gourmet cookies with chocolate and mint that a person would buy for a treat. Sometimes I bought them myself—that's why I noticed them in his cart—just so I could have one after supper from time to time.

As he stood in the middle of the aisle, he lifted his eyebrows and gave just the least bit of a nod of his head toward the front of the store. It was spring, and outside the sun was shining, and, when I stepped out there, as I knew I soon would, that sunshine would warm my face and the air would smell of the earth thawed from its winter freeze.

The man took his time walking across the parking lot. Blue and orange pennants swayed from the light poles, lifting and falling in a lazy breeze. The sun glinted off windshields and chrome bumpers. I shaded my eyes with my hand and saw the man open the door of a blue Ford Galaxy. He paused a moment, one hand on the door, one reaching in for the steering wheel. He kept his eyes on me, and I knew that I was to get into my own car and follow him.

We drove out into the country, into Lukin Township, and then the Galaxy turned down a gravel road. The man slowed down, and I knew he was being mindful of the dust he was throwing up behind his tires, trying to spare me.

That kind gesture makes it difficult for me to say what happened next. I got to thinking about Dewey and the kiss he gave me the night we walked down the alley behind our houses, holding hands. A sweet kiss. From that point on, though I didn't know it at the time, I'd never be able to feel a man close to me with the same sweetness that I had that night with Dewey.

The Galaxy turned down a lane that led back to a deserted farmstead. I stopped my car on the gravel road, idling there at the mouth of that lane, unable to turn the wheel and follow. The Galaxy's brake lights came on, and the man stopped, waiting for me. Then I pressed down on the accelerator and went on up the gravel road. I found my way to the blacktop and went back into town. I went back to the IGA, and, believe it or not, our carts were still there right where we'd left them. I could barely stand to look at his—that Wonder Bread and lunchmeat and those cookies I'd never be able to buy for myself after that day. If I knew where that man was now, I'd tell him I'm sorry I left him there in that lane.

I can barely stand to think of all this as Stump and I take our walk. The only person we meet is Arthur. He's at the corner, so much in a rush that he almost steps out into the path of a car. I have to take his arm and keep him on the curb.

"It's Maddie." When he looks at me, his eyes are wild. "She's gone again, and I can't find her."

"Again?"

"She came home, and I told her all right, we'll have tinsel *and* icicles. Everything was shipshape. Then I told her to open her present."

"The skirt and top."

Arthur nods. "Let's just say here's one time when Vera didn't quite make the right recommendation."

I see the fear in him, and, no matter how much he hurt me earlier, I'm ready to offer my help.

Then he looks down at Stump, and for the first time he takes in that French sailor's outfit, and he says, "Jesus Christ," says it as if he's just seen the most pathetic thing in the world, and all I can bring myself to say is, "I hope you find her," before turning, tugging on Stump's leash, and heading off down the street.

I go around the block, circling back to my house.

Arthur's house is dark. His Chrysler isn't in the driveway, and I imagine he's driving the streets now, looking for Maddie.

I open the gate to my side yard, and as Stump and I pass his ship, I smell cigarette smoke. Stump strains against his leash, and I let him take the lead. He pulls me toward the ship, where he sniffs at the pet door that leads into the hull. Then he tugs harder at the leash and he begins to bark.

Something scrabbles around inside the ship. It takes some doing on my part, but I get down on my knees there in the snow. I pull the door away from the hull, and that's when I see the fire of a cigarette, and I say, "Maddie, is that you?"

"No," she says, "it's Santa Claus taking a smoke break."

I can only see her when she puffs on her cigarette and its fire spreads a dim light over her chin and the tip of her nose. "You can't stay in there," I tell her.

"Seems pretty cozy to me."

"Your grandfather's worried about you. He's out looking for you right now." She has nothing to say to that. She only draws on her cigarette again, and I hear her breath as she exhales the smoke. "It's Christmas Eve," I say.

She starts crying in earnest now, hiccupping sobs she couldn't hide if she tried. She tries to say something between the hiccups. "Do . . . you . . . know . . ."

"Do I know what?" Although the sound of her crying is something I feel in my throat, I keep my voice patient and calm. "What is it, Maddie? Go on, you can tell me."

"It's him," she says. "He doesn't know anything about who I am."

Something comes flying toward me, a piece of cloth that strikes me on the chest and then falls onto the snow. I pick it up, and from the feel of the material and from what Arthur told me earlier, I can make a good guess at what I'm holding in my hand.

"The skirt or the top?" I ask.

"Half of the top," she says. Several more pieces of cloth come fluttering out the pet door. "Here's the rest of it, and most of the skirt. Why would he ever think?"

"He was just trying," I say. "You can't blame him for that."

"We're strangers," she says in a tired whisper. "That's what we are. I see him maybe once or twice all my life, and then, bam, I'm living with him. How would you like it?"

I imagine she's right. How hard it must be for the two of them tossed together now because her mother's in trouble with dope and her father is incommunicado south of the border. "I guess you'll have to get to know each other," I say. "What choice do you have?"

"I could stay right here."

"No, I think eventually you'd freeze."

"You should have heated this place."

I don't tell her that I'm thinking about it. I've been studying up on how to wire the ship's hull with thermostat-controlled electrical heating elements. I don't tell her because I don't want her to think I'm being ridiculous about Stump, who has started to chew on some of the scraps of cloth that Maddie threw out of the hull.

"Looks like Stump agrees with you about that outfit," I say.

Maddie crawls over to the pet door and sticks her head outside. She starts that baby talk. "Stumpie-Wumpie," she says. "Yes, that's a good boy. What a good boy. You old Stumper-Wumper, you." She reaches out to scratch his ears and that's when she notices the French sailor's outfit. "Oh, look at you. You handsome devil, you. *Très chic. Oui, oui.*"

"It's his Christmas present," I say. "Too much, you think?"

She has her arms around Stump's neck, and she's pressing him to her with a tenderness I can feel in my chest. "Not a bit," she says. "It's just perfect."

I can't tell you exactly what comes over me, only to say it's a feeling I haven't had for a long time, a sense that here's this girl who will let me be who I am, and I say to her, "Come inside my house. Get warm. We'll figure something out."

She pulls away from Stump and looks at me. Here we both are, kneeling in the snow on Christmas Eve, and there's that music off in the distance at the city park—"Silent Night" is playing now—and Maddie says to me, "All right. Just for a while."

Then she stands up and reaches her hand out to me, and I let her help me to my feet.

INSIDE MY HOUSE, MADDIE FLOPS DOWN IN MY RECLINING chair and picks up the remote control from the end table. She kicks up the leg rest and clicks on the television. Music swells: the *I Love Lucy* theme song.

"TV land," Maddie says with a smug nod of her head. "Yep. That suits you."

I'm stooped over, taking off Stump's leash. "How do you figure?"

Maddie mutes the sound. "Look."

I straighten and watch the TV. Everything's in black and white, of course. There's Lucy in their New York City apartment, playing the piano, the flared skirt of her dress fanned out about her legs. Ricky is standing beside the piano, and he's wearing a Santa Claus suit, at least the coat and the pants and the boots. He doesn't have on the hat or the fake white mustache and beard. His glorious black hair is perfectly combed, and he's snapping his fingers as he sings. The Mertzes are there. The Mertzes are always there. Fred's trousers are up high on his big belly, and he rests his hands on its shelf. Ethel has that angelic look on her face that says even though she's married to an old poop like Fred she still thinks her life is wonderful.

Without the sound, it's as if I'm watching someone's home movies. Lucy finishes the song with a flourish, her hands coming down hard on the keys. Everyone holds that last note—whatever the song is—mouths wide open, and then Fred pats Ricky on the back, and Ethel puts her arm around Lucy's shoulders and gives her a squeeze, and everything's all right there. You can tell that even without any words. Everything is A-okay, hunky-dory, apple-pie grand.

Then the feeling starts to come to me, the way it always does when I look at old photographs or when I daydream too long about something that happened way back when, that there's this whole life that these people don't know about. This inevitable life. It's just waiting for them. Sooner or later, Cal will come back—his things are still here, so he has to come back, right?—and I'll ask him about that map, and then who knows what will happen next.

I want to explain the feeling I have to Maddie, but it's hard to find the right words, and all I can manage is, "There they are."

"Exactly," she says. "It gives me the shivers, too."

The telephone rings, and Maddie clicks off the TV, puts down the chair's leg rest, and springs to her feet. She looks at me and puts a finger to her lips.

"I have to tell him," I say.

"You could let it ring."

"Maddie, he knows I'm home. He can see the lights."

"I don't want to go back there."

"We'll work it out," I say. "You'll see."

But it isn't Arthur on the phone. It's Vera. "Our boy's over here." For a moment, I wonder whether she means Cal: maybe he's gone to pay her a call. Then she says, "He can't find his granddaughter," and I know she's talking about Arthur.

"Yes," I say, "that's what he told me earlier. I was out walking my dog. It was that time of evening, you see, that time when Stump . . . that's my dog . . . needs to go for a walk." I'm not sure why I go to such pains to explain how I happened to be out at the same time Arthur was looking for Maddie. As if a man can't take a walk with his basset hound, who just happens to be wearing a French sailor's suit on Christmas Eve. "I was walking my dog," I say again, "and I ran into Arthur."

"He's plenty worried." Here Vera's voice shrinks to a whisper, and I hear her heels clicking over the floor as she moves, so I assume, out of range of Arthur's hearing. "Oh, ducky. He's out of his head with worry. He's sitting in my living room right now, and he's crying. A man like him. Sam, it breaks my heart."

Maddie stands close to me, close enough so she can tilt her head toward my ear, trying to hear every bit of my conversation with Vera. I smell a faint tang of cigarette smoke from Maddie's hair and the wool from her sweater and a trace of vanilla—a shampoo or powder or lotion, I assume. All in all, it's a pleasant smell. What I'm saying is, I don't mind it. A strand of her hair tickles my neck. She comes up on her toes, trying to get even closer to the receiver. She has to lay her hand on my shoulder for balance, and this intimacy makes it seem that we've lived comfortably together in this house for years.

"I'm sorry this is happening," I say to Vera. "Sorry for Arthur."

"He's thinking he should go to the police, but he wanted me to call you first to ask if you could see any lights on in his house. Maybe the girl's come home."

"No. No lights."

"Then I guess it's going to have to be the cops."

"Vera, wait." Maddie draws away from me. A stir of air passes over my face, a last sniff of vanilla. She crosses her fingers.

She mouths the word, *please.* I don't have time or the nerve to tell her I don't want to do this, to explain that I'm glad for her company, that I wish we could pretend a little longer. I don't know how to explain that I have no right to her, that family, no matter how shaky, is always more important than one person's loneliness. "Tell him she's here," I say to Vera. "Tell Arthur I've got her."

I hang up the phone, and Maddie bangs her hand down on my kitchen counter. "I can't believe you ratted me out," she says.

What was I to do, I ask her. Lie? "He's worried about you," I say. "Vera says he's over at her house right now, crying. That's how worried he is."

"He *should* be worried." Maddie crosses her arms over her chest and makes her head do a sharp bob, the way that Jeannie did on that old television program whenever she wanted something to change. She crossed her arms, blinked her eyes, nodded her head, and presto: a grown man shrank to the size of a snap pea, a dog became a camel, people traveled back in time.

But nothing changes for Maddie. Here she is, still in my house on Christmas Eve, mad at her grandfather, who, I'm sure, is on his way to get her.

"He loves you," I say. "Look at what he's doing for you. Taking you into his home. Taking care of you until your mother gets well."

"Gets well?" Maddie's arms come undone, and she puts her hands on her hips. She opens her mouth and stares at me as if she's trying to make sure that she just heard what she thinks she did. "What kind of sick joke are you trying to pull? Last time I checked, Sam-You-Am, no one 'gets well' "—as she says this, she lifts her arms and curls the first two fingers on each hand into air quotes— "from being dead."

Now it's my turn to question whether I've heard correctly. I go back over the story Arthur told me about Maddie's mother and her methamphetamine addiction.

"Your mother," I say.

"Dead."

"But . . ."

"Dead." Maddie is shouting now. "Dead, dead, dead."

Stump comes to her. He noses around her legs, barks at her until she stoops down to pet him. *Don't shout*, he tells her when he licks her face. *Don't shout. I'm here.*

I have stones in my throat. Sorry that I've hurt her. I try to explain. "Your grandfather told me your mother had a drug problem, and that's why you're here."

"Is that his story?" She gives Stump one last scratch behind his ears and then straightens up to face me. "It doesn't surprise me. That's how ashamed he is."

She tells me the real story. Her mother died of AIDS, which she caught from having unprotected sex with a man who used heroin. "Shot up smack," Maddie first says, and I have to ask her to please speak in language a man like me, one who doesn't know the lingo of this and that, can understand. *Heroin*, she says. *IV drug user. Exchange of bodily fluids.* She thrusts her pelvis forward. "You know," she says. "The old humpty-dumpty."

I hold up my hand in protest. "Please," I say. "This isn't my business."

She puts her tongue to her front teeth, and her jaw juts out and her lips curl with what I can only call disgust. "Too much for you?" she asks.

"Please," I say again. "This is a matter of your family's. Something now between you and your grandfather. It's not for me to be a part of."

"But you *are* a part of it," she says, her voice now overly sweet, the way Vera's can be when she's telling the Seasoned Chefs how to prepare a dish or when she's on her radio show. "You know the story," Maddie says. "The *real* story. It's yours now, Sam-You-Am. It's up to you what you do with it. You can ignore it. You can tell it to someone else. You can shake your head and say, *my, my, my.* You can think, *oh, how fucked up these people are.* Pardon my French. Choices, Sam. We all make choices." She moves to the kitchen window and looks out across my side yard to a set of headlights sweeping now into Arthur's driveway. "Here he comes," she says. "Here comes the Pope. What's it going to be, Sam?" She turns back to me, and I see tears wet on her cheeks. "Are you going to let me stay here with you or not?"

"Here?" I say.

"Choices," she says. "Sam, I don't have too many left."

Arthur doesn't knock on my back door. He opens it and comes marching in. "Maddie," he says. He doesn't bother to close the door behind him, and the storm door, once it claps shut to the frame, clouds over with condensation, the warm air inside my house meeting the cold on the other side. "Maddie," he says again. "Good Christ."

His face is red, and despite the cold, sweat beads up on his forehead. I can smell liquor on him. This isn't to say that he's drunk. I don't believe he is. But it's clear that he's had a drink or two, something I imagine Vera offered to brace him while he told her about Maddie.

"You're drunk," Maddie says to him.

"Maddie," he says, "don't be like that. You know it isn't true. Now let's go home. Let's get out of Sammy's hair."

She stares at me and lifts her eyebrows as if to say, *Well?*

I remember what she's just told me about choices and how I

can ignore her or judge her or make her the subject of gossip. She's right. Once we know the hidden life, the secrets someone carries, how can it not be ours? How can it not be something we live? I think of Cal and all he told me. I think of that map and all that's about to become mine. My life used to be so simple, no one expecting anything of me, no one but Stump—and he's always easy to please. Now here are all these people. Now I have all their stories.

"Arthur," I say. "Let's all sit down. It's Christmas Eve. Please. Let's sit down and talk."

Sometimes all we can hope is that someone will come forward and say, *Here. Listen. This is what you should do.* I know this to be true because it's what I did once upon a time when I was friends with Dewey Finn. I was young and stupid. I was Cal's little brother, and I didn't understand that I could determine what happened next.

So I tell Arthur. I tell him that he and Maddie are like oil and water right now—not a good mix. "I don't believe that's anything to be ashamed of," I say. "That's just the way families are sometimes." If he wants, he can think I know nothing about what it is to be a family, but once upon a time I did. I could tell him, if I chose, that I know what it is to always feel this strain in the heart, this ache that he feels now. Instead, I say, "Anyone can see how much you love each other."

Maddie, who's sitting on the couch chewing on her fingernails, spits one into her palm and says, "Ha!"

"You see?" Arthur comes up from his chair and points a finger at her. "Sammy, do you see the thanks I get from this one?"

"Why did you lie?" Maddie's on her feet now, too. Her fingers curl into fists. "Why did you lie about Mom being dead?"

Stump is barking.

"Please," I say. "Please, let's calm down."

Arthur turns away and storms across the room to the library
table in front of the picture window. He stands with his back to us,
his head bowed. Maddie sinks back down on the couch.

"It's not the kind of thing you talk about," Arthur finally
says, and his voice is so low it seems to come from somewhere in
the distance. "The thing that killed your mother. It's not something to admit to people."

"It's the truth," Maddie says. "And it's part of us, part of who
we are." She looks at me. "You see the problem?" Then she stands
up and moves across the room to Arthur. She takes him by the
shoulders and turns him so he has to face her. "Look at me," she
says. "Why can't you just look at me, at us? Why can't you admit
how fucked up everything is?"

"Don't swear," he says.

"Fucked up," Maddie says again. "That's exactly what we are.
We're smack-dab in the middle of—'Oh, no, Toto'—Fuckville. We
could book ourselves on one of those slimy talk shows. Maury
Povich, Jerry Springer." She opens the thumb and pinky on her
right hand and, keeping the other fingers curled, she pantomimes
talking into a phone. "Hello, Maury, Hello, Jerry. It's us."

Something about the way she says this last part—*it's us*—
grabs me by the throat. I can see from the way Arthur's shoulders
stiffen that he feels it as well. She says it with a catch in her voice
as if she can barely stand to admit that we have the lives that we
do. Though Arthur and Maddie don't know this about me, I know
it plain enough myself. Yes, I'm one of them. Yes, we're the ones
people look at and wonder how in the world we ever came to be
who we are. Yes, it's true. Yes, it's us.

Outside, it's started to snow again. I can see the flakes drifting
down past the streetlight, sticking to the sidewalks. It's so quiet in
my house I can hear the music from the city park, though I can't

make out the tune. Suddenly I feel a great tenderness for Maddie and Arthur, and, yes, even for me, because we're ruined, and it's Christmas Eve, and here we all are, together. Even though I'm embarrassed by how much we need, I'm not ashamed enough to stop myself from saying, "Arthur, listen to me. I think I have a solution, something to help you through this—what shall we call it—this rough passage?" I tell him that he and Maddie need time for the waters to calm. "It's a stormy time," I say. "The seas are rough."

"Can the sailing talk," says Arthur. "Say it to me plain."

"The truth is." I clear my throat, gather my breath. "The truth is Maddie would like to stay with me for a while."

"With you? Why would she want to stay with you?"

I tell him how I found her in Stump's house, hidden there because she felt she couldn't be in Arthur's home. "The two of you need time to get to know each other. With this arrangement you'll both be right next door but not underfoot. You'll have a place to go to let in some air. Like I said, even an idiot can see how much you mean to each other. You just need to go slow. You just need time. That's what I'm offering."

"Is it true?" Arthur asks Maddie. "Is this what you want?"

"Gramps," she says, and for a moment I can see the little girl she was, trusting and eager to please, before the world got hold of her. "Just for a while. Please. It won't be so bad. You'll see."

"You won't even come home with me tonight on Christmas Eve? Am I to be alone tonight?"

"No, you don't have to be alone." Maddie takes his hand. "Here we are, the three of us." Stump lets out a bark and a whine. "No, wait," she says. "The four of us. You and me and Sam-You-Am and Stump the French sailor. Merry Christmas. *Joyeux Noël!* What more could we want?"

My kitchen door opens, and in walks Cal. He stops, his hand still on the doorknob, looking through the archway to the living room, sizing up the situation: Arthur and Maddie and me, more people than he expected to find.

"Cal," I say. "You're back."

"I went shopping," he says. I notice, then, the blue plastic Wal-Mart bags in his hand. "Tomorrow's Christmas." He closes the door. He comes into the living room and sets the bags on the coffee table. Inside them are peanuts and chocolate drops and hard ribbon candy in wavy strips of red and white and green. The last bag he opens holds tangerines. He puts them out on the table. Tangerines like my father used to buy for Christmas back in the days when we were still a family. Cal tosses one to me, and I catch it. "I hope they're good and juicy, Sammy," he says. "I know you always liked them when Dad brought them home." He hands me the last bag. "And here, this is for you." I peek inside the bag and see a flannel shirt of green and black forest plaid. A shirt to keep me warm through winter. "I didn't know what to get you," he says, "but I thought you'd like what I'd like. After all, we're brothers, right?"

For an instant, it's like we're alone in the house, just the two of us speaking a private language. Maddie and Arthur must sense this. She clears her throat; he looks down at his feet. Both of them are shy now that Cal has come in and reminded us how blood, no matter if we want it to or not, runs to blood.

I wonder how to break the news to Cal that Maddie will be living with us for a while. Am I an idiot? Of course I am. What was I thinking when I made this offer? There's Cal and his Ruger Single Six, and now this map of downtown Chicago and whatever this is all adding up to. On top of that, I can't predict what's going to happen with Duncan and the way he's got his nose on the trail of that night at the tracks when Dewey died. There's a story there—forgive me for not being able to tell it just yet—that I wouldn't want Maddie to know.

"I'm afraid I don't have anything for you," I say to Cal.

"Aw, Sammy. It's better to give than to receive, right?" He turns toward Maddie and Arthur. His eyebrows rise slightly. "Arthur," he says, "I don't believe I've met this young lady." I know he's calculating his odds—this has become his life since the day he met Leonard Mink—trying to figure out whether Maddie is someone he can trust or whether she'll have to go.

"I'm Maddie," she says. Then she does the most surprising thing. She steps forward and gives Cal a hug. He raises his arms, hesitating, not sure what to make of this affection from a stranger. Then he puts his arms around her shoulders, and they stand like that for a moment. I don't know how it happens, but I can tell that they sense that they come from like cloth: two people, eager for someone to tell them they're safe.

"Maddie," he says, and I can hear in his voice that she's won him.

VERA CALLS TO MAKE SURE ARTHUR GOT TO MY HOUSE ALL right. "Just between you and me and the doorpost," she says, "he had a little bit to drink."

I tell her yes, he got here just fine and we've had a good talk and we've decided some things. I'm in the kitchen on the phone, and Arthur and Cal and Maddie are in the living room, playing with Stump. I hear Maddie toss the rubber horseshoe and tell him, "Get it, get it boy, fetch."

"You two really hit it off," Cal says to Maddie, and I can tell from the tone of his voice that he's pleased.

Even Arthur has something to say. "He's a good dog, but good Lord, look at that sailor suit he's wearing. We ought to make Sammy walk the plank for putting that on him."

Then everyone laughs, and why wouldn't they? A basset hound in a French sailor's suit, a rubber horseshoe hanging from his mouth.

"Looks like he's drunk on shore leave," Arthur says, and the laughs get louder.

I tell Vera that Maddie will be living here with me for a while.

There's a long silence. Then Vera says, "Isn't your brother still there? Two old bachelors and a teenage girl? You know, Sam, people might talk."

"There's no reason."

"Oh, there hardly ever is. Still, people in this town, well, you know."

I don't want to think about people and the fools we are more often than not. Instead I want to linger on the image of Stump and that French sailor's suit and that horseshoe; I want to listen to the har-de-har-har coming from my front room. I try to make my feelings as plain as I can to Vera. "I've spent years living too much inside my head. Just me and my dogs. Now there's this girl, Maddie. Having her in my house means something to me, something I can hardly put into words. She lights things up. Just having her in the house tonight makes everything different."

"But what about Arthur? He lost his dear Bess and now this? Sam, do you really want to be in the way of him and Maddie? Don't you think she should be living with him?"

"Eventually she will." I feel the truth of this slice through my heart. "I just mean to smooth the way. Provide a buffer zone so the two of them can get comfortable with each other. But sooner or later, well, of course, she'll go back to Arthur. I know that, Vera. But for now . . . well, now is now. That's as far as I can see."

Vera sighs. I hear ice cubes rattling in a glass, and I figure she's having some Christmas Eve cheer of her own. "Have you thought as far as Christmas?" she wants to know. "You and your makeshift family? What will you do tomorrow?"

"Tomorrow?"

"Just like I figured. You've got no idea, do you, Sam?"

"I guess not."

"You'll all come to my house for dinner. There, how about that, ducky?"

"All of us?"

"The whole gang. Now say good night. Very Vera needs to get very busy."

"But don't you already have plans?"

"Oh, ducky." There's a catch in her voice. "My daughter and her family live in Stockholm. Sweden for God's sake. They haven't been home in years. Please, come to dinner, the four of you. We find family where we can find it, yes? We'll have a nice meal, and we'll all feel . . . well, ducky, we'll all feel a little less alone."

I wouldn't have thought of Vera being lonely. After all, she's Vera of *Very Vera* fame. I see her about town, always waving a hand to say hello to this person or that. *Hello, Mr. Man Who Slices Meat in the Wal-Mart Deli. Good Morning, Miss Girlie Behind the Window at the Bank. Hello, to you and you and you. Hello.* That's Vera. And now here she is, stuck with us misfits for Christmas dinner.

"Tomorrow," I say.

"Thank you, Sam. Until tomorrow."

Arthur's on board right away. "Vera," he says, "cooks like nobody's business. Food from heaven. Not like the short-order fare old galley cooks like us slop together, right?"

"Speak for yourself," Cal says. He bristles, taking pride as he does in his culinary skills. "What time are we supposed to be there? Noon?" I nod, and I can see him calculating the time. "All right, then." He slaps his hands together. "I've got to get into the kitchen and start rattling those pots and pans."

"What's he talking about, Sammy?" Arthur wants to know.

"You don't think I'm showing up empty-handed, do you?"

Cal gives Arthur a smirk. "And it won't be galley fare, Mister Wisenheimer. No shit on a shingle, bub. Savvy?"

He doesn't wait for an answer. He hits the kitchen, and I hear the refrigerator door swing open. Soon I hear him putting a pan on the stove, chopping something on the cutting board, then I smell onions sautéing and hear him singing something in Italian.

Maddie takes some convincing. She's sprawled on the couch, which will be her bed as long as Cal is still using the spare room. She's watching a program on television—some sort of kooky game show where Japanese people wearing safety helmets try to do certain stunts and end up falling in a river. "That woman," she says. "That Vera. She drives me ape."

I turn down the volume. "What is it about her you don't like?"

"She's just so . . . so . . . ." Maddie bites her lip trying to come up with the right word. "So . . . oh, I don't know what she is, but I know I don't like her."

"So perfect?"

Maddie snaps her fingers. "That's it. Yeah. Perfect."

"And there's something wrong with that?" Arthur says.

I hold up my hand, signaling him not to push this toward trouble.

"She's just so Martha," Maddie says.

"Stewart?" I ask, finishing the name of the renowned life-style guru.

"Yeah, she's the Martha Stewart of Podunk Town, Illinois." Maddie puts on her Vera voice, soothing and musical. "Crocheting a toilet tissue cozy is as simple as snapping beans or dressing your favorite stone goose lawn ornament for the holidays."

"You shouldn't make fun."

"Oh, please," Maddie says. "Making fun is so much fun." She clicks the remote control and the House and Garden Network comes on. A perky red-haired woman is telling us how to brighten dark rooms and give our lives more pizzazz. "You see?" Maddie says. "These people just want to remind us exactly how shitty we've got it. *That's* what I don't like about Vera."

ONCE ARTHUR HAS GONE HOME AND MADDIE HAS FALLEN asleep on the couch, I go into the kitchen, where Cal is running dishwater. Dirty mixing bowls and utensils litter the countertop. His creation—some sort of casserole with potatoes and onions—cools on the stove.

I don't know any other way to do this, but to put it to him straight out. "You want to explain this?" I say, and then I show him the map.

He glances at it and bows his head over the sink. He plunges his hands into the dishwater; a few soap bubbles float up and drift awhile before they bump together and pop. "I don't like you seeing that," he finally says. "I mean it, Sammy. I'm ashamed."

"It's Chicago," I say. He still won't look at me. He washes a bowl, dips it into the rinse water, and sets it in the drainer to dry. "It's the Sears Tower." I see him close his eyes for just an instant. He squeezes them shut as if he's felt a pain in his head. "Who drew this map, Cal?"

"Mink," he says in a whisper. "That night we were drinking at the VFW."

"Cal?" I say, afraid of where this may be heading.

He looks at me, and I can see the tears welling up in his eyes. "Mink drew it when he was telling me how it would all happen. 'You better believe me, buddy,' he said. 'This is the real deal.' I told him, hell, yeah, I knew it. Remember, I was drunk, Sammy. I was talking out of my head. Mink finished his Wild Turkey and got up to leave. 'Your map,' I said to him, and he told me to keep it. 'Souvenir,' he said. Cal wipes at his eyes with his shirtsleeve. "Sammy, I sobered up the next morning, and I saw that map, and I got scared to death."

"How come you kept it?"

"I thought if all hell broke loose in Chicago, I'd have that map, and I'd be able to go to the police and tell them all about Leonard Mink."

"But wouldn't they suspect you were part of it?"

"It's Mink's handwriting. Not mine."

"So did you tell the police all this after Mink was dead?"

"I couldn't." I wait for Cal to tell me more, but he doesn't. "Trust me, Sammy, by that time, I couldn't say a word. I just let the police think what they wanted to think, that I was a hero, and then I got the hell out of town."

"What about this address?" I show him the back of the paper where at some time he wrote *5214 Larkspur Lane.* "Is that somewhere in Chicago?"

"No, not Chicago. That address doesn't have anything to do with Mink or Zwilling or Chicago." He dries his hands on a dish towel. "I wrote that address down so I wouldn't forget it. If trouble comes and I have to run, there's something I want to make sure I take care of, and that's the place I'll need to go to see to things."

"Where is it, Cal? What city?"

He shakes his head. "You don't want to know that. Trust me, Sammy. If the shit hits the fan, I don't want any of it getting on you."

I understand that he's trying to protect me. I've reached the point where I'm afraid to know more—this story threatens to run to places too frightening to consider—so I don't press him about the address. When he motions for me to follow him, I do.

We go out into the living room, taking care, I notice, to be as quiet with our steps as we can, so we won't wake Maddie. She sleeps on her side with her hands folded under her cheek, the way I imagine people do when they lie down to rest in heaven. I notice, too, that for a moment Cal and I both stop and watch her, the way fathers must when they look in on their children at night. I'm seized with how, for just this instant, everything else has fallen away and all that matters is the fact that Maddie is here with us, that we now have this girl to watch over.

I take a step, meaning to move on down the hall, but Cal grabs hold of my arm and stops me.

He goes to the couch, bends over, and with great care, he pulls the blanket up over Maddie's shoulders, so she won't feel the cold and stir from sleep.

I'm grateful that I'm here to see this, my brother's tender concern. I want to linger inside it, but, of course, time is marching on ahead of us, and soon, I know, Cal will turn away from Maddie, and I'll follow him.

He moves down the hall, and together we go into his bedroom. He closes the door. Then he opens the closet and finds his duffel bag. He reaches his hand down inside it and takes out a manila envelope, wrinkled and soft with wear, one of those oversized envelopes, bigger than a piece of paper, the flap held with a metal clasp.

"Open it," he says, and I do. Inside are copies of the map I found in the garage: downtown Chicago and the Sears Tower and the route to the getaway car. "I made copies," Cal says. "Just in case I lost the first one like I did tonight. So much junk in my truck. I'm a careless man, Sammy. You've always known that. I wish I'd never laid eyes on Leonard Mink." Cal takes the maps from me and puts them back in the envelope. He lays the envelope in the top drawer of the bureau and slides it shut. "If you ask me, Sammy, we've all got at least one moment we wish we could go back and fix."

It takes me a long time to fall asleep, mulling over the story Cal's told me and the part he hasn't, whatever it was that made it impossible for him to show the police that map and tell them the whole story. When I finally doze off sometime toward morning, I dream that he and I are in Jerusalem. Brilliant sunshine glinting off white stone. A warm breeze from the Mediterranean Sea. We enter Gethsemane where Christ spent his last night before he was taken for the crucifixion, and there amid the gnarled olive trees and the rocks, Cal takes my hand, and I feel I'm at the place where the world had its chance and then let it go, and all its troubles began. That's what I feel in my dream, this tremendous sense that once there was a time when we could have made a bargain to love one another, when we could have saved ourselves from every misery to come.

Then everything is moving, the way it does in dreams, and Cal and I are running—our legs are the legs of boys—down narrow alleyways, our feet pounding on cobbles, our shoulders brushing stone walls, and though I don't know who's chasing us, I know it's my job to run as fast as I can, to keep up with Cal who goes on before me. And I do. I run and run until I wake, my heart hammering in my chest, and I have to talk myself back to the world I know, the one we keep trying our best to ruin, the one that tests the depths of our love. I lie awake, saying to myself, this is my bed, this is my house, this is my life for better or worse.

I find my bathrobe and slippers, and then I go out into the living room. The sky is brightening in the east, and there's enough light for me to see Maddie on the couch and Stump stretched out beside her. He grunts in his sleep. Maddie's arm is out from under the blanket and draped over his back. For now it's enough, the sight of them huddled together. It's enough to make me glad for all the days and months and years that have added up to this.

Here I am on Christmas morning, and for the first time in longer than I can remember, I have a place to go and people's company to enjoy.

I2

MADDIE DECIDES, GIVEN THE CHOICE BETWEEN GOING TO
Vera's or staying home alone with a hot dog and a can of pork and
beans, it won't hurt her, at least this once, to put her feet under
Vera's table. "It's probably a very nice table," she says. "A very
Vera table." She tries to be a wiseacre, but as she does there's a
tremor to her voice—that and a furrow to her brow, a weakening
around her eyes—that tells me she doesn't dislike Vera as much as
she tries to let on.

Cal warms up his Russian potato casserole, and Maddie begs
him for "just a teensy bite." He tells her she'll have to wait until
it's served at Christmas dinner.

So we go—Cal and Maddie and Arthur and I. We wish one
another Merry Christmas, and we get into Arthur's Chrysler, and
we drive across Christy to the part of town known as White Squirrel Woods. Magnificent old homes sit far back from the streets on
heavily treed lots where squirrels—white, gray, and somewhere in
between—scamper and dart.

Soon we're gathered around the table. Here is the roast duck,
the cranberry sauce, the yams, Cal's Russian potato casserole.

"You've put caramelized onions on top," Vera says. "Now that can be tricky."

"Oh, not so hard if you know the secret," Cal says. "You must know what I mean. An old pro like you."

"Well," Vera begins, but he won't let her finish. He's too eager, I can tell, to show off what he knows.

"A piece of parchment," he says.

"Exactly," says Vera. She reaches out and squeezes his hand.

He says, "Right after you put a dot of butter and pinch of sugar in the saucepan."

She says, "It keeps the moisture from evaporating. Cal, you're a gem."

He smiles, and it does me good to see how pleased he is.

And why shouldn't he be. Here is the fir tree trimmed and lit. The smell of bayberry candles aflame in their pewter holders. The light reflecting off the crystal water glasses, the wine goblets brimming with sparkling cider, the china. The logs crackling in the fireplace. Here are the miniature dollhouses that Vera collects displayed on occasional tables and bookshelves and on the sideboard behind where Maddie and I sit next to each other. While Vera and Cal chatter on about parchment paper and caramelized onions, I catch Maddie turning to look into the small windows at the tiny people and dishes and chairs, the precisely patterned quilts on beds no bigger than postage stamps.

"It's all something, isn't it?" I whisper to her.

She shrugs her shoulders. "It's all right," she says, but I can tell she's quite taken, as I am, with the miniature ice skates and bars of soap and anything you can think of—all the exquisite details of our living.

"Merry Christmas." Vera holds her goblet aloft, and we all raise our glasses.

"To the hostess with the mostest," Arthur says, and I add my modest appreciation.

"Thank you for thinking of us," I say.

We eat without much chatter, polite guests feeling just a tad strange to one another, speaking from time to time to compliment Vera on the duck or the chestnut stuffing, to say how pretty the snow is, to comment on the New Year's Eve Murder Mystery Dinner.

"A real whodunit," Arthur says with a grin. "What to you think, Maddie? How does that sound?"

"Boring," says Maddie, picking at her stuffing with her fork. "Snooze City. That's how it sounds."

"Well, I think it'll be a hoot," Arthur says.

"Indeed," says Vera. "Cal, you must come. It's a costume party. You should see the one I picked out for Sam."

Arthur wants to know what sort of costume I have. "I hope it's nothing swishy," he says, "like the getup you had on your dog."

Vera smiles at me. "Oh, a costume for your dog? How fun. Please, tell me all about it."

"Just a sailor's outfit," I say, embarrassed. "Just something I ordered in the mail. You know, for laughs."

"Oh, it was a riot," Arthur says. "Sailor Stump all fou-fou. All ribbons and bows."

"He was cute," Maddie says.

"I don't know. If you ask me, the whole deal was swishy."

"Swish-pish," Vera says with a wave of her hand. "I get tired of talk like that. Like the story of that boy. You know the one I mean. That Dewey Finn? Duncan came by the other day—Dewey was his great-uncle, you know—asking me what I remembered about when he died. I wish people would just leave it alone. Ancient history. Kaput."

"Dewey Finn?" Maddie says.

"A boy from Rat Town," Vera says. "It was a long time ago. Cal, you remember, yes?"

"Dewey Finn," says Cal, and then he goes back to eating.

When I speak, I do my best to keep my voice even like I'm trying to call to mind something I heard about and then forgot. "Yes, there was a boy from Rat Town, but that's not a story for a day like this. Not a Christmas story at all."

Vera says, "It was a train that killed him. The National Limited. He was lying on the tracks on the trestle just north of Rat Town. I guess he got what he wanted. Folks said it was because he'd been tormented so—you know, because he liked boys—he just couldn't bear the thought of living anymore. Isn't that the way you remember it, Sam?"

"That was a long time ago," I say.

"I think Sammy is right," Arthur says. "Maybe this isn't a story to hear on Christmas."

I do my best to steer the conversation to another topic. "Vera, I don't know how you manage to be so relaxed and natural on your radio program." I balance my knife on the rim of my plate. "I'd think of all those people listening to me, and I'd be scared to death."

"Oh, it's nothing, ducky." She winks at me. "It's just chit-chat. I just talk into the microphone. La-di-dah. I've always been able to gab."

TONIGHT, WHEN MADDIE AND I ARE ALONE IN MY KITCHEN, Cal gone to bed, she says, "You knew that boy, the one Vera talked about. He was your friend, wasn't he?"

We're in the kitchen drinking cocoa and having a slice of spice cake I bought from the Wal-Mart bakery. Compared to the feast we had at Vera's, this is puny doin's, but still there's something to love about the fact that here we sit on this Christmas night, the cake on our paper plates, the cocoa steaming in our mugs, and Maddie waiting for me to answer her question.

"Yes," I say. "He was my friend."

This is the time of night when ordinarily I feel the dark close in around me—another day nearly gone—and I find myself thinking about the way time runs out and leaves us wishing we had more. What will it be like, I wonder, when it ends for me the way it did that spring evening in 1955 for Dewey? There are times, to be perfectly honest, when I'm ready to be done with it all, to just disappear into the darkness, to let all the sounds of the living slip away, and to be nothing more than a name said on occasion by someone trying to recall the old man who lived by himself and kept a succession of dogs—basset hounds, every one of them—for company.

Then there are moments like this—Maddie speaking to me in soft, soothing tones; Stump on his belly by my feet, chewing on his rubber horseshoe—when I wish it could all go on and on, when I let myself believe for just a moment that there might really be a heaven where every sin gets washed away and the dead live forever in paradise.

"Is it true?" Maddie asks. "What Vera said? Did it happen like that? Did that boy lie down and wait for that train?"

The easy answer is, yes, it's true. Yes, it happened exactly like that. But really there's so much more to it, so much I can't bring myself to say.

"It was a horrible thing." I try to take another sip of my cocoa, but my hand is trembling and I have to set the mug back on the table. "It's something you'd never want to know about."

But she does want to know. "Did he want to die because he couldn't stand being different?"

"He was just a boy," I say. "We both were."

I bow my head, afraid I've said too much, afraid I've given myself away. After all these years with no one in my house but the dogs, I don't know how to talk to people about the things that matter. I've spent a lifetime hiding myself from the world. I look up at Maddie and she has such a kindness in her face that I can't speak. My throat closes and I feel the ache. Then I have to stand up and move away from the table so she won't see how shaken I am. I go to the sink, where I pour out what's left of my cocoa and rinse out the mug.

It isn't long before Maddie joins me. She puts her hand on my back. She says, "If you loved him. If he was special to you, it's okay."

Then she leaves me alone. She goes down the hallway to the bathroom to get herself ready for bed. She'll sleep on the couch again tonight and who knows how many nights to come, and I'm glad for that—as glad as I've been in some time.

STILL, I CAN'T GET DEWEY OUT OF MY HEAD. I REMEMBER THE night when Arthur and two of his friends were uptown in front of the pool hall. This was in 1955, and Mt. Gilead was celebrating its centennial. The men were growing chin whiskers, trying to win the beard-growing contest. "Buddies of the Brush," they called themselves. Some of the older boys like Arthur and his buddies were sporting beards, too, and that gave them even more swagger than usual. That night in front of the pool hall, they were lighting matchsticks and tossing them at one another and sometimes at people walking by on the sidewalk. They were bored and more than a little mean, the way teenage boys can be, and they were putting a little jazz into the way they lit the matches. They struck them on their belt buckles, the soles of their shoes. They snapped them with their thumbnails, flicked them from their front teeth. I guess you'd say they were lighting those matches with flare—please excuse the pun.

Certain facts I'll never forget. They're burned into me. I know this isn't the time to be funny, but sometimes the words are just there and I can't stop myself from saying them. Just like I couldn't stop myself that night from saying what I did about Dewey. He went walking by on the other side of the street, and, because I didn't know what to do with that kiss he'd given me in the alley behind our houses, I said, "Look at that queer. Ain't he a sweetheart?" That caught the other boys' fancy and Arthur called after him: "Dewey! Oh, Dewey. Come over here, sweetie." I said it again. "Queer," I said, the way I'd heard it said so many times in our town.

One of Arthur's friends wore a white T-shirt, a package of Lucky Strikes rolled in one sleeve. The other boy was lanky and he belted his trousers high on his waist. He had a pencil behind his ear. These are the things I remember.

A few days later, Dewey was dead, and I can only imagine, as I have for years, what misery I must have started for him when I called him a queer, and Arthur and his friends picked up on it. How did I make the last days of his life when I said that, said it to protect myself, afraid that eventually people like Arthur would figure out the truth about me?

As my father finally did a few years after Dewey died. It was, as it so often is with the moments that change our lives, a small thing that made him understand the truth he had surely sensed but hadn't been willing to accept. Perhaps this truth began to gnaw at him the night Dewey died. Or maybe Cal, before he left town a few days later, told him what he'd seen the evening Dewey kissed me in the alley, and my father did his best as long as he could to believe it didn't mean anything.

Whatever the case, my secret became clear on a Sunday in August when my mother and father and I drove out to the state park to have supper at the Lakeview Inn. We were celebrating. I was nineteen, and I'd just hired on with the janitorial service. I'd had my first payday on Friday, and now I was taking my parents out to eat.

"A regular Rockefeller," my father said with a sneer, but I knew he was putting on. I could tell he was happy for me.

My mother was happy, too. Cal's infrequent visits since coming home from Germany had taken the heart out of her, and, as we sat down to supper that night at the Lakeview Inn, I could see that she was glad to have something to lift her spirits. She took my arm as we walked to our table, and I made a big show of pulling out her chair for her. "Ooh-la-la," she said. "My son, the gentleman." I shook out the cloth napkin and laid it in her lap. She leaned across the table toward my father, who hadn't taken off the summer-weight, woven straw fedora he was wearing. "Are you taking notes, Bill? Are you watching this? Maybe you could learn something?"

"Mr. Fancy-Pants." My father pushed the fedora back on his head and squinted at me. "So tell me, Cary Grant, how come you don't have a girl?"

I didn't know what to say. It was something he asked me from time to time, teasing, and I always said, well, you know, gee, Dad, I guess I'm picky. That's all right, he always told me. It was better to do a little living first and not get tied down too soon. "Forty," he said. "That's the best time to get hitched. You'll be all used up by then, and you'll need someone to look after you."

That evening at the restaurant, I said to my father, "If you want the truth, I don't hold much faith in that lovey-dovey, happily-ever-after jazz." I was full of myself. Nineteen and money in my pocket. I was, as my father sometimes said of me, just talking to hear myself roar. "Oh, it might be fine for some folks," I said. "But me?" I held my arms away from my body, as if someone were frisking me. I invited my parents to give me the once-over. "Come on. Seriously." I turned my face first left and then right, displaying each profile. "Do I look like the kind of guy a girl would go ga-ga over?"

I knew my mother had no reason at all to suspect me. I wasn't a swish; in fact, I didn't believe there was anything effeminate about me at all. I was a skinny kid, normal-looking enough, but not striking by any means. Not pretty. Sometimes I studied the other boys in town, the ones who chased girls, strutted around jacked up with hormones. The ones like Cal and Arthur. Even they had a feature here and there that, under the right circumstances, might come across as womanly: long eyelashes, slender tapered fingers, delicate collarbones. But no one thought a thing about them, just like I imagined no one thought a thing about me when they saw me out and about. I was just a young man, seated now in this restaurant, doing monkeyshines for his parents. No one would have thought anything at all about me and the secret I had.

My mother said, "You're very handsome, Sammy."

She reached across the table to pat my hand, and, when she did, a raveling from the sleeve of her dress floated out into the air and landed on my arm.

I brushed it off, not with the flat of my hand the way I had seen my father sweep the powdery dust from the mill room off his clothes on our wash porch after work, but with my fingertips—a breezy, back-handed flip like that, and I saw the way my father looked at me as if something had come clear to him, as if he had finally worried a splinter up through his skin.

That's what did it. That loose thread. The way I brushed it away with a motion my father perhaps had never seen me make, and suddenly he couldn't ignore the boy I was. It should have been nothing, that motion I made, but right then, given all that my father must have surely suspected, it was everything.

"I'm hungry," he said in a voice that was too loud and full of bluster. "My God, I'm starved. I swear I could eat a moose."

My mother laughed. "You don't have to tell the whole joint about it. Honestly, Bill." She glanced back over her shoulder. "Folks will think we don't know how to act."

He wouldn't take off his hat. Not even when our food came, nor when my mother asked him in a quiet voice, "Bill, please."

"A man ought to be able to wear his goddamn hat." He tugged on the brim of the fedora. "Yes, sir. Wherever he damn well pleases."

I felt sorry for my mother. The air had gone out of the evening—a festive night out she'd been enjoying—and she couldn't understand why.

Only my father and I knew. Our shame was all around us: in the way we both kept our heads bowed over our plates, barely saying a word; in the puny answers we gave to the questions the waitress asked ("More iced tea? Coffee? Save room for dessert?"); in the defiant way he kept his hat pulled down close to his eyes as if he hoped he could shade out the truth that was glaring now between us.

But he couldn't deny it, and later that night, when I was getting ready for bed, he came into my room, and he said to me, "Dewey Finn."

"Yes," I said.

I was buttoning my pajama shirt, and my father couldn't watch, couldn't tolerate, suddenly, the sight of my bare chest. He looked down at the floor. He stuck his hands in his pocket. He rocked up on the balls of his feet.

"The two of you," he said, and I couldn't avoid it any longer. I told him yes, it was true; I was the same as Dewey. That's why I didn't have a girl. That was the real answer to the question he'd asked me at the restaurant.

He took a sharp breath. He ran his hand over his head, forehead to crown, taking his time, as if the right words were there in his brain and if he touched himself in the right way he would call them up and give them to me like a gift. He let his hand slide down to his neck and rest there. He lifted his face to me, a look in his eyes I can only describe as helpless.

"Christ, Sammy," he said. "What do I do with this . . . this thing you're saying? This way of being? It's something I don't know."

You have to remember this was 1959, and my father was a man, like most men then, who had no idea how far love could reach.

"Can't you just let it be?" I said. "Why do we have to do anything with it at all?"

You have to know I didn't blame him—not then. I was willing to let him be the man he was, someone who had trouble with the idea that his son was queer. All I wanted was the same from him; all I wanted was for him to allow me to be who I was. The problem, of course, was that we were at cross-purposes. How could either of us be who we really were around the other as long as my father carried in him the smallest grain of disgust, or, as much as it still hurts me to say it, hate?

He nodded his head. He took his hands out of his pockets and clapped them together once as if to say, all right, yes, okay. He turned and started to walk out of my room. I was anxious for him to be gone. But he paused at the doorway. He reached up and

grabbed the top of the jamb, as if he had to stop himself from taking another step.

"Whatever goes on in your life in this town from here on."
For a long time, he stood there, head bowed, shoulders slumped.
"You've got no one to blame but yourself."

He slapped the door jamb with his palm. Then he left my
room. The quiet settled around me and I could barely stand to put
out my light and close my eyes and slip off into sleep, my ears on
fire with the ugly thing he'd said, which I imagined was the way
he felt about what had happened to Dewey, that he had lain down
in front of that train because he hadn't been able to live with the
fact of who he was—that he had made his own end.

When my father died in 1973, he was a widower, my mother
having gone on ahead of him. The last words I spoke to him were
at her funeral.

"I can look after you," I told him. By this time, his heart had
failed him once and it wouldn't be long before it stopped for good.

He gave me a fierce look, one that said he had no use for me.
Whatever love he'd had for me went away as soon as he found out
I was queer. "You don't need to come looking after me," he said.
And that was that.

13

THE SUN IS BRIGHT THE MORNING AFTER CHRISTMAS WHEN I take Stump for his walk. Some folks, anxious to be done with the holiday chores, have left their Christmas trees at the curb for the garbage men to pick up. Here and there, a few strands of icicles still cling to the trees and sparkle in the sunlight. Bits of ribbon—green, red, silver, and gold—flutter in the wind, which comes this morning from the south, promising a warm-up and the melting of all this snow.

The neighborhood kids are enjoying it while they can, building snowmen in yards, hurrying by toting sleds, bound for the hills at the city park. Their woolen scarves unfurl behind them as they run. Their shouts ring out on this clear, bright day. "Wait up, Enis McMeanus," one boy shouts to another, and right away I recognize the boy—the one who shouts—as the boy who told the pirate joke to Stump. Enis McMeanus—I delight in the whimsy of that made-up name.

A red woolen scarf slips from the boy's neck, and I snatch it from the air. Stump strains at his leash, eager to follow the boys as they hurry past.

But we have our own day ahead of us: this brisk walk, smartly once around the block, and then back home to make breakfast. A special turkey and lamb for Stump; Belgian waffles, a recipe I got from listening to Vera on the radio, for Maddie and Cal and me. He's done almost all the cooking since he's been here, and it's time for me to get off my duff. I've decided that I'll go to Vera's New Year's Eve party. I'll even try to convince Cal and Maddie to go. I'll play the role of Happy Mickey Finn.

I wave the scarf in the air. "Hey," I shout. "Your scarf." But the boy keeps running. Then I do it, and the sound of my voice both thrills and frightens me. "Hey, Enis McMeanus," I say, and the boy stops, turns back to me, his mouth open in amazement, stunned that an old man like me has been listening to this private talk of boys and now has been so bold as to use their language as if it's his own.

I reach out the scarf to him. He walks back to me, his steps at first hesitant. Then he grabs the scarf from my hand and runs to join his friends, who are speeding on ahead of him. He stops once, nearly halfway down the block, and he calls back to me. "I like your dog." He waves the scarf in the air. "Thanks, Enis McMeanus," he says, and then he runs on down the street, leaving me to laugh to myself, to appreciate this one, simple moment of joy. Oh, for a world of days like this and one Enis McMeanus after another.

WHEN I GET HOME, CAL AND MADDIE ARE DANCING. SWEAR to God. My brother, still spry enough to stomp the boards and show her some of that rockabilly swing dancing he was always so good at. Maddie has her portable stereo—a boombox, I guess she'd call it—in the living room, and Cal's put on a Carl Perkins CD. "Blue

Suede Shoes" is blaring, and Cal's showing Maddie how to spin and bounce and turn.

Stump looks up at me as if to say, "What in the devil," and, like him, I'm amazed.

Cal and Maddie try to do a figure-eight turn, but they both lose their balance and tumble onto the couch, laughing.

Stump starts barking, and that's when they see me.

"Oh, Lord, Sammy," Cal says. "You been there watching me make a fool out of myself? I used to be able to swing with the best of them."

"It looked all right to me," I say. "A little more practice and you'll be ready for Vera's party."

"I don't hardly think so." He holds up his hands and shakes his head. "No, I think I'm going to keep quiet on New Year's Eve."

"Come on." Maddie tugs at his shirtsleeve. "We'll show everyone how to dance."

"You go ahead, little lady," he says. "I'll stay home and you can tell me all about it after it's done."

"No dice," she says. "If you're not going, neither am I."

"All right," I say, deciding for the time being not to press the issue and risk the high spirits we all have. "Now I'm going to make us some breakfast."

Cal snaps to attention. "That's my job, Sammy."

"Not this morning," I tell him.

Then I go out to the kitchen and get to work.

When everything's on the table, Cal pours maple syrup over his waffle. Maddie spreads strawberry jam on hers. She sits cross-legged, her feet drawn up beneath her knees. She's wearing a pair of black sweatpants and a man's flannel shirt over her white T-shirt. It takes me a while to realize that the flannel shirt is mine, the green and black forest plaid Cal gave me for Christmas. I'd left it still folded on my dresser, and now here's Maddie wearing it as if it's her own.

"It's all right, isn't it?" she says when she realizes I'm studying the shirt. "I got a little chilly."

And here's the thing. I don't mind at all. In fact, I'm overjoyed because this is one of the rare times in my life when someone has needed something and I've been able to supply it. Like I did when I gave the boy his scarf. This is what I'm learning. These small gifts, these simple ways of finding love.

"It's all right," I tell her. "It looks good on you. It matches the green in your eyes."

She gives me a skeptical look. "Jeez, Sam-You-Am," she says. "Shake off the pixie dust and come back to planet Earth. We're just talking about a shirt."

I can't help but notice, then, the way she's so neatly folded back the cuffs of my flannel shirt—it makes my heart glad to know that she was cold and now the shirt has warmed her—or the care she takes with each bite of her waffle, chewing slowly, her eyes closing sometimes with bliss. How happy I am that I made these waffles that so obviously please her, that Cal is here, and we are, at least for the time being, a family.

When we're finished with the waffles, Maddie takes Stump out to his ship. I watch her light a cigarette, something I won't let her do in my home, and she stands there, smoking, looking over at Arthur's house.

I let Cal help me with the dishes. I wash and he dries, and for a good while we don't say much. There's only the noise of the water and the dishes bumping around in the sink and the squeak of Cal's dish towel as he dries the plates.

Then he says, "You're doing a good thing, Sammy. With Maddie, I mean."

I go to work on the silverware, scrubbing the syrup and jam off the knives and forks. "I'm not sure Arthur sees it that way."

"Maybe not now, but he will. Just be patient." Cal takes a handful of silverware from the rinse and shakes the water from them. "You're a good man, Sammy. You always have been."

I don't know what to say to that; I've spent so much of my life believing otherwise. To hear it, though, from Cal, means something to me, and I stand there lingering in the glow of his compliment.

Through the kitchen window, I can see that Arthur has come outside and that he and Maddie are standing at my fence, talking. He has his hands stuck in his pockets, and he hangs his head as if he's having a hard time saying what he came to say. But he does, and then Maddie reaches across the fence and throws her arms around his neck and gives him a hug. I'm happy for Maddie and her good heart and happy for Arthur, who means to do right by her. My throat fills with an ache, sensing as I do that I'm this much closer to not having her in my home, but hasn't that been the plan from the git-go? So why should I feel anything but glad?

Cal's cell phone rings. He dries his hands and takes it from his pants pocket. He flips it open and holds it to his ear. The odd thing is he doesn't say a word, doesn't say "hello," doesn't say "Cal Brady." He just listens. Then he says, "Right. Got it. I'll be ready. I'll wait for word."

He puts the phone away, and we stand there a good while just looking at each other.

Finally, I can't stand the silence, so I say, "Ready for what?"

"That was Mora Grove," Cal says. "The woman from Herbert Zwilling's grain elevator."

"About that Coca-Cola glass? Is that why she was calling?"

Cal narrows his eyes at me. "I made that up, Sammy. I read about that blind man in the *Daily Mail*. I had no idea you actually had that glass."

"Why would you do that?"

"Because I couldn't stand to tell you the truth." He takes a breath and lets it out. "The truth about Herbert Zwilling and me."

I hold my hands in the dishwater until I can barely stand the heat. Then I lift them out and stare awhile at the red, wrinkled skin, and it seems as if they aren't my hands at all. Then, I say what I've come to suspect, that Cal and Zwilling knew one another longer than Cal has let on. "Is that the case, Cal? Were you already hooked up that day you took Mink to the grain elevator to get that Volare?"

Cal hesitates. Then he says it, the thing he hasn't been able to bring himself to say. "Me and Zwilling," he says. "We'd known each other for some time."

I don't know what to say because I fear where this is leading, and finally Cal goes on. "I wasn't part of that militia, but Zwilling was wrapped up in it. Still is. That Michigan Militia, Sammy. Conspiracy to overthrow the government. That's what we're talking about here, and he knows at any minute I could decide to go to the police and tell them everything I know."

"And Mora Grove?"

"She says Zwilling's making noise about trying to hunt me down. If he finds me, Sammy . . . well, he'll kill me if he gets the chance. That's what he'll do. He'll put me where I can't say a word. That's how men like him operate, the ones that think they're above the law. They show up one day and tap you on the shoulder. Then it's too late. Then you're done. Mora will let me know when it's time for me to run."

The back door opens, and I feel my heart in my throat. It's only Maddie coming in from the yard, breezing into the kitchen, singing "Blue Suede Shoes." "The Pope has given me his blessing," she says, and she goes on to explain that she and Arthur are starting to see eye to eye. "Zippity doo-dah," she says. She stands with her hands on her hips, a smile on her face. "Look at that sunshine, gents. What a glorious day, and here you stand, both of you looking like you've seen a ghost."

ARTHUR TAKES HER TO EVANSVILLE TO BUY HER ANOTHER Christmas gift, to let her pick something out at the mall, and, when it's just Cal and me in the house, I say to him, as much as it pains me, "I won't let you stay here unless I know everything there is to know. You'll have to tell me everything, Cal. Otherwise, I'll turn you out."

He paces around the living room. He tells me to get comfortable because what he has to say is going to take a while.

I do what he says. I sit on the couch, and while he talks I rub my hand over the quilt and blanket Maddie has folded. I think of her out enjoying the sunny winter day with Arthur, and though I don't begrudge her that, I realize that what I'm fearing most of all is the likelihood that soon she'll be gone from my house and Cal, who works up the nerve now to tell me the rest of his story, will follow and here we'll be again, just me and Stump, the two of us alone.

It was true, Cal says, what he told me about drinking with

Leonard Mink that night at the VFW, but what wasn't exactly true was that it was the first time he knew of the plot to bring down the Sears Tower. He knew about it years before because he knew Herbert Zwilling, and Herbert Zwilling had been involved with other plots, even Oklahoma City.

"There's all sorts of people in on these things," Cal says. "People in the government, even. Folks you wouldn't suspect. Just people like Herbert Zwilling, running his business and up to no good on the sly. Trust me, Sammy. I know."

He knew because he'd made the mistake of getting chummy with Herbert Zwilling at a gun show. "We got to talking," Cal says, "and he asked me if I'd like to make a little extra money by helping out at his grain elevator. So I did. I'd go down there a few days a week during harvest season and run the scales and write up the tickets and sell fertilizer and the like, just a part-time job like that. Then one day, I was the only one there—Zwilling and Mora Grove had gone uptown for lunch—and the mailman delivered a box that was coming return receipt requested. I didn't think a thing about it. I just signed like the mailman told me to do. Then, when Zwilling and Mora came back from lunch, I gave him the box. He studied the return address, and he said to Mora, 'It's from Hendrik. It's what we've been waiting for.' I didn't know who this Jacob Hendrik was, but I figured what he'd sent in that box had something to do with the business. Once I knew that Zwilling was part of that militia, I remembered that the box had come from Cadillac, Michigan, and I figured that it had something to do with what finally happened in Oklahoma City: blasting caps, fuses, something like that. Do you see what a stupid thing it was for me to do? Now someone has that return receipt with my signature on it—someone Zwilling knows—and it's the proof they need to claim I've been in on all these plots all along. It's that receipt, don't you understand, that made it risky for me to say anything to the police even after Mink was dead."

Cal stops pacing and stands at the picture window, his hands flat on the library table, his head bowed. "You believe me, don't you, Sammy?" Cal turns to face me. "If anyone would believe me, I figured it'd be you. Sometimes things just happen, things we never intended, and there we are. You know that, don't you, Sammy? I know you do."

14

ALL WEEK, I GO OVER CAL'S STORY IN MY HEAD, TRYING TO figure out whether I believe him. To tell you the truth, I'm not sure what I can trust, and he and I don't talk about Zwilling or Mora Grove or anything that happened in Ohio. I ask Cal again to go to the New Year's Eve party with me, and he says, no, he doesn't think so.

Come New Year's Eve, the Cabbage Rose Bed and Breakfast, where Vera is hosting her party, rings and clangs with ragtime jazz. I stand on the wraparound porch, about to ring the bell, and for a moment longer I convince myself that I can step through this doorway and call out the names of my fellow guests and meet them with a smile when they in turn say, "Sam, Sammy. Hey, how's the boy?" I pretend that I'm capable of this. I wish that Cal and Maddie were with me to make this easier, but he's kept to his bedroom, not even coming out for supper, and Maddie's held true to her promise to stay home with him. "He'll come out sooner or later," she said just before I walked out the door, "and I wouldn't want him to be alone on New Year's Eve."

So it's just me, here on the porch listening to the screech of clarinets, the rollicking notes of a piano, the blare of horns. I know I have to make myself do this or else I'll lose my nerve and turn around and go home. I don't even ring the bell. I open the door and step inside.

Vera is in the foyer wearing a flapper's dress—sleeveless and covered with fringe. Strands of silver beads hang to her knees.

"Sammy," she says, stretching out her arms to me. "Look at you. You're a real cake eater."

"Excuse me," I say.

"A cake eater." She gives me a wink and grabs onto my hand. "You know. A ladies' man."

I try to pretend that I could be exactly that, a man comfortable with the ladies, a man who might, as Cal came close to doing once upon a time, take up a life with Vera. I lean over and kiss her on the cheek. "Sister," I say, "you ain't bad yourself." I see the twinkle in her eye, and for this brief moment I know what it's like to be a flirt.

She shows me where to hang my coat. Then here comes Arthur, or, as he'll be known tonight, the Big Lucky. Here he comes in his dark pinstripe suit, a gold chain draped from his vest pocket, his eyes shaded by the sloping brim of his white fedora, a fat cigar screwed into the corner of his mouth.

"Shammy," he says, the cigar giving him a lisp. "You're lookin' schwanky. Where's Maddie and your brother?"

"Homebodies," I tell him, and Arthur shrugs his shoulders as if to say he won't let it bother him, the fact that Maddie has chosen Cal's company over his.

"So your brother's given me the cold shoulder." Vera helps me off with my coat. "You two. Look at you. Happy Mickey Finn and the Big Lucky." She gently lays a hand against each of our faces, and she gets this look in her eyes as if she's recalling what it was like to have a man in her life. "You big lugs." She gives us each a pat on the cheek. "Go join the others. I mean it, boys. The game's about to begin."

The others are the Seasoned Chefs, some of them with lady friends. "Vamps," they call them. Or "skirts." Or as I hear one gent put it, his "sheba." I turn toward that voice and see that it doesn't belong to any of the Seasoned Chefs but to Duncan Hines. I recall the note he left asking me to call him, the note I tore up, and now I'm afraid to face him.

He's all arms and legs in a three-piece suit, and he has a straw boater on his head, the sort I saw in *Déjà New* the day I went there with Vera to pick out my costume. I stand in the entryway, watching the other guests as they bunch together and chat—women in evening attire, white gloves running up to their elbows, cigarette holders waving like wands; men shouting *hot socks* and *jeepers creepers* and *Now you're on the trolley*—and I wonder whatever made me think I could be one of them.

"Mr. Pope," Duncan calls to Arthur. Then he slaps his forehead with his palm, reminding himself to speak the twenties lingo someone must have taught him. "Geesh, I'm sorry. Hey, Big Lucky. Come over here and check out the chassis on my sheba. But hold onto your dough. She's a real gold digger!"

For a moment, I'm left alone, as Arthur—excuse me, the Big Lucky—joins Duncan, who's now offering his sheba a drink from a silver hip flask. She's coy, pretends she's shocked, puts her hand to the flask and pushes it away. She's a woman with short red hair, spit curls trailing along her temples and coiling over her cheekbones, hot with rouge. She's a woman much older than Duncan, a woman my age. She wears a silver-beaded flapper dress and a black satin choker around her throat, a shiny brass button in the center. Duncan tips the neck of the flask toward her again, and this time, she shrugs her shoulders, giggles, and takes a sip.

Now that this piece of theatrics is complete, Duncan is embarrassed, not knowing how to continue. He caps the flask and slips it back in his pocket. He fiddles with his boater, taking it off and twirling it by the brim. Then he puts it back on, setting it far back on his head so the brim points up to the ceiling.

The woman with the red hair catches on that she's gone too far with the acting. "Oh, come on, Duncan." She takes his hand. "Can't an old dame have a little fun on New Year's Eve?"

Duncan lays an arm across her shoulders and gives her a clumsy hug. "Sure, Grandma," he says, and I feel a flutter in my chest.

"Nancy," Arthur says to her. "It's been years and years."

I know that I'm looking at Nancy Finn, and I can't for the life of me imagine getting through the evening.

So I turn away to find Vera, to tell her I must have my coat. I must go home—suddenly I miss Maddie with an ache that almost brings me to my knees—and then I hear someone calling my name—*Mr. Brady*—and before I can make a move, Duncan is tapping me on the back and I have no choice but to turn to him and say hello.

"Mr. Brady," he says. "Long time, no see. Didn't you get my note?"

I play dumb. "Note?"

"I stuck it between your front door and the frame. There's something I need to tell you."

"The wind must have got it." I try to make a joke. "Or maybe Stump ate it."

It's enough to distract Duncan. "He's quite a dog. Still sailing the high seas?"

"Aye," I say, eager to stay anchored in this good-humored small talk.

Duncan hooks his thumbs in the watch pockets of his vest. "I'm a G-Man," he says, and I understand that he's once again assuming the character that Vera assigned him for the evening. "Melvin Purvis. I'm here to get to the bottom of things." His shirt collar is too loose around his slender neck and his bow tie droops a bit. "Now what's your name, fella, and what do you know about John Dillinger's missing doily?"

I remember the character sketch that came with Vera's invitation. *Happy Mickey Finn*, I'm supposed to say. *I was playing piano for Mr. Dillinger that night. He was necking with that doll.* Here, if I were really saying this, I'd point to Vera and use her character name. *That Lotta Love. They were getting chummy, and Mr. Dillinger had just run dry of gin.* "I'm outta coffin varnish," *he said, and I told him I'd make everything copacetic. Then I went to get him another drink.*

But I can't bring myself to play the game. Duncan looks at me with such expectation and hope, his eyes opening wider. I could say, at least, *my name is Happy Mickey Finn*, but I can't even manage that. I stick my hands in my trouser pockets, imitating the way Duncan stands with his thumbs hooked in his vest pockets, thinking this will make me appear at ease, but instead it makes me feel too guarded, so I take my hands out of my pockets, and I'm surprised to see that I've taken out my coin purse.

"Don't think you can buy your way out of this," Duncan says, still in character.

I stuff the purse back in my pocket and then fiddle with my sleeve garters. "I'm sorry," I say. "Parties are difficult for me. So many people. So much noise."

"Then come say hello to my grandma. She's visiting from

Indiana." Duncan puts a hand on my back and starts shepherding me toward Arthur and Nancy. "I bet the two of you haven't seen each other in forever."

The last time I saw Nancy Finn, she was working uptown at Beal's Newsstand. It was the first Christmas after Dewey died, and Arthur had joined the Navy. I'd seen his picture in the *Daily Mail*, a formal portrait taken when he was in uniform, his hair cut close to his scalp, his spine ramrod straight, his jaw set. He seemed like someone I didn't know anymore, someone who was moving out into the world, a world that had barely taken notice of what had happened to Dewey.

That Christmas, I stepped into Beal's and there was Arthur. He was leaning against the counter, flipping through a *Saturday Evening Post*, while he chatted with Nancy, who stood behind the cash register. She was a pretty girl with a narrow face and that red hair she kept in curls. She fetched a package of Lucky Strikes from the cigarette rack behind her and took a fifty-cent piece from Arthur.

He was on leave, he told her, but soon he'd be overseas.

"Golly," she said. "Aren't you scared?"

"No, darlin'." He reached across the counter and laid his hand on her hip. "Life's too short for that."

She didn't move away from him. She let him keep his hand right where it was, and I thought it was the most amazing thing, that he could touch her like that. By this time, everyone knew she was sweet on Grinny Hines, and he wasn't the sort who would take kindly to Arthur touching his girl like that. It wouldn't be long before Grinny and Nancy would marry and end up, so Snuff Finn would tell my father, living in Detroit, where Grinny had established what Snuff called "a little business."

That day at Beal's, Nancy and Arthur both looked up and saw me standing just inside the door, my hands balled up in the pockets of my corduroy coat, snow melting on my sock hat.

Arthur winked at me, and that wink said he had the world on a string. He turned back to Nancy. "Darlin'," I heard him say again. "You're about the sweetest thing I've seen in a good while. Hon, you're one sweet piece of cake."

I'm thinking about that moment as Duncan pushes me toward Arthur and Nancy, and, when I'm here, standing right in front of her, I can't help but hear again the sound of her sobbing the night my father and I went to the Finns' house to see if there was anything we could do.

"Sam Brady," she says. She even reaches out and takes my left hand in hers. "Sammy, it's been such a long time."

It amazes me, no matter how old I get, how little it takes to make me feel I'm still fifteen. A door opens and I step through it; even here at the end of the year, I go spinning back to the night I listened to Nancy and her mother and sisters wailing with grief because Dewey was dead.

"Nancy Finn," I say, and that's all I can get out.

She squeezes my hand, and I look in her eyes, and I understand there's no words for what happened to us when Dewey was no longer in our lives.

"We're putting another year to bed," she says.

I nod. "Where do they all go?" I look beyond her, taking note of all the men at the party, trying to figure out if Grinny Hines is one of them. "Is your husband with you this evening?"

"My husband? I'm afraid I'm a widow. Grinny passed early on in our marriage."

"And you never remarried?"

"There was another man in my life. Henk—that's what I called my second fella. We never married, but we were sweethearts a long time before he died just a few years ago."

"Granny moved to Evansville then," Duncan says. "That's where my folks live."

"Where did you live before that?" Arthur asks.

"Henk and I were in Michigan," she says.

"Detroit?" I ask her, but before she can answer, Arthur interrupts.

"Boy, I could eat a whale," he says.

Nancy ignores him. It's as if he and Duncan and all the others have vanished, and it's just the two of us talking.

"One look at you," she says, "and I'm right back in Rat Town. You know what I mean, don't you, Sammy?"

I tell her I do, and that's how we acknowledge Dewey without ever saying his name.

Arthur reaches out and touches his finger to the brass button at the center of Nancy's choker. "Where did you get this button?"

He pulls his finger away, and Nancy puts her hand to her throat. "This? Oh, I found it in some of Henk's things when I moved. I sewed it on this satin band just to complete my costume."

She takes her hand away, and I see that the button has a flag engraved on it, unfurled and split at the end like a snake's tongue.

"Don't you know what that flag means?" Arthur asks. "That's the White Star Line, the cruise line that the *Titanic* was part of."

"The ship that sank?" Duncan says.

"They've been recovering relics from the site for a good while." Arthur raises his eyebrows and looks around at all of us. "Nancy," he says, "that just might be a piece of history."

"From the *Titanic*," she says. "Now where in the world would Henk have gotten something like that?"

Then Vera is here, taking Duncan by the arm. "Mister G-Man," she says. "It's time for you to get things started."

"Twenty-three skidoo," he says, and together they move toward the grand dining room, leaving Nancy and Arthur and me behind.

Nancy puts her hands on her hips and acts peeved. "Looks like I've been deserted." She takes Arthur's right arm, and on her other side she takes my left. "Gents, I need an escort," she says, and I have no choice but to go with them into the dining room where the ragtime coming from a stereo gets louder and Vera instructs everyone to find their place cards at the table. "Quickly now," she calls out. "Get a wiggle on. The fun's about to begin."

Arthur pulls out Nancy's chair. "What a gentleman," she says, allowing him to seat her. He grabs the chair to her right and I'm left to sit next to him.

Here we are in a line, and Nancy leans across Arthur and says something to me. The music's so loud and the other guests are shouting out things like, *Don't be a dumb Dora.* Or: *Aw, go tell it to Sweeney.* The noise is such that for a moment I'm not sure what she says. Then I realize it's, *Are you happy?* She reaches across Arthur and points to my name card. "Are you Happy?" she asks, and I know now she's referring to my character. "Yes," I tell her. "I'm Happy."

Vera escorts Duncan to the head of the table. She nods to one of the Seasoned Chefs, and he turns off the compact disc player that's been blasting out the ragtime. "Gals and gents," she says in her bright Vera voice, and everyone falls quiet. "Welcome to *Very Vera's Vice and Vamp Valhalla.*"

"You got a swell gin-mill here, baby," Arthur calls out. At the same time, his hand slides from the table, to his lap, and apparently to regions beyond because Nancy squeals and says, "Go chase yourself, goof." She lifts his hand and puts it back on the table. "The bank's closed."

Everyone laughs, and then Vera says, "Easy, there, Big Lucky. It's time to cut the static and get down to brass tacks."

She nods to Duncan, and he clears his throat. He reaches for his water glass and takes a long drink, getting ready, I assume, to deliver the speech Vera has given him, to become the G-Man, Melvin Purvis.

"Here's the goods," he finally says. "I'm here to find the rat who made off with John Dillinger's doily because once I find him, I'll be one step closer to Dillinger himself. All I need is a little help from you. So I've asked Vera here to prepare a little feast, something to put you more in the mood to spill the beans."

Vera claps her hands together twice, and the servers, young men and women, in black trousers and white shirts and long white aprons tied around their waists, carry gleaming silver serving dishes to the table. Steam rises from the dishes, and several of the guests lean over the table, taking a deep breath through their noses, smelling a meaty spice.

"Hoppin' John," Vera says as if she's reading a new recipe on her radio program. "A zippy mix of rice and bacon and black-eyed peas to bring you luck in the new year. And oh, yes, just enough crushed red pepper to give it some zing."

"Zing-a-ling-a-ding," says Arthur.

Duncan clears his throat again. "Cool your heels. Have a good dinner. Pretty soon we'll be talking turkey."

Again, Vera claps her hands and this time the servers carry out meat platters. "Campeche Turkey Filets," she says. "Turkey breasts tossed in olive oil and rubbed with cilantro and cumin and served over corn tortillas with fresh slices of mango. *Feliz año nuevo.*"

"You'll have to mind your potatoes," Duncan says, and Vera

announces the baked potato skins sprinkled with paprika and served with sour cream. "Then, when you start to talk, you'll know your onions."

"Glazed onions," Vera says with a sweep of her hand toward the servers. "Garnished with mint leaves and grated cheese."

The food keeps coming: fruits and salads and breads. "Enjoy the grub," Duncan says. He walks around the table, lingering behind the guests. "But remember I'm keeping my eye on you. Especially this one." He stops behind me and lays a hand on my back. "Happy Mickey Finn," he says. "A sly one with the knockout drops. If I were you, I'd think twice before I asked him to make me a drink."

"That's right," says Arthur. "He's a tricky one."

"Tricky Mickey," says Nancy, and as everyone laughs, I feel the heat and blush come into my face.

Duncan returns to the head of the table where Vera waits. She leans over and whispers something to him.

"Right," he says. "I almost forgot." He takes another drink from his water glass. His Adam's apple slides up and down his long throat. "The thing is," he says. "The most important thing." Suddenly, he seems nervous. He hooks a finger inside his shirt collar as if it's too tight and he's trying to get more air, but as I've already noted the collar is too loose the way it is. He clears his throat again, leans over with his palms flat on the table. He takes off his straw boater and fans his face. "What you see," he says, "isn't always the clue you think it is. There's always another clue you'll have to find. And remember, you're all suspects. You're all hiding something. But sooner or later you'll talk. You won't be able to help it. You'll get scared. You'll come clean. You'll tell your story just to hear your own voice, just to know there's someone out there listening. So you'll know you're not alone. Oh, you'll talk all right. Like you, Big Lucky." He points the straw boater toward Arthur. Then the boater swings toward me. "And you . . ."

Before he can say Happy Mickey Finn, the boater drops from his hand and he clutches his chest. His head goes back, and his knees buckle, and he collapses to the floor.

ALL THE WAY HOME, I TRY TO IMAGINE TELLING THE STORY to Maddie. The story of how, after Duncan collapsed, I rushed to him. I cradled his head in my hands. I shouted, "Is there a doctor here? Is anyone a doctor or a nurse?"

"Oh, that's a scream," someone said. "That's right out of a movie. Is there a doctor in the house?"

People were laughing. Later, they'd say they thought what I said was part of the script. They never for once thought that Duncan was really in trouble. They didn't think, like I did, that his heart had seized up or a blood vessel had burst in his brain. They thought it was all part of the act, part of the story that Vera had arranged for the party.

Only Arthur took it seriously—Arthur who had watched his wife fall to the floor with an aneurysm. He knew how someone could be here one minute and then be gone in an instant.

I need to tell Maddie about the way he knelt on the floor with me and started performing CPR, the heel of his hand pumping Duncan's chest. "There he was," I'll tell her, "your grandfather. Right there when he thought someone needed him." I'll try to explain what this should mean to her, the fact that her grandfather is someone people can depend on. Someone *she* can depend on. "Your grandfather," I'll say. "Your family." Then I'll let her see the truth of things. "He wants the best for you," I'll say. "You should give him another chance."

At the Cabbage Rose, Duncan opened one eye. I was still cradling his head, looking down at his face, and he winked at me. I'll have to tell Maddie that as well. I'll have to say that Vera started laughing so hard the fringe on her flapper dress shimmied, and then Duncan was holding up his hands, and he was shaking with his own laughter, sputtering out words of protest to make Arthur stop pressing on his chest. "Enough, enough," he said. "It's . . . all . . . part of . . . the game."

So it was. A little surprise to throw us a curve. We hadn't gathered to solve the mystery of John Dillinger's Disappeared Doily at all. We'd come to figure out who killed the G-Man, Melvin Purvis, and how.

"Poison," said Nancy later. "That much is clear. Someone fed him arsenic or something."

Vera told her she was right. "It was Happy Mickey Finn. He was the one who did it. Arsenic. Mixed it into his drink and made him go to sleep."

"Sammy, I always wondered about you," Nancy said very gravely, and I wondered whether she was serious or only pulling my leg.

Everyone was in high spirits the rest of the evening as the mystery unraveled. They kept repeating what I'd shouted. One of the Seasoned Chefs would get weak in the knees and clutch his heart. "Someone call nine one one," he'd say. Then his date would put her hand on his chest or give him a kiss, and he'd say, "Oh, doctor."

"What a hoot," said Vera as I was getting my coat. "For a minute, ducky, even I thought Duncan was in trouble. You and Arthur. I guess you were the suckers tonight."

I could barely look at Duncan the rest of the evening. Not only had he had a part in making a fool out of me; I was afraid he would now remember that he had something he wanted to tell me, whatever it was that had caused him to leave me that note and to mention it when I first arrived at the party.

The other thing I'll have to tell Maddie is that Arthur wasn't like me, wasn't hurt or embarrassed by how he'd been duped. He thought it was a riot, the way he fell for everything. "Hooked me and reeled me in," he kept saying with a big smile. "I guess I'm just about as dumb as they come." He was a good sport. "You see," I'll tell Maddie. "He can take what life throws him and not lose his balance. He can keep sailing ahead. That's the sort of man you want to love you. Someone steady like your grandfather."

But what I won't tell her is this: After I had my coat and was trying to slip out of the Cabbage Rose, I saw Duncan and Nancy on the porch. I opened the door and heard Nancy say, "I remember it was spring and the water was up."

Right away, I knew they were talking about Dewey, and I lingered in the doorway, eavesdropping. Duncan said, "When I interviewed Mr. Brady for that *It's Us* feature, it came out that you were a Finn from Rat Town, and he never said a word about being friends with Dewey."

"That doesn't surprise me," Nancy said. "He's like that."

"Tight-lipped?" Duncan asked.

Nancy set her jaw. "Tight-lipped with reason," she said, leaving me to wonder exactly what she meant.

Arthur came up behind me. "We really fell for it, didn't we, Sammy?"

At the sound of his voice, Nancy stopped talking. She and Duncan turned to look at us there in the doorway. I had no choice, then, but to step out onto the porch.

"You were quick on the trigger tonight, Mr. Brady," Duncan said. "If I'm ever really in trouble, I hope you're somewhere nearby."

"Arthur's the one who knew what to do," I said.

"Aren't you going to stick around until midnight?" Arthur asked me. "Pop the cork? Drink some bubbly?"

"No, I need to get home. It's late for an old dog like me."

I went down the steps, shrinking from the glow of the Cabbage Rose's lights, as I slipped farther into the darkness.

Arthur called after me. "Tell Maddie I said Happy New Year. Tell her I'll see her tomorrow."

"Happy New Year," Nancy said.

"And to you," I said.

I won't tell Maddie what Nancy said to Duncan—*tight-lipped with reason*. That's mine to mull over.

Duncan said, "Mr. Brady, wait." He came down the steps to where I was standing. "I want you to know something." He glanced back over his shoulder to where Nancy and Arthur stood on the porch. Nancy shaded her eyes with her hand and leaned forward, trying her best, I imagined, to see us there in the dark. Duncan said, "I got to looking at those clothes again, those clothes of Dewey's." He closed his hand around my bicep as if he sensed how close I was to drawing away from him and wanted to keep me right where I was long enough to say the thing he'd come to say. "That belt, one piece of it with a ragged edge. That belt wasn't cut like we thought, Mr. Brady. An edge like that. It was torn away." He squeezed my arm with more pressure. He turned to look at Nancy, who was still on the porch, chatting with Arthur. "Do you know what it's done to my grandmother to think all these years that Dewey was so miserable he went off and killed himself? I'll do anything to prove that's not what happened. I'll do that so she can have some peace."

So I decided to tell him, then, about the night in front of the pool hall when I said what I did about Dewey, and Arthur and his friends picked up on it. I told Duncan I'd always wondered what harm I might have brought Dewey because of what I said.

"Mr. Pope?" Duncan said, and I knew he was trying to put two and two together. "Do you think . . . ?"

I interrupted him. "I'm just telling you a story. That's all. A story about what I said that night when Arthur could hear it. Maybe you should talk to him."

"Why would you say it, Mr. Brady? I thought Dewey was your friend."

"We were on the outs," I said, and then, before the silence demanded I say more, Nancy came down the steps, calling my name.

"Sammy," she said, "don't go just yet." Duncan let go of my arm, and we both dummied up, waiting for her to join us. She opened her handbag and took out a notepad and a pen. "I want to give you my address in Evansville," she said. "In case you're ever down that way. Maybe you could drop by, and we could chat." She scribbled something on the notepad, tore off a small sheet, and pressed it into my hand. "Will you do that, Sammy? Please? We could catch up on old times."

There was a little light from the porch spilling out onto the walk, just enough for me to make out the address she'd written: *5214 Larkspur Lane, Evansville, IN.* The address, the same one I'd seen written on the back of that map of Chicago. The place Cal had said he'd go to take care of things if trouble found him.

15

I HURRY HOME, KEYED UP, BECAUSE SURELY THE REASON Cal has Nancy Finn's address is because he means to make good on his word, to stand up and tell her the truth about Dewey, the truth I wish we'd told the night he died. I pull into my driveway and before I open my garage door, I close my eyes and listen to the courthouse clock uptown, chiming twelve. Then the chiming stops, and I open my eyes to the New Year. The first thing I see is the gate to my side yard wide open, and in my house, all the lights ablaze.

I get out of my Jeep and make time as quick as I can into the yard. When I come up my back steps, I see that the storm door is standing open, cockeyed on its hinges, the pneumatic closer that allows it to open and close easily broken away from the frame. Whoever came through that door last, opened it with force. I can see that for sure, and right away I'm thinking that it's finally happened, that just like Cal feared, Herbert Zwilling has found him and taken him away despite his best efforts to resist. Then, a second, more urgent thought comes to me—Maddie—and I hurry into my house.

She's there—thank God—curled up on the couch, crying.

I kneel on the floor beside her. "Maddie," I say, and she throws her arms around my neck and clings to me. "Maddie," I say again. "What's happened? Are you all right?"

She's trying to tell me, but her face is pressed into my neck and she's sobbing, so all I can make out at first is, "He's gone."

I ease her away from me. "Did Cal say where he was going?"

"Not Cal," she says with a wail. "Stump."

At first, the news doesn't sink in. Stump gone. Those two words. What can they mean?

"Where's Cal?" I ask.

"Gone to look for him," she says, and then I know this is really happening.

It was her fault, she tells me, when she's finally calm enough to give me the whole story. She went over to Arthur's house just a few minutes before eleven because she wanted to watch the ball drop at midnight in Times Square and Cal didn't want her to have the television on. In fact, he wanted all the lights out, too, so it'd look like no one was home. "He was acting funny like that," she says. "He kept peeking out the curtains, and when I asked him what was going on, he just told me to never mind."

So she went over to Arthur's, and Stump whined to go with her. She let him out into the side yard, thinking he could nose around out there awhile, maybe cozy up in his ship, and then she'd collect him when she came back.

"I guess I didn't get the gate latched," she says. "When I came back, it was wide open, and Stump was nowhere to be seen."

The confession starts her bawling again, and now I don't have the patience to comfort her. I grab a flashlight and start for the back door.

Before I can step outside, I hear a phone ring, but it's not the old-time jangle of the dial phone on my kitchen wall. It's a musical series of electronic beeps, and I realize it's coming from Cal's cell phone, which, in his haste to find Stump, he's left on the kitchen counter.

My first thought is to ignore it, but then I wonder if it might be Cal calling from a pay phone, calling to say he's found Stump.

I pick up the cell phone and take it to Maddie. "Quick," I say, "how do I answer this?"

She flips it open, punches a button, and reaches the phone out to me. I put it to my ear and before I can say a word, a voice is speaking to me. A woman's voice, and I know it's Mora Grove. "Cal, it's me. Listen . . ."

I interrupt her. "This isn't Cal. It's his brother."

"Jesus," Mora Grove says. Then there's a long silence. "Where's Cal? Where is he?"

"Out," I say. "I don't know where."

"Listen." Her voice is sharper now. "You find him. You find him quick, and you tell him it's time."

Then the line goes dead.

OUTSIDE, I STOP AT THE GATE AND SHINE THE FLASHLIGHT on the tracks in the snow—Stump's tracks. They trail out into the driveway, across the corner of Arthur's yard, and down the sidewalk farther than my flashlight beam can stretch. Out there, is all I can think. Maddie left the gate open, and now Stump is wandering somewhere, following a scent the way basset hounds will do, noses to the ground, any thought of distance and effort covered over with the desire to keep moving, to find out what this and that is until they're exhausted, in need of food and water, so far from home there's no way for them to ever get back.

I hear the door close behind me, and here's Maddie coming toward me, buttoning her coat.

"Is Cal on foot?" I ask her.

"No, he took his truck."

Better to be on foot, I think, to follow Stump's tracks, but I'd have a better chance of finding Cal if I took my Jeep. "When did you say you left the gate open?"

"A little before eleven."

Over an hour. An hour for Stump to sniff after whatever scent he took a fancy to.

"Here's his tracks," I say.

Maddie nods. "I'm coming with you."

As angry as I am, at least I can allow her this chance to stand with me and face her mistake.

"All right," I say, and then we set out.

We make it to the corner, and in the streetlight's glow, I can see that Stump's tracks circle the street sign pole and then head east toward Cherry Blossom. So far, we're lucky. He's stayed off the cleared sidewalk where he'd leave no prints and stuck to the snow-covered grass. But now the wind's up, blowing north to south, and soon those tracks will cover over and Stump will be out there in the night and I'll have no way to find him. I tell Maddie as much, and that sets her to crying again. She does her best to hide it, but I can hear her sniffles, and the catch in her breathing. Then she gets the hiccups. Everything's a mess: Maddie crying, the wind scattering snow, and Stump gone, his tracks petering out here where Cherry Blossom intersects with East Street, the main north-south artery on this side of town. The stoplights are blinking—red for the traffic headed east and west, yellow for the northbound and southbound lanes—and though there's no cars in sight (Mt. Gilead is mostly quiet as the New Year begins, only a few firecrackers going off somewhere in the distance), I can't help but imagine Stump sauntering out into the path of some New Year's party hound, too drunk to find the brakes in time.

Maddie starts to step off the curb to cross East Street, but I grab her by her sleeve and hold her back.

"It's no good," I say. "The tracks are gone."

The wind is even stronger now; the street signs shake. "It's all my fault." Maddie bangs her fists against her thighs. "I should have made sure that gate was latched."

She's sobbing now, great choking sobs that remind me of the noise Nancy Finn made when she sat in the muddy yard crying on the night she found out Dewey was dead. Then, I had no idea of anything I could do to comfort her, but on this night I don't even have to think about it. Sad as I am that Stump is gone, and worried as I am about Cal and the call that's come, I can't bear standing witness to Maddie's misery. I put my arms around her and pull her to me. She wraps her slender arms around my waist, and we stand here, holding on.

What can I tell her about mistakes, about the things we shouldn't have done? They're ours forever. We carry them just under our skin, the scars of our living.

"Let's go back home," I say to Maddie because where else is there to go when trouble comes but to the place where night after night you lay your head? "Stop that crying," I tell her. "We'll go home."

Then, as if we've sent a prayer to heaven, a truck comes from the east. The headlights catch us in their glare, and I have to shield my eyes with my arm. The truck, Cal's Explorer, slows. The window goes down, and I can see, on the other side of Cal, Stump sitting on the passenger seat, his muzzle lifted a bit as if he's the navigator, keeping close watch on the road ahead.

"I found him," Cal says. "Thank God. I found him."

I take Maddie's hand, and we step out into the street, meaning to go to Cal and get into the Explorer, relieved, and go home. In some better world, this is what would happen.

But then I hear another car, and I see it coming from the east. Cal must hear it, too. He pokes his head out the window to get a peek at the car coming up behind him. Then he looks at me, and I can see the fear in his eyes. He's told me that, when it happens—when Herbert Zwilling comes for him—it will happen in an instant. The look in his eyes tells me that he's afraid it's come to this now, the car closing ground behind him. He keeps looking at me, and I get this odd feeling that he's waiting for me to tell him yes, it's all right, go.

"It's time," I shout, as if I've spent all my life preparing for this moment I didn't even know would come. If I could say more, I'd tell Cal that Mora Grove called. She said, "Find him quick." But I sense that Cal understands all this. He does a quick, frantic search of his coat pockets, and I know he's looking for the cell phone he left on the kitchen counter. I can't give it to him. It's in my house, on the coffee table where I left it. I can't give him his phone, and I don't even have time to fetch Stump from the Explorer. It's speeding away now, Cal desperate to get to safety.

My throat closes with the cold and the knowledge that nearly drives me to my knees. I know this may very well be the last I'll see of Stump, who is with Cal now, for better or worse, the two of them on the run.

Red at night, I think, as I watch the Explorer's taillights disappear. Be well, my sailing friend.

The car coming from the east slows and stops in the street. It's one of those little boxy cars that's popular these days, one of those toy cars you expect a load of clowns to get out of. This one's a

Scion, I see, made by Toyota if I remember the correct commercials, a Toyota Scion the color of a black cherry. The window goes down and I see that it's only Duncan Hines driving the car and that Nancy Finn is with him. My legs tense. I take a few steps toward the west, toward Cal and Stump, wanting to cry out, *wait*, *wait*, but it's too late. They're gone, gone, gone.

"Is everything all right?" Duncan asks. "Mr. Brady, do you need a ride?"

"My dog," I say. I can't tell them the whole story, the one about Cal and Zwilling and Mora Grove's warning, so I tell them the one fact I wish I could bury in the snow, cover it over and all the tracks that lead to it, and have the life back I had before Cal arrived. "Stump," I say, and an ache comes into my throat. "He's gone."

16

DUNCAN DRIVES ME HOME, AND HE SAYS NOT TO WORRY.
Surely Cal will be back soon with Stump. "Why did he take off
like that, anyway?"

"I don't know," I tell Duncan, and Maddie doesn't say a word
about what I shouted to Cal, *It's time*. She sits on the far edge of
the backseat, as far away as she can get from me, her hands in her
coat pocket, her shoulders hunched so her hood comes up around
her face.

"Cal's always been in the middle of something," Nancy says.
"I remember that about him. I remember one time when he
punched Grinny between the eyes and put him on the ground.
Right in front of the Verlene Café. In broad daylight, no less."

"Try not to worry too much about it, Mr. Brady," Duncan
says. He glances at me in the rearview mirror, and I take stock of
his pointed, buzz-cut head. His eyeglasses are slipped down on his
thin nose, and I wish I could reach out and gently push them back
in place. I get it, then, the truth of him, that he tries his best to
hide. He's been an oddball all his life, a clumsy, gawky kid, and

now every time he writes an *It's Us* profile on someone with an eccentric talent or hobby—people like me with Stump's ship, and Vera with her dollhouse collection—he's thumbing his nose at all the people who ever made fun of him, a boy named after a cake mix. His talent is with the words it takes to turn all of us oddballs into the sorts of folks everyone would love to have as their neighbors. His good heart overwhelms me, and I feel guilty about keeping things from him when it comes to the truth about Dewey. On this night of sadness, I'm thankful for Duncan's optimism. "Maybe your brother just went on back to your house. Mr. Brady, I bet he's there right now."

OF COURSE, HE ISN'T. MADDIE AND I GO INTO MY HOUSE, where the lights are still blazing but there's no Cal, no Stump. Maddie picks up the quilt she left in a tangle on the couch. It seems as if there's nothing to say between us. Any word will lead back to the fact that she left that gate open, and now Stump's gone.

I tell her the story of the New Year's Eve party and how her grandfather, when he thought Duncan was in trouble, came to the rescue. "He was right there," I say, "ready to do what he could." I tell her what a good sport he was after the real story came out and everyone knew Duncan's collapse had been staged. "Your grandfather can roll with the punches," I say. "Whatever you need, he's going to do his best to help you out."

I help her fold the quilt. We fold it in half lengthwise, then turn it flat. I carry my end to her and she takes it from me, hugging the quilt to her chest.

"You want me to leave, don't you?" Her voice is shaking. "I left the gate open and now you want me to go back to the Pope."

I have to steel myself in order to do what I know is right. "You left that gate open," I say, and she lets the quilt drop from her fingers and slide to the floor.

SO SHE GOES BACK TO ARTHUR, AND I STAY UP MOST OF THE night, unable to sleep. I empty my pockets to change from my Happy Mickey Finn costume into my own clothes, and I find the slip of paper on which Nancy wrote her address. I lay it on the library table and anchor it with the Brulatour Courtyard paperweight. Once I'm changed, I lie on the couch where the pillow still smells of Maddie's vanilla scent. I put the quilt over me, and sometime toward morning I finally doze off.

When I wake, the sunlight is coming into my eyes, and the telephone is ringing.

It's Arthur calling. "You home?" he says. I can look out my kitchen window and see him at his. I give him a little wave. "Have you eaten lunch yet?" he asks. "Hold on. I'm on my way over."

In a tick, he's here, and Maddie is with him. She carries a casserole dish: Arthur's specialty, andouille jambalaya. I can smell its spice as soon as I open the back door and the two of them step inside my kitchen.

"I made a sweet potato and apple salad." Arthur pops the lid off a Tupperware bowl and moves it back and forth beneath my nose. I smell the tang of citrus juice and the spike of garlic. "Vera should be here any minute."

"Vera?"

"She's bringing Cajun crawfish cornbread," Maddie says, already setting the casserole dish in the oven and turning it on low heat to keep it warm.

I catch no hint of mockery in her voice, nor any anger with me because I made her go back to Arthur. If anything, she seems comfortable. She wipes her hands on a dish towel and then opens the cupboard and takes down four plates. She sets the table and finds the silverware.

Arthur puts the lid back on the Tupperware bowl and sets it in the refrigerator. "You hadn't ought to be alone, Sammy." If he harbors any grudge because Maddie once chose to live with me, he doesn't show it. He speaks with a gentle voice. "Not now," he says. "Not at a time like this. Trust me, Sammy. I know what it is to lose someone you love. You and Stump had years together. I know what he meant to you. Now we'll have a good meal, just the four of us. We'll eat, and we'll be together."

Sometimes, I'm learning, that's what it takes—just the nearness of people—to make you feel there may be a good reason for all we suffer. Maybe for moments like this when Vera breezes through the door and I smell her flowery cologne, and she hugs me, not a quick, how-do-you-do hug, but a true embrace. She holds me to her as if right now I'm the most precious thing in the world.

"Sam," she says, "I've brought bread."

So we sit around this table, and as we eat, I'm thankful to Arthur and Maddie and Vera for knowing what I need.

Vera says to Maddie, "I'll take you shopping tomorrow. We'll go to *Déjà New*."

"That vintage clothing store, right?" Maddie smoothes her napkin over her lap.

Arthur rolls his eyes at me. "Girl talk."

It delights me, this chit-chat that's a sign of life going on—this and the fact that something about Stump's disappearance has made Maddie open her heart to Vera. Maddie will be starting school here in a few days—a new kid in the middle of the year—and she'll need friends, a little advice from time to time, the sort of commiseration Arthur won't be the best equipped to offer. It's good, then, that she's started to make room for Vera, who is as close to a mother as she may have for some time.

"You're such a pretty girl," Vera says.

"Really?" Maddie smiles.

"Oh definitely. You're a knockout."

We finish our meal, but no one makes a move to get up from the table. None of us wants to break the spell, the belief that we can get beyond the sadness of Stump and Cal being gone, but of course, that fact isn't far from our minds. In our silence, it works itself up through the good food and conversation we've just now put an end to.

Then Arthur, unable to keep quiet any longer, says, "So your brother's ducked out again." It's clear that Arthur takes some degree of pleasure in saying this. I imagine he still remembers how the girls went crazy over Cal when he was a young buck, and most of the boys in Mt. Gilead wished they could be him. Old feelings die hard, and I imagine Arthur's still smarting from the way Vera took so easily to Cal that night at the Seasoned Chefs. "Doesn't surprise me a bit."

"What do you mean by that?" I say.

"He doesn't spend too much time in port. That's your brother, the kind to leave and not think about how he might hurt someone else. Isn't that right, Vera? Just the way he walked out on you back when you were starting out."

I know now that sometime, maybe the night Arthur was looking for Maddie, Vera told him the story of her and Cal and how there was a time when she swore she loved him. Then he went away from her, and now here she is, a widow stuck with the company of men like Arthur and me.

She stands up from the table and starts clearing dishes. "When Cal showed up that night at the Seasoned Chefs, I thought it might lead to something." She lets her hand trail over Maddie's back. "See how foolish your heart can be no matter how old you get?"

Arthur turns his palms up. "Now he's run out, just like he did then. This is what I'm saying."

I feel an anger rising in me, one born not only from the indignation I feel to hear Arthur so smugly cast suspicion on Cal, but also from the fact I can't deny, the horrible feeling I have that perhaps Cal has more to answer for than he's let on.

"Maybe we're all guilty of something," I say to Arthur. "Maybe it's like that."

"Not me," says Arthur. "I sleep good at night."

I could go on. I could say more, but there's danger in words. They can lead us to places we'd rather not go.

"Do you, Arthur?" I finally say.

"Like a baby," he says, but I see the way he braces himself with his hands flat on the table, like he'd spring up and run away if he could. I see that, and I see his head tip back just the slightest bit and the skin around his eyes crinkle as if he just felt the worst pain behind them, and I know he's lying. I know he lies awake in the night, thinking about Bess, wishing that she were there with him, playing over in his head, perhaps, all the things he might have done wrong in his life, the things he has to pay for now by being alone.

"Gents," Vera says. "Is this really the time for this kind of talk?"

Arthur and I shut our yaps, and we help tidy up the kitchen. We sit in the living room, with the television on, and Vera says she hopes we have a short winter. I feel an ache for summer and its long light. I let myself dream that Stump will come back, and in a few months' time, we'll be taking our evening walks, the sun brimming red on the horizon. He'll sniff at the air, tip his face up to me, and give me that look that says there's nowhere in the world he'd rather be, and this time, these days of winter, will be far behind us.

We all sit in my living room until dusk starts to fall, and Vera and Arthur and Maddie have to get back to their own lives. Vera kisses my cheek as she leaves. Arthur pats me on the shoulder. Maddie gives me a hug and says, "I'm sorry."

"I know you are," I say, and she hugs me again. Then I'm alone.

IN THE EVENING, NEARLY TEN O'CLOCK, I HEAR A TIMID TAP-ping at my back door: "Shave and a Haircut." I turn on the hall light and then I go to open the door. Arthur steps inside, and he says to me, "You know I saw him that night. The night that Dewey died. I saw Cal. He was heading down the tracks."

I close the door behind me. I turn around to face him, my hands on my hips. I take a deep breath, and then I say it: "I know you did. I saw you off in the woods. You were following Dewey, weren't you? It was because of what I said that night in front of the pool hall."

For a good while, Arthur doesn't speak. He glances behind him into the living room, as if he's making sure there's no one eavesdropping on us. "That was a long time ago, Sammy." His voice, hushed, is full of embarrassment. "I was just a kid," he says, as if that fact alone can absolve him.

"Like I said," I tell him. "Maybe we're all guilty of something."

He sits at the table, and bows his head. He tugs on the hem of the tablecloth, straightening its edge. I wait until he works up the nerve to lift his head and look at me. Then he says, "You're right. It started that night in front of the pool hall. I was there with Ollie

Scaggs and Wendell Black." The names align themselves with the boys I remember: Ollie, who wore a white T-shirt; Wendell with a pencil behind his ear. "Dewey was walking by," Arthur says, "and you called him a queer. That got us going, Ollie and Wendell and me, and one night we got him in my car and drove down into Lukin Township. We parked back up one of those oil lease roads, and Ollie took Dewey's face in his hands, and he said, 'Boys, look at that pretty mouth. You ever seen a mouth as pretty as that?' We undid our blue jeans, and, well, do I have to say more? Am I making myself plain? We showed Dewey exactly what he was."

I take a chair across the table from Arthur, a sick feeling rising in my chest, knowing for certain now the torment I brought to Dewey at the end of his life. It happened sometimes, just the way Arthur said. Boys in our town—boys who weren't "like that"—made another boy take them in his mouth, and then threatened to beat him if he ever breathed a word.

"Dewey said he'd tell," Arthur says, "and I believed him. I couldn't have that happen, Sammy. I was already in love with Bess then." Here, he closes his eyes tight, and he swallows hard. "Jesus, Sammy. What if she'd found out?" He opens his eyes and looks right at me. "So when I saw him going down the tracks, I followed along there in the woods, thinking I had my chance to get him off by himself and show him what would happen if he ever told. Then I saw Cal, and I saw you. That's the way it was, wasn't it?"

"Yes," I tell him, and in my mind I travel back over the years to that April evening. "That's the way it was. There we were, you and me and Cal and Dewey, the four of us at the tracks."

17

MY BACK DOOR OPENS, THEN, AND A MAN I KNOW IS HERBERT Zwilling walks into my house. I remember the beefy face from the photograph on CNN during the hostage crisis. That face is red now, red with cold and the rage he's carried with him from Ohio. He's sweating, and he runs his hand over his forehead up through his flattop haircut.

"Where is he?" he says. "Where's Cal Brady?"

I get up from the table and turn on the overhead light. Herbert Zwilling blinks his eyes. Then he stomps through the kitchen to the hallway. He flips on the light and goes down to the bedrooms. I hear him opening the closet doors.

"Sammy?" Arthur says. "You know this guy?"

"Cal," I say, and that's all I can get out because then Herbert Zwilling is back in the kitchen, and now he's pointing a gun at me. A handgun with a steel-blue barrel and a chrome grip. He motions for me to join him.

"Both of you," he says, meaning Arthur, of course.

What choice do we have? When we're in the hallway, Herbert Zwilling steps up close to me, the way I imagine Cal crowded

Leonard Mink the day he popped that Ruger Single Six up under his chin.

"Tell me," Herbert Zwilling says, and I know that what Cal has claimed is the truth: This man wants him dead.

"He's gone." I do my best to keep my voice steady. "He took my dog," I say, and right away I know how ridiculous that sounds.

"I don't give a good goddamn about your dog." Herbert Zwilling sticks the barrel of the gun into my ear. I know it's a fool thing to do, but I try to move away from it. I stumble into the living room, and he comes with me, grinding that gun barrel into my ear, until I bump up against the library table, and he says, "What kind of an idiot are you? Don't you know you don't mean anything to me?"

It's true. I know that. I'm nothing to this man, nor is Arthur, who's taken a few steps into the living room and stands now, bent over, his hands on his knees. "Jesus," he says.

A prayer, I think. One word before the slaughter begins.

I stand still, and finally Herbert Zwilling says again, his voice calm this time, "I want to know where your brother is."

We could stand here a while longer with the truth unsaid. If I had any thought in the world where Cal might be, I'd have been after him in an instant.

But what's the use? Even with the barrel in my ear, I hear the hammer on that gun ratchet back. Herbert Zwilling starts counting—"One, two, three"—and I understand, without him having to tell me, that he's giving me till ten to tell him what he's convinced I know.

I glance down and see that the paper with Nancy Finn's address on it has worked its way out from under the Brulatour Courtyard paperweight. I know this is where Cal has said he'll go if trouble comes, so I try to cover the paper with my hand. Herbert Zwilling jerks it away. He picks up the paper and studies it.

"All right." He motions toward the door with his gun. "Both of you," he says. "Let's go."

WE GO OUT INTO THE NIGHT, AND JUST AS WE STEP THROUGH my gate, Maddie comes out the side door of Arthur's house. She's in a long, white nightgown that falls to her ankles—a nightgown, I imagine, that belonged to Bess. Her feet are bare, and I think of the first time I saw her sitting on the deck of Stump's ship, saw her naked shins and worried over her out there in the cold. Now here she comes, barefoot, through the snow, as if it isn't snow at all, but puffs of clouds she glides over, the high clouds just below the golden light of heaven.

I watch her, my tongue gone dead in my mouth. That's how taken I am by the sight of her, ghostly in the night, that white gown billowing and falling with each step she takes through the snow.

I won't speak for Arthur or Herbert Zwilling, but me? I'm thinking there must be a land—yes, I'll call it heaven; you call it whatever you'd like—where the dead are never cold, never want for love, never look back and regret their time among the living or call us to answer for the wrongs we did them. They leave that reckoning to us, and when the time comes for us to join them, they open their arms, the way Maddie now lifts her slender arms toward Herbert Zwilling. I can tell she's sleep-walking. She's coming directly toward him and the gun he holds, as if nothing in the world can hurt her, or as if everything already has.

If I ever stand with Dewey in paradise—I have to believe this—he'll put his arms around me. "Sammy, sweetheart," he'll say. And that'll be that.

But for now, I'm here on this cold night, heaven far beyond

the stars above me, and I see the situation for what it is: a young girl not knowing she's walking straight toward disaster.

I reach out—it's that easy, really, ridiculous as it may seem—and grab the gun from Herbert Zwilling. Just like that, it comes out of his hand and I hold it on him.

Arthur lays his hands on Maddie. Just the softest touch on her shoulders to let her know she's still among the living. "Honey," he says, his voice barely a whisper, the sound of every breath that ever left this world. "Honey, it's okay. You're right here."

Maddie lets him hold her. He wraps his arms around her and gathers her in.

I HAVE ROPE IN MY BASEMENT, AND ARTHUR, THE OLD SAILOR, knows knots: cat's paw, Turk's head, sheet bend. He learned them all in the Navy and is quite eager now to put them to use to restrain Herbert Zwilling, while Maddie is safe in Arthur's house.

"Don't waste time with that," I tell him. "Call the police."

"No, we need to tie him down," he says, and I can see there's no use arguing with him.

"Sit," I tell Herbert Zwilling, stunned by how little this shakes me. I've never held a gun in my life, but I've watched Cal and I know how to make it look like I mean business.

"Mister," says Herbert Zwilling. He sits on the wooden folding chair and lets Arthur pull his arms back behind him. "You don't know what you're getting yourself into."

"Don't talk," I tell him.

"I mean it," he says. "This is way too big for the likes of you."

The likes of me? The words get inside me, and I can't stop myself. I stick the barrel of the gun into Herbert Zwilling's throat, jam it hard against his Adam's apple. He tips his head back, but I won't let him go. I keep bearing down, and I can see him swallow, can hear a little gurgle in his throat.

"You don't know anything about me," I say, and I hold that gun there while Arthur goes to work with the rope. When he's securing the last of the knots, I tell him I'm going upstairs to call the police.

Just as I reach for the phone, Maddie comes through my kitchen door. She's dressed now in jeans and a sweater and dragging a coat by one arm. "I want to know what's going on." She sits on a kitchen chair, her coat draped over her lap. She squints at me as if she's trying to make sense of everything. "Sam?" she says.

I imagine what she sees when she looks at me. This old man holding this gun, this man who took her into his house when she was desperate to escape her grandfather. She trusted me with the story of her mother—"the real story," she called it. She knew what Dewey meant to me without me even having to tell her. "If he was special to you," she said, "it's okay." Now, here I am. Now here's this gun. I can barely look at her, not wanting to be this sort of man. I remember the moment when I saw Cal on the television, coming out of that grain elevator, the danger over. The reporter on CNN called him a hero, and right now, standing here with this gun, looking at Maddie, I know how that made Cal feel, like an impostor.

"You were walking in your sleep," I tell her.

That's what it feels like now—this night, my whole life after Dewey—a sleepy fog. I've always been trying to find the boy I was. I left him back there on the railroad trestle singing with Dewey. One of the last times I truly felt joy.

My phone rings. Its shrill noise shakes me.

What can I do but answer? This is the way it is, isn't it? You can think you don't have a prayer, and then a phone rings or a door opens, and you feel your life shooting on ahead of you. Maybe it was going that way all along but you didn't know it, and now all you can do is hang on and wait to see what's waiting on the other end.

I pick up the phone, and suddenly I can't find my voice, the events of the evening too much for me.

"Sammy?" the voice on the phone finally says, and I know it's Cal. "Sammy?" he says. "You asleep?"

This is my brother, somewhere in the night, somewhere on the run. I want to tell him to come back. *Come home,* I want to say, *and we'll lie in the dark and talk our quiet talk the way we did when we were boys. Blood to blood. You'll tell me everything there is to say, and I'll hold it inside me forever. Hold your secrets until I'm dead and gone.* But I know he can't come back. Nothing here is safe. Herbert Zwilling is bound and gagged in the basement, but are there others, men like Leonard Mink, out there tonight looking for Cal?

"No, I'm not asleep," I tell him. "Cal, I'm right here."

"I wanted to make sure you're all right." I hear the noise of highway traffic, the blare of a horn fading as a diesel truck goes by. Cal's voice is jazzed up with fear. "Sammy, I'm sorry."

"About the way you left with Stump? It wasn't your fault. You didn't have any other choice."

"I had choices all up and down the line. You know that. I could have come out a different man than I am now." For a good while, he doesn't say anything. There's only the traffic noise, and what sounds like the wind pushing a can across pavement, and what I guess is the squeal of a metal sign rocking on its hinges. I imagine him at a pay phone—you can still find them here in the middle of the country—maybe at a truck stop, maybe at a gas station closed now for the night. I think of him braced against that wind. "If I'd stayed home." Now his voice is barely a whisper. "If I'd never left Rat Town, Sammy. If I hadn't been hotheaded like the old man."

"Dad," I say. "He could never make room for who I was."

"He loved you."

"You, too," I tell him.

The basement door flies open and bangs back against the kitchen counter. The noise startles me so badly I drop the phone.

Then everything speeds up.

Arthur stumbles up from the basement, Herbert Zwilling behind him, his arm barred across Arthur's throat, the knots of rope, somehow ineffectual, loosed and gone.

I swing the gun toward them.

"Grandpa," says Maddie.

Herbert Zwilling tells her to shut up.

"Put that gun down," he says to me. "Put it on the table where I can reach it. I mean it. Do it now, or I'll break your buddy's neck."

He tightens his arm, and Arthur's head goes back. He shuts his eyes tight.

I line up the pistol's sight with Herbert Zwilling's left temple. I try to convince myself I can pull the trigger. One shot clean to the brain. But here's Arthur's face so close to Herbert Zwilling's. No room for error, and, of course, even as my finger tightens on the trigger, and I tell myself to squeeze it, I know I won't. I know the only thing I can do is to lay the pistol on the table exactly how Herbert Zwilling has told me. He picks it up.

Then it happens: A bullet to Arthur's head, and he slips to the floor.

This is the way it is. Why should I be surprised? We can think our lives are removed from it all, quaint and safe. We build a dog-house that's the replica of a ship, learn recipes at the Seasoned Chefs, dress up and play tough guy at a New Year's Eve party. Then a door opens and the evil comes inside and suddenly, the terror we've read about in headlines, watched on the evening news, is ours.

My ears ring. I smell the blood, feel its odor settle on my tongue. The sickness rises up into my throat, and I choke it down.

Maddie is crying. She's put her coat over her head so she won't see the bullet she's sure is hers.

Then I say to Herbert Zwilling, "She's just a girl." I say it like a prayer. "Please leave her be. She can't hurt you."

He takes a few steps toward her, and that's when I move. I lift her up from her chair and I wrap my arms around her, turning my back to Herbert Zwilling, doing the only thing I can, shielding her with my body.

I hold her, and I wait.

Then I feel the pistol's barrel against the back of my head.

"Put your coats on," Herbert Zwilling says. "Both of you, and don't say a word when we walk out the door. Just keep your mouths shut and do everything I tell you to do."

I DRIVE. "NICE AND EASY," HERBERT ZWILLING SAYS. "YOU get me to where your brother is. No tricks. Anything shaky and I'll kill the girl."

He sits in the backseat of his Chevy Blazer, leaning forward, his gun held at Maddie's head. She's fidgeting with the strings that hang down from the hood of her coat. She's flipped the hood over her head, as if that piece of insulated material can protect her.

She's still crying a little, a few whimpers and sniffles muffled inside the hood. When she speaks, her voice shakes.

She says, "How fucked up is this?"

And Herbert Zwilling shoves her head forward with the pistol's barrel. "I'm back here, Mouth," he says. "Remember me?" Again, he taps her head with the pistol. "The only reason I don't shut you up right now—I mean forever, Mouth—is you're going to come in handy soon."

"She's just a girl," I say like I did a few minutes earlier in my house, a house where I know Arthur's body waits to be found, a house I can't imagine ever seeming like mine again. "What could she possibly do?"

"You," Herbert Zwilling shouts, and he knocks my face a little with the pistol. "Drive."

Then it's like we've all dissolved into a silent movie. I think of the episode of *I Love Lucy* that was playing the night I found Maddie in Stump's house and told her to come inside. There they were—Lucy and Ethel and Ricky and Fred—gathered around the piano, singing, and watching them, Maddie and I understood something: the shadows looming ahead.

Now we glide along Highway 130 on our way to Evansville. In the middle of the night, there's hardly any traffic at all, but from time to time we meet a car and the headlights come into the Blazer, and I imagine what the other driver must see for just an instant: an old man, his jaw set; a girl with a hood over her head; a man in the backseat, each of them staring straight down the road.

AT GRAYVILLE, WE GET ON INTERSTATE 64, AND SOON WE'RE in Indiana, heading east to Highway 41, which takes us south to the city. It's here, at a stoplight near Dress Regional Airport, the lights of the city spreading out before me, that I realize I have no idea where Nancy Finn lives, wouldn't begin to know how to find Larkspur Lane.

Evansville isn't Mt. Gilead—no sir, not by a long shot—not a one-horse town where you might drive up and down streets until you hit a neighborhood that seems like it might be right. You'd hit Orchard Farms, maybe, and see those streets—Peach Tree, Apple Blossom, Cherry Blossom—and you'd think, hallelujah, Cider Court must be just around the corner.

No, here in Evansville, this river town nestled in close to the Ohio, the streets spread out, east from the inner city to Highway 41 and beyond to Green River Road and out to the Warrick County line, and west along the Lloyd Expressway to Posey County, and south past Ellis Park Race Track before the high arching bridge crosses the Ohio into Kentucky, and north up here to the airport, where I sit at a red light, wondering what to do.

Herbert Zwilling is getting nervous. "So where is it?" he says. "Where's this place we're going? Where's this Larkspur Lane?"

And I tell him the truth. Sometimes that's all you can do. "I don't know."

"How can you not know? What do you mean you don't know? You've got the address."

I lie. "My brother. Cal. He wrote down that address. That's all I know. What do you want with him anyway?"

"Like you don't know? Like he never told you." Herbert Zwilling laughs—an exaggerated laugh, the way people used to write in letters when they wanted to call attention to a joke or a teasing tone of voice. "Ha," he says. "Ha, ha." Then he leans over the front seat. He puts his mouth next to my ear, and he whispers. "He's the one, Pops. The one I've got to find."

The light turns green, and for a moment I can't bring myself to accelerate through the intersection. I glance over at Maddie, who still has the hood over her head.

"We're not getting out of this, are we?" I say.

"Pops, I don't think you've got a prayer."

Then Maddie says, "Turn left."

Herbert Zwilling laughs. "So you calling the shots now, Mouth? Is that it?"

Maddie's voice is calm now. "It's not far. Larkspur Lane. Just on the other side of the airport. Turn left." A car behind me honks, and I make the left turn. Then I narrow my eyes and look at Maddie, wondering how in the world she knows anything about Larkspur Lane. Then I remember the trip she and Arthur made to Evansville after Christmas so she could go to the mall. "I've been there," she says. "I was there with . . ." Here her voice breaks and she goes dumb. I know, then, that when Arthur took her to Evansville, they must have stopped in to visit with Nancy Finn, and now Maddie is choked with the truth that her grandfather is dead.

Herbert Zwilling won't let her be. "Who lives there, Mouth?"

"Duncan Hines's grandmother," she says.

Herbert Zwilling slaps her head with the palm of his hand. "Don't fuck with me. Duncan Hines, my ass, and I suppose his grandmother is Betty Crocker. Now who lives there?"

"She's telling the truth," I say. "Nancy Finn lives there. As hard as it may be to believe, her grandson's name is indeed Duncan Hines."

Herbert Zwilling shifts his head over close to mine. I feel his breath on my face, turn away from its sour smell, something close to old milk. "So now we're all telling the truth. That's good. You know what they say about the truth making you free. You believe that, Pops?"

What I want to ask Herbert Zwilling is this: what good is the

truth when it never brings back the dead? When more often than
not it only makes clear our failures of courage and heart? That's
what I should have told Duncan that day he took me to the police
annex and showed me that box of Dewey's clothes. No, the truth
doesn't set us free. Not when it traps us in the moment where we
failed to love someone enough. It leaves us stagger-blind, feeling
in the dark, trying to find our way back to our living.

I wish I could agree with Herbert Zwilling. I wish I could say,
"Yes, the truth will make us free." But I can't. Not now. Not on
this night when Arthur is dead, and I'm here with Maddie and
Herbert Zwilling on our way to Nancy Finn's where God knows
what will happen.

"Sure, I believe it," I tell Herbert Zwilling because I think it's
what he wants to hear.

"Then you're an idiot," he says, and I keep driving, listening
as Maddie tells me where to turn.

We drive through a neighborhood of ranch houses and Cape
Cods, set off along the open fields that surround the airport and
its landing strips. Picture windows and second-story dormers
sometimes frame rectangles of light that I glimpse through the
branches of the leafless trees along the curbs. The streets have
names like Foxglove and Coneflower and Delphinium, and what a
sweet joy it would be if I lived here and were coming home to one
of those houses where there was a light in the window and someone waiting up to welcome me.

At the end of a street, I see the runway lights at the airport
stretching off to the horizon. A small plane is setting down. The
prop engine buzzes and hums in the otherwise quiet night.

"Right," says Maddie, and I see the sign for Larkspur Lane.

The house numbers are painted on the curbs, black numbers
on white rectangles. I creep along, thinking what would have

happened if Maddie hadn't admitted she knew exactly where Nancy Finn lived. Would Herbert Zwilling have made me stop somewhere—an all-night convenience store, perhaps—to ask directions? And what if the person I asked didn't know how to find Larkspur Lane, or the next person, or the one after that? What if no one on this night could tell us where it was? Would Herbert Zwilling have let us go? Or would he have shot us dead? That's one thing we'll never know because now I see 5214, and parked in the driveway is Cal's Explorer, the driver's door open, the dome light on. In an instant, I feel so much love for my brother because I see I've been right all along. I imagine him inside that house telling Nancy exactly what happened with Dewey that night at the tracks.

"Park on the street," Herbert Zwilling tells me, "and douse the lights. No need to announce ourselves just yet." He pulls the hood from Maddie's head. "That's where you come in, Mouth." Her hair is mussed and tangled, and her face seems so small to me—small and pale and full of fear. I want to reach over and pull the hood back up over her head, anything to keep her safe.

But Herbert Zwilling has his hand closed around her neck. "I want you to go up there," he says. "I want you to knock on that door, and ask for Cal Brady. He's scared. He's on the run. If he knows he's cornered, it's hard to tell what he'll do. I'd rather put him in a place where he doesn't have a choice. That's where you come in, Mouth. I want you to give him the fact of the matter. Tell him his brother is out here in this truck. Tell him he's got a gun to his head. Tell him to come out here, or his brother's dead." Herbert Zwilling chuckles. "He wouldn't want that, would he, brother? Hasn't he always loved you?"

The question drives to my heart, and for a moment I can't make an answer. Then I say, "I guess we'll see."

Herbert Zwilling is laughing hard now. "You've got a sense of humor, Pops. I'll give you that. What else can you do, right?"

Maddie reaches up and tries to pat her hair down. For just an instant, I see her fingers trembling. Then Herbert Zwilling slaps them away. "Move," he tells her. "Now."

She opens the truck door and steps out into the night. I think of the story Arthur told me about the time she was barefoot, and her mother locked her out of the house. She slept in the garage with rags tied around her feet. I'm about to roll down my window and shout for her to run. *Run*, I'll tell her, hoping that she'll understand that she can vanish into the night and let whatever's going to happen go on without her. *Go*, I'll tell her, meaning, *it's all right, you owe us nothing, Cal and me. That day I found you on the deck of Stump's ship, you were stepping into bad luck, and you didn't know it. Run.*

But before I can say a word, Stump climbs down from the front seat of Cal's Explorer. He eases himself out the open door, and the dome light lets me see him clearly just an instant before he's in the dark.

Lordy, what a feeling goes through me. The sight of Stump, ambling along about his business, no thought in the world of how cruel people can be, makes me yearn for those days when it was just the two of us, no one else for me to have to answer to. His duck and potato, his house, a stroll through the neighborhood each morning and night. If I hadn't built that house, Duncan wouldn't have featured it in *It's Us*, would never have found out that I knew Dewey, and Cal wouldn't have seen my picture in the paper and come back to me when he was in trouble. Maybe Arthur wouldn't have gotten involved with me, giving up on ever convincing me to attend the Seasoned Chefs, and Maddie wouldn't have made my acquaintance and wouldn't be out here now in the night kneeling down in the street, saying, "Here, Stump. Come on boy. Come here."

"What the hell's going on?" Herbert Zwilling says.

"It's my dog," I tell him.

I imagine Stump snoozing in Cal's Explorer, then waking and seeing the open door and setting out to investigate. Now here's a scent he recognizes, the scent of Maddie, and he starts to bark, that deep, baying gump. *Hel-loo*, it says. *Hel-loo!* It's as if a gong is sounding or a church bell ringing. I haven't heard this racket in too long—have feared I wouldn't ever again—and before I have any thought of what the consequences will be, I'm out of the truck, stepping into the street.

"You." I hear that one word from Herbert Zwilling, but it doesn't stop me. Call me a fool. Call me an idiot in love with his life, in love with this dog, Stump, and this girl, Maddie, and my brother, Cal, who—I'm vaguely aware of this now—has come out the door of Nancy Finn's house to see what all the hullabaloo is about. Call me a man who has the crazy thought that he can walk away from trouble, just walk away and be safe and happy on the other side of the world's madness.

Then Herbert Zwilling has me. He grabs my coat at the back of my neck, balls the fabric up in his fist. The top of the zipper cuts into my throat. He yanks harder, and I come up on the tips of my toes.

"Hello, Cal," he says. "It's been a while."

We're shadows in the dark street, no more than a few feet apart, Maddie now hunkered down between us, her arms around Stump. There's just enough of a moon so I can clearly see that Cal has come outside without his coat or hat and stands now, bareheaded, wearing jeans and a hooded sweatshirt, the kind with a pouch pocket in the front. He takes his left hand from that pouch and scratches his head.

"Sammy?" he says. "Is it you?"

Herbert Zwilling loosens his grip a little, and I say, "Cal." Just that. Just his name to let him know that, yes, it's me.

And we stand here awhile in the cold and dark, waiting for someone to make the next move.

It doesn't take long. Herbert Zwilling says to Cal, "I've got your brother, and you're the only one who can save him." Herbert Zwilling pushes me forward, his fist between my shoulder blades. "Tell him, Pops."

"He killed Arthur," I say. Maddie is sobbing now. She's on her knees in the street, holding onto Stump, and she's sobbing. "He shot him inside my house."

"You had no call," Cal says to Herbert Zwilling. "He didn't have anything to do with you and me. My brother either. He's got nothing at all to do with us."

"Wrong place," Herbert Zwilling says. "Wrong time."

"Let him go," Cal says.

"I can manage that. All it takes is for you to come over here." Herbert Zwilling puts the gun to my temple, and I hear the hammer ratchet back. "You don't want me to hurt him, do you?"

"Don't do it," I say to Cal. "Get Maddie and Stump and go back in the house. Call the police. Let him kill me. I'm ready."

And I mean it—at least I persuade myself I do. Ready to cross to the other side. Ready to stand with my mother and father, and Arthur, and, yes, ready to face Dewey in whatever by and by awaits me.

But Cal says, "Hey, you asleep? Don't be an idiot."

"Maybe that's what I need. A good, long sleep."

A cloud passes over the moon, and Cal recedes into the dark. Then he's standing in front of me. He finds my hand and squeezes it, the way Dewey did that night in the alley when we were fifteen and just walking home, no thought of the world around us.

Then Herbert Zwilling has his gun in Cal's face. "All right," he says, and Cal lets loose of my hand. For an instant, I try to grab it again, but I only grasp air, and then he's gone.

At Herbert Zwilling's truck, Cal turns back to me. "I took good care of your dog," he says, and I swallow hard at this ache that comes into my throat. A line like that at a time like this.

Herbert Zwilling doesn't stop at the truck. He shoves Cal ahead, and they go around the front, up over the curb and into the open field that surrounds the airport. They walk off into the darkness so far I can't see them. For a good while there's no noise save the wind and Maddie's sobbing turned now to whimpers, and Stump's toenails clicking over the street as he comes toward me. He's got Cal's scent, and he's determined to follow it, but I reach down and grab his collar and make him heel.

Nancy Finn comes out onto her porch, calling for Cal, and at that moment, in the distance, a gun goes off. One shot, and then another.

I know I should move, should gather up Maddie and Nancy and Stump, hope there are keys in Cal's truck, and drive us all away from this place. A porch light flips on at a house at the end of the street, but other than that there's no sign that the neighbors have heard anything to give them alarm.

"What in the world?" Nancy says, but still, I don't move.

I stand in the middle of the street, peering off into the darkness, and finally I see a figure coming from the field and I know right away from the set of his shoulders and the swing of his arms—the way I'd know him in heaven—it's Cal.

"Call the police," he says, when he's standing in front of me, the Ruger Single Six in his hand. "I'll tell them everything I know."

18

THERE ARE, AT THE END OF EVERY STORY, EXPLANATIONS to make.

"I tried to keep Zwilling from knowing you were here," I say to Cal, and for the first time I have a chance to tell him about Nancy Finn giving me her address at the New Year's Eve party. "The notepaper she wrote it on was lying on the library table, and I tried to hide it from Zwilling, but he saw it."

We're standing outside, Cal now wearing his coat and hat. Nancy and Maddie and Stump are safe inside. Nancy has put the teakettle on the stove. What else do you do in the middle of the night when worry comes and you wait for the police to give you some sign that you can try to go back to your living?—and I've told her as much as I can stand to say. I've told her the man dead in the field was a man Cal had trouble with in Ohio. I've told her about Arthur. "Oh, Sammy," Nancy said, and she wrapped her arms around Maddie and called her dear one. "Oh, dear one," she said. "I know where you are right now. I know what it is to lose someone."

"I didn't mean for you to get into the middle of this," Cal says. "Really, Sammy. I didn't, but things happen, don't they?"

"I'm just glad you're all right. I'm glad it's over." I reach out and put my arm across his shoulders. "I can't tell you what it means to me that you've finally told Nancy the truth."

Cal draws back, and my arm falls to my side. "Told her?"

"You told me if trouble came, you'd come to this address to take care of something." The cold air stings my eyes. "Didn't you come to tell her the real story about Dewey?"

"I came for that postal receipt," Cal says. "The one I signed when that box came to Zwilling's grain elevator, the one that went back to the sender. I thought if I could get that receipt and destroy it, maybe I could go to the police, and they'd save me from Zwilling."

My head swims with the thought of how foolish I've been. "Why would you come here after that receipt?"

"You're not going to believe this, Sammy, but Mora Grove figured it all out, exactly where that receipt might be." He pauses, giving me time to take this in. Then, finally, he goes on to explain that Mora recalled that Jacob Hendrik, the man who had mailed that box, was involved with a woman named Nancy Hines. "Mora poked around," Cal says, "and found out that Hendrik was dead, and this Nancy Hines had moved away from Michigan, had left Cadillac, for Evansville, and maybe, just maybe, she had that receipt packed away with all of Hendrik's things."

I remember now, the story Nancy told at the Cabbage Rose on New Year's Eve about living with a man she called Henk—a nickname, I imagine now, for this Jacob Hendrik. But as knotty as Cal's stories have been, I'm slow to buy all this.

"Henk?" I say.

Cal nods. "That's what everyone called him."

"Did Nancy know about the militia?"

"I can't say what she knew." Cal glances behind him at the

lighted window, trying to catch a glimpse, I imagine, of Nancy Finn. "I just know she was with this Hendrik, and then he died, and now here she is. I thought it was worth a shot to see what might be what. I came here on New Year's Eve as soon as I left Mt. Gilead, but she wasn't here. Her house was shut up tight. I got a motel and waited until tonight to make my move."

Something still puzzles me. "Cal," I say, "Mora Grove told you about Nancy Hines. How did you know she was talking about Nancy Finn from Rat Town?"

"I didn't know for sure, but once I was back in Mt. Gilead and there was that boy, that Duncan Hines, and he said his grandmother was Nancy Finn, I started to wonder. I remembered a time when Hendrik stopped by in Edon, and I saw a woman in his car, a woman with red hair, and I thought, well, that looks like Nancy Finn, but wouldn't that be crazy? I almost went out and said something to her, just to get a closer look."

It is crazy, I want to tell him, everything that's adding up on this night, but all I can do is listen, curiosity getting the better of me.

"Then, right before I left Ohio to come to Mt. Gilead, Mora told me that Nancy might have that receipt." Cal folds his arms across his chest and stomps his feet to try to stay warm. "I'd have come down here right away to see about it, but I was afraid if I did I'd tell the story about Dewey. I wanted to do that for your sake, Sammy. Believe me, I did, but every time I tried to imagine it, I couldn't face the truth any more than I could back in 1955. I hoped we could go on living there in your house—you and me and Maddie and Stump, you know, a family—and I'd never have to try to get that receipt to protect myself. Then you told me it was time, and I understood." Cal curls his fingers into fists and bangs them together. "Damn it, Sammy. Now I wonder what would have happened if I'd gone out to that car that day in Ohio and said something to Nancy. Who knows? Maybe I'd have told her every-thing about Dewey, and then something would have changed in me, and I'd have gotten myself out of that militia."

I let the word hang in the air, the cold air that stings my throat when I take a breath. "The militia," I finally say. "Cal, were you in it?"

He lets his head hang for a moment. Then he lifts it and looks me in the eye. "I was in it," he said, "but, Sammy, I was trying my best to get out."

"Oklahoma City?" I ask.

"No, nothing like that."

The wind is up now, coming through the trees. I watch the bare branches shake. I feel like I'm at the point of no return with Cal, that point where he won't matter to me at all in just a while. I'm tired of lies and stories that turn back on themselves and questions of what he did or didn't do. I'm tired of waiting for him to do the right thing and tell the truth about Dewey. I know I could have done it myself, but I let Cal tell me what we should and shouldn't say.

"Did you get what you came for?" I ask him. "Did you get that receipt?"

"I never had the chance. I remembered I'd left the truck door open, and I stepped outside and there you were."

I see Nancy pass by the window, carrying a cup of tea to Mad-die, who sits on the sofa, Stump stretched out across her lap. Nancy is in her robe. She hasn't taken the time to put in her den-tures, and her mouth is caved in like it was the night my father and I went to the Finns' to pay our respects over Dewey and she was there on the couch with her mother and sister, their mouths twisted with their wailing.

"Cal, if we tell her, we should tell her together."

"You're right," he says. "The both of us." He rubs a hand over his face. "I'd be a fool if I didn't know it after this mess with Zwilling. You can't run away from what you do in your life, Sammy. I tried to after that night at the tracks. That's why I joined the Army and went away. I couldn't stay in Rat Town with that secret. I was afraid sometime I'd say something—maybe I'd have too much to drink some night at one of those juke joints— and I wouldn't be able to keep it in." He pauses, and I can tell he's thinking this all out, trying to decide what he's ready to do. "I know it's time for both of us to own up," he says, "but I'm not sure I can do it. Sammy, I told you. I'm no hero. I expect you know that now."

A police car comes up the street, its red lights swirling and lighting up the houses all along Larkspur Lane. Cal hitches up his pants and squares his shoulders. He steps out toward the police car, and I watch him go.

He turns back to me. "I didn't want anyone to ever know how it came to be that you and Dewey ended up at that trestle. When I left, Sammy, I carried that part of the story with me, too. Remember that. I wasn't just looking out for myself. I was looking out for you."

YOU CAN'T KILL A MAN, NO MATTER WHO THAT MAN IS, NO matter the evil he's done, and not have to answer the whys of it. We all know, don't we, that the snares and traps in our passways are only the doors to the crumbled-up folks we are when we're alone with ourselves? We know this truth no matter how much we'd like to say we don't. We know the responsibility for the world and its hurts always lies with us.

So I find my voice, and I say to the two policemen who come, "There's a man dead in my house in Illinois."

"Did you kill him?" one of the policemen asks. He's a man with loose, wrinkled skin on his throat, a man who's been around long enough to size me up and make the assumption he does.

It takes me a while to answer, trying to figure what to make of the fact that my life has come to the point where this man can take one look at me and assume such a thing.

"I didn't pull the trigger," I finally say. "It was that man. The one out in the field."

Then we start to sort it out, the story of Herbert Zwilling and why he was in my house and how he came to kill Arthur.

An ambulance comes, and the other policeman—this one younger, his cheeks and nose red with the cold—points the way. He's already been out in the field with his flashlight and now he uses it to direct the ambulance driver to Herbert Zwilling's body. The ambulance pulls up over the curb and rocks across the ruts in the frozen field.

Maddie and Nancy are on the porch watching.

"Who are they?" the older policeman asks, and I have to tell him that Maddie was with me when the murders took place in my house. "A witness?" he says, and I tell him, yes. I tell him the man dead in my house is her grandfather. I say that her mother is dead and no one knows where her father is, and the truth is she's got no one in the world except me and Vera—"A nice lady back home," I say. "A lady who didn't have anything to do with all of this."— and Nancy Finn, who stands now with her arm across Maddie's shoulders.

"Sorry," he says, "but we'll have to talk to her. The girl. We'll have to go downtown and sort this all out."

Which we do. We sit in an interrogation room with detectives— Cal in one room and me in another, each of us telling our stories.

And Maddie tells hers, too. I get a glimpse of her walking

down the hall with a female police detective, and another woman, this one in sweatpants and sneakers, a long wool coat draped over her arm, her blonde hair back in a ponytail, crease marks on her cheek from being too recently asleep. I imagine she's a social worker or whatever they call the folks who come in at a time like this to try to make everything less traumatic for a young girl like Maddie.

I try to tell my story as plainly as I can, but there's so much to put in about Arthur and the ship we built for Stump, and then Cal showed up, and he told me the story of Leonard Mink and the plot to blow up the Sears Tower, and now I know he was more involved than he first let on. I imagine him in his own interrogation room trying to tell his story in a way that will allow him to walk away, free.

Of course, the detectives ask me why Cal was at Nancy Finn's, and I can't bring myself to say anything about what Cal's told me about that postal receipt. I want to believe that Nancy had no knowledge of Hendrik's involvement in the Michigan Militia, and I can't stand the thought of bringing more trouble into her life.

"Old friend," I say. "Someone we both knew when we were boys."

By now, the detectives have been in touch with the police in Mt. Gilead, and I assume that officers have gone to my house and confirmed that yes, indeed, there's a body there, a man with a bullet in his head.

One of the detectives is flossing his teeth. "You've got a mess in your house." He throws the strand of floss into a metal trash can. "A dead man just like you told us. The girl tells the same story. A hell of a thing for her to have to go through."

"I'd like to see her," I say. "Maddie." For an instant, I believe that the sound of me saying her name will be enough to tell the detectives exactly how much love I feel for her, how sorry I am for everything I've brought into her life, how I want to be there for her now to let her know she can count on me. Then I see that I have to say more, so I tell the detectives about the trouble that she and Arthur had and how for a time she lived in my house. Then I went to Vera's New Year's Eve party at the Cabbage Rose and saw how Arthur should be the one she depended on. Now that he's gone, I have to be that person for Maddie. That's what I promise myself sitting here in the interrogation room. That's what I tell the detectives, and the one who hasn't been saying much, the one sitting slumped in his chair, tapping a pencil on the desk, says, "The courts will decide guardianship."

Then I say the thing that's been rising in me ever since the day Maddie appeared on the deck of Stump's ship. "She brought something to me. Maddie. Some joy I hadn't known in years." I'm embarrassed to say the rest, how she made me remember what it is to know love, so I say her name again, "Maddie," hoping that will be enough this time to make everything clear.

"She's a tough kid," the pencil-tapping detective says.

"But still a kid," I say, and here I break down and can barely say what I know I must. "I feel responsible for what I've brought into her life."

"Here's the truth of the matter," the detective says. "I've been investigating homicides a long time, and the one thing I know is sometimes innocent folks just get in the way of trouble."

I wish I could be satisfied with that, but I'm not. After everything I've gone through on this night—this night that should convince me of the haphazard devilry dancing all around us—I still can't get cozy with the notion that, as the detective says, sometimes we just get in harm's way. Think about it. We touch the world—we stoop to pick up a penny, build a fancy doghouse, follow a boy down the railroad tracks—and sooner or later the world touches back. We're not even safe in our dreams. We come out into the cold night, our sleepwalking flinging us to the devil's den.

Everything—the noble intention and the ragged heart—is all tied up together like the knots Arthur surely thought he'd made strong enough, secure enough, to keep Herbert Zwilling in my basement. That's what breaks me, the thought of how close we were to avoiding all that happened from that point on.

"Please," I say to the detectives, and they finally agree that, for the time, there's nothing more to ask me. They're convinced I had nothing to do with the body in my kitchen or the one in the frozen field.

The detective who was flossing his teeth accompanies me to the door. He even lays his hand on my shoulder in a gesture I understand is meant to be a comfort. "If anyone's responsible for anything here," he says, "it's your brother."

They won't let Cal go, not tonight. He's killed a man, and even if it was in self-defense, as I know it was—Cal with that Ruger Single Six in the pouch pocket of his hooded sweatshirt, just waiting for the right time to make it do its business—it'll take a while to prove that, and there's all these connections to Leonard Mink and the Michigan Militia to sort through.

There will be months and months, I imagine, of investigators coming to ask me questions, but for now, nearly dawn, there's no call for the police to hold me. I step out into the hallway, and at its end I see Maddie. With her are Vera and Duncan and Nancy Finn, and, yes, even Stump, on a leash someone has rustled up.

"How did you know to come?" I ask Vera and Duncan.

"I called Duncan," Nancy says.

"And I called Vera," says Duncan. "I didn't know what else to do."

Of course, it would be Vera who would be here to ease us back to the living. She's even convinced the social worker that Maddie will be all right with us, that we'll take care of her. I remember the way Vera rubbed my back that first night at the Seasoned Chefs. Vera who has always counted on decorum and hospitality to carry her through the lonely times since her husband died.

"We're going back to Mt. Gilead," she says. "I've got rooms ready for you and Maddie at my house. You'll stay there as long as you need to. You won't want to go back to your house for a while, Sam. Maybe not for some nights to come. Don't worry. You and Maddie are welcome as long as you need to stay."

"What's going to happen to me?" Maddie says.

Vera takes her hand. "We're not going to talk about that right now," she says. "We're just going to go home."

But first I have to have a word with Nancy Finn. I wait until Duncan has driven us back to her neighborhood, where now the sky is brightening in the east, planes are taking off from the airport, and neighbors are dragging garbage cans to the curb. A few folks gather in a driveway and watch Duncan's Scion glide by, and I know they've been witness to the comings and goings of the police working the crime scene after Cal and Maddie and I were already downtown. Now there's only those neighbors following us with their curious stares—even Cal's Explorer is gone from Nancy's driveway, towed into a police garage, I imagine, for searching—to bring back the horror of the night now past.

I insist, despite Duncan's protest that he'll see to it in a snap, on escorting Nancy to her door. She gives him a kiss on the cheek and turns from her position in the front seat to grab Maddie's hand one more time—Maddie who's sitting in the back between Vera and me.

"Dear one," Nancy says to Maddie. "You let these good folks see after you. You'll do that, won't you?"

"Yes, ma'am," Maddie says, her voice a whisper that tells me she's at that point where Cal was the evening he came to my house and said, "Sammy, it's me. It's your brother." That point of sur-render to the kindness and care of others.

I get out of the car and hold the door open for Nancy. I offe her my hand and she takes it the way she did that night at t' Cabbage Rose. She squeezed my hand then, just as she does n and I walk her to her door and wait until she's unlocked it ' her key and is about to step inside. I want to tell her every' about that April evening when I followed Dewey down the t' , and how later I had the foolish notion that I could walk aw; d find a life that would one day have nothing to do with wh ad happened, but I can't find the words, so I say, "Thank you for being so kind to Maddie."

Nancy hesitates, the door half open, her hand on the knob. It's like she can't bring herself to step inside, and I can tell she's trying to make up her mind about something. Then she looks me in the eyes, her own narrowed against the sun up full on the hori-zon now, its glare slanting across the front of the house.

"Sammy, you broke Dewey's heart when you turned away from him."

Here we are, at this point I've tried to avoid, this moment of truth where I tell Nancy the first thing—*he kissed me, he called me his sweetheart*—and then everything unravels from there. But I can't tell her that. I can't have that kiss, sweet and as full of love as it was, lead from there to here—from the innocent to the ugly. So I say, "I was a kid. A stupid kid." Then the memory of the two of us that night in the alley becomes too much for me, and my throat closes up and I can't say another word.

Nancy says, "I know how much Dewey loved you."

I find my voice long enough to acknowledge that, yes, I loved him, too, only I was afraid. "Duncan hinted that you knew about Dewey and me. You never let on. I hope it wasn't because you were ashamed of him."

"I loved him." She gives me a fierce look. "Whoever he was, I loved my brother. I didn't want his life to be any harder than what it was. I'm sure you know all about that, Sammy. Even today, in a small town like Mt. Gilead, it can't be easy."

I bow my head. I'm close now, so close to telling her everything. I feel the trembling in my legs as if at any second the earth will give way and I'll disappear forever. "Nancy," I say, but before I can go on, she stops me.

"People can be good, Sammy. Sometimes all we can do is believe in that." She's telling me, I know, to keep looking forward, as she must have somehow learned to do after Dewey was dead—to keep looking ahead and hold faith in a good life to come. "Go home now, Sammy." She steps across her threshold and turns back a final time to face me. "That dear girl needs you. Even if you've never been able to manage it before, now's the time to believe in your own good heart."

19

AT VERA'S, THE BEDSHEETS AND PILLOWCASES ARE CRISP and hold the soothing scent of lavender from the sprigs she hangs to dry in her linen closets. "Just a little touch I like," she says. "It calms the jitters. Puts the heebie-jeebies to rest."

She has pajamas for me. Freshly laundered and ironed, she points out. "They were my husband's," she says.

I put on a dead man's pajamas and stretch out in bed, Stump beside me. He sniffs the pajama shirt, then my face, relying on his memory of my scent. Then he gives my chin a lick, reclaiming me, and the two of us drift off to sleep.

Maddie sleeps in a room across the hall, and when I wake, so late in the afternoon the winter light is fading, her door is still closed.

I tap on it. "Maddie," I say. "Are you all right?"

"You can come in," she says, and I open the door a crack and see the bed, the covers tossed back, and then Maddie sitting on the window seat, wearing a chenille bathrobe, her knees drawn to her chest the way they were the first time I saw her sitting on the deck of Stump's ship.

"I didn't hate him the way I let on sometimes," she says, and I know she's been thinking about Arthur. I know the regret that'll be hers from now on.

So I tell her there's no profit in dwelling on the should'ves and could'ves and what-ifs. I tell her the truth. Her grandfather loved her—that's a fact—loved her no matter the bumps and scrapes between them. I tell her the story of that evening before Christmas when he and I came back from shopping at Wal-Mart, and we saw her peeking through the sheers at the picture window, and he told me the story of the time her mother turned her out of the house. "The night you were barefoot," I say. "The night it was snowing and you had to wrap rags around your feet and sleep in the garage. Your grandfather told me that and how much it broke his heart to think of it."

I hold in my mind the picture of him on that evening and how he told me he intended to stick by Maddie and love her no matter what troubles might lie ahead, and I tell her all this, too. I sit beside her on the window seat and together we watch the dusk come on.

Vera lives on Silver Street in one of the stately two-story federal houses featured each year at Christmas during the Holiday Tour of Homes. Gaslights still line the streets here in White Squirrel Woods, the way they did years ago before electricity, and it gives me a peaceful feeling to look down on their glow and to see the light they throw on the cobblestones.

"He said that?" Maddie says. "He said he loved me?"

I think of what he told me those days in autumn when we measured and cut and nailed the planks for Stump's ship—how the ancient Egyptian and Chinese shipbuilders carved eye goddesses into the bows so the ships could better find their way. I think of Arthur's Bess and how much I want to believe that when

Herbert Zwilling put a bullet into his head, she called him to her. I hope Dewey had someone to do the same for him. I like to think the spirits of the dead keep watch for us, and when the time comes to join them, they shine a light to carry us across the river of heaven.

But here's what I wonder. What happens to the ones like Leonard Mink and Herbert Zwilling—anyone who's deliberately done evil against the tribe we are on this earth? Do they have someone on the other side calling them home, someone who re-members them when they were innocent, the way I remember Cal when he was a boy and we slept in the same room, and I whis-pered to him one night, "Are you asleep?" If it happens that I cross over first, will my mother and my father—the old hurt be-tween him and me forgotten—be there to greet me? Will we be a family again the way we were in Rat Town before Dewey's death, and then, together, will we wait for Cal to come home?

"Yes, he said that," I tell Maddie. "Your grandfather loved you with all his heart."

"I loved him, too," Maddie says. "He took me in when I didn't have anywhere else to go."

For a good while, I don't say anything, knowing that we're up against the hard truth that here Maddie is, no family to call her own, only what we can cobble together for the time—me and Vera, who moves about below us in her kitchen, the smells of din-ner beginning to fill the house.

"I guess you're stuck with us for a while," I tell Maddie.

"Guess so," she says, and for the time, we leave it at that, waiting, as I know we will for some months, to see what the end of our story will be.

• • •

SOMEHOW, WE GET BEYOND ARTHUR'S FUNERAL AND BURIAL.
We pay attention, as Vera insists, to the details, and that's what gets
us through. She's there to offer advice about flowers, and the musical selections for the service, and the headstone for the grave. When
it all gets too much for Maddie, Vera's there to comfort her, and
Maddie gives herself over to her care. I watch as Maddie reaches for
Vera's hand at the gravesite, and I'm glad that the two of them are
at ease with each other, glad that Vera is there for Maddie the way
Bess would have been.

In the days that follow, the courts want to put Maddie in foster
care, but I won't let that happen.

"I can't," I tell Vera. "She's been kicked around enough in
her life."

Vera nods her head in agreement. "We'll fight it," she says. "I
have an attorney. I told you, Sam. You and Maddie can stay here
as long as you want."

So we do. Then one evening, Vera and I are sitting in the living room while Maddie takes Stump for a walk. Vera has a fire
going, and we sit in armchairs close enough so I can feel its heat
across my legs. She gets up to stoke the fire, and the logs crackle
and pop.

"I'm thinking I'd like to adopt her," I say, an inclination I
didn't even know I had until I heard it find words. As soon as I say
it, I'm terrified and delighted.

"Oh, ducky," Vera says. "Do you think that's a good idea?"
She speaks to me in that soothing voice she uses when she's intent
on helping the Seasoned Chefs prepare a dish. "Sweetie, if you try
to adopt Maddie, they'll dig around in your business. Are you sure
you want that?"

"My business?"

"Who you are. What you've done. The way you live your life.

I'm just saying you better make sure you don't have anything you'd rather folks not know."

She pokes at the fire again and leaves me to think about what she's said. I wrestle it around, coming to the conclusion that Vera has always known the truth about me. I know how it would play in court, particularly in this small town, if an aging homosexual came forward to say he wanted to adopt this sixteen-year-old girl. I feel in my bones how unfair it is. From the time I called Dewey a queer until the moment Cal came back and tossed everything willy-nilly, I kept to myself and did no harm to anyone. I lived a private, sensible life. A lonely life, to be sure, but one I chose. Now, at the time I most want to reach out to someone else—most want to express this love I feel for Maddie, the greatest affection I've felt since my boyhood with Dewey—I'm forced to admit what I should, by all rights, be able to keep to myself.

"Vera," I say, and I'm so taken with anger and embarrassment, I can't go on.

"Sam, please understand I'm not sitting in judgment of you." She pauses as she puts the screen back in front of the fire and hangs the poker on its rack. "I just want to save you from trouble on down the road. Some people just aren't meant for how ugly this world can be. I felt that about you the first night you came to the Seasoned Chefs. I rubbed your back and felt the curve of your spine, and there was a nerve just below your shoulder blade, and it was trembling. I could tell you were someone who needed TLC." I look at her, not knowing what to say, overwhelmed by the fact that she touched me and knew right away the life I had. "Yes, sir," she says. "A lot of Tender Loving Care."

"You know about me," I say, and it's a relief to finally say it to someone after all the years I've kept it a secret. "You know what I am."

She comes to me, then, and she touches me again, this time a brush of the back of her hand across my cheek. "It's not a wrong thing to be, Sam. It's just that now . . . well, if you try to adopt Maddie, I'm afraid they'll send her to foster care for sure."

"Do you have a better idea?"

As I ask the question, I understand that Vera, ever since her husband died and her daughter left to live in Sweden, has been living her own lonely life, filling it up with her radio show, and her cooking lessons for the Seasoned Chefs, and her miniature dollhouses. One of them is on the table by the window. Although it's less spectacular than most any other house in Vera's collection, this bungalow happens to be Maddie's favorite. I've seen her in this room looking at the front porch with its swing where a girl sits, a tabby cat on her lap. "It looks so cozy," she said one day. "So ordinary."

Where else, I think, should Maddie be, but here, cared for and loved, having, finally, the sort of easy living she once upon a time pretended to detest, but secretly longed for? A life where she'd never have to go barefoot into the snow, or have her father leave, or watch her mother or grandfather die—exactly the sort of life Bess would have given her if she'd had the chance.

"Sam," Vera says, "I believe I do."

Then Maddie is coming through the door, announcing that the temperature is falling and she's frozen. And hungry. "Man, I'm starved," she says, kneeling to let Stump off his leash. He comes over in front of the fire and flops down on the hearth rug. "Really, Vera," she says. "I'm just about starved to death."

Like this, we make a family. Then one night at bedtime, I linger on the upstairs landing, listening to Vera and Maddie talking in Maddie's bedroom. The door is open just a crack, enough for me to see that Maddie is standing by the side of the bed. The hem of her nightgown falls to her ankles. I see her bare feet on the floor.

Vera, whom I can't see, says, "Do you think you'd like that?"

I know I should go on to my own room and leave them in private, but I can't stop myself from eavesdropping.

"You mean for always?" Maddie says.

"I'd be your guardian," says Vera.

Maddie doesn't say a word. I see her feet move over the floor until she's out of my sight, and I imagine her going to Vera to give her a hug, to let her know that, yes, this is where she'd like to live.

Then she says, "What about Sam-You-Am?"

"Oh, sweetie," Vera says. "I meant it when I said the two of you can stay here as long as you want. Both of you."

In the morning, Vera tells me that her attorney will file the proper papers and argue that since the court can't locate Maddie's father—and even if they could, how responsible has he proven himself to be?—and since no other relatives, no aunts or uncles or her mother's parents, have any interest in the matter, Vera should be Maddie's legal guardian.

"So it's settled," she says.

And I tell her, "Good."

After breakfast, I take Stump out on his leash and we walk a ways with Maddie, who's now going to school.

"Did Vera tell you?" she asks.

"It's the right thing," I tell her, and she says she thinks so, too.

Then she says, "You know you can stay with us."

"I know," I say, and then I tell her to go on, she shouldn't be late. I tell her I'll be there when she gets home. Then I say to her the thing I've always wanted to say. "Maddie," I say, "I love you."

She comes up on her tiptoes and kisses me on the cheek. "I

love you, too," she says. "Geez, Sam-You-Am, I thought you always knew that."

I CAN'T BRING MYSELF TO GO BACK HOME, UNABLE TO BEAR the thought of stepping into the kitchen and seeing where Arthur last lay. Days pass, and the police are in and out of my house. When they want to talk to me, they come here to Vera's, and I tell them what I know. I tell them how Cal came to stay with me, how he said he was on the run because he knew too much about the people who had a plot to blow up the Sears Tower, people who even had something to do with the bombing in Oklahoma City. I don't tell the police that he was in the Michigan Militia, and I'm surprised that I'm inclined to protect him. I guess he was right when he told me that the years couldn't change what ran between us. Blood to blood. I tell the police instead that Herbert Zwilling showed up, and everything exploded and Arthur was dead.

One day, an FBI investigator comes to talk to me. It's a sunny day, one of those winter days when the temperature gets up to fifty, and folks allow themselves to dream of spring. The FBI man is bareheaded, and he hasn't bothered with a topcoat. He's wearing a dark suit and a white oxford shirt, the collar button undone and his necktie loosened. He introduces himself as Agent Schramm, and he says he's come to talk about my brother.

We sit on Vera's sun porch, where she prunes her bonsai trees and tends to her orchids. We sit in the brilliant sunlight streaming in through the walls of glass, and she brings us tea to drink: tea in china cups on a tray with a small dish of lemon wedges, another of sugar cubes, and a cruet of milk, all this and a platter of shortbread cookies.

"How can I help you?" I ask Agent Schramm after Vera leaves us to our business.

"Mr. Brady, here's the thing." Schramm lifts his teacup to his mouth, purses his lips, and blows across the cup to cool the tea. "Your brother told us a story that was pretty far-fetched. This story about Jacob Hendrik and Leonard Mink and Herbert Zwilling. Lots of holes in that story. I can tell you that much." Schramm sips from the teacup and immediately pulls back his head, the tea still too hot to drink. "Boy, that's on fire," he says. He sets the cup back on its saucer, and when he lifts his head to look at me, his jaw is set and his eyes are narrowed. "We've talked to Mora Grove, and she's told us another story, one that checks out." I wonder what sort of story she's told to save herself from any suspicion. Schramm pours a little milk into his tea. He stirs it with the dainty silver spoon. "Zwilling and your brother had been involved in a dispute for a good while. Sooner or later, it was bound to boil over."

Schramm tells me a story of greed and hate so deep they can lead a man to violence. This Herbert Zwilling, he says, was a collector of unusual objects. "One-of-a-kind things, mainly," Schramm says. "Things he could turn a nice profit on. Passion or money, Mr. Brady. So many murders come down to one of the two."

In this case, he says, Cal was one of Zwilling's finders, one of the people who kept their eyes out for rare objects, anything they knew Zwilling would be interested in selling. He paid them a ten-percent commission. Then Cal found an item that Zwilling especially coveted, only Cal wouldn't let him have it.

"That's why your brother was on the run, Mr. Brady." Schramm folds his hands in his lap as if to say the matter is settled. "Zwilling was after him. He wasn't a nice man. He wasn't a patient man. He'd been in prison once for manslaughter. Let's just say he was used to having whatever he wanted, and your brother knew he was in danger if he stayed in Ohio. We've talked to the right people, and we've found an item in your house, the object your brother was trying to keep from Zwilling. A gold-plated Coca-Cola glass. Only one like it in the world."

"No," I say, and then I'm rushing to get it all out, the truth of how the glass was in that box of odds and ends I bought at the blind man's auction. All the while I'm speaking, I'm thinking of how Cal first told me that Zwilling was a collector, that he had his eye out for just such a glass, and, Lord God, what a miracle it was that I had it. Then later, Cal said he'd made up the whole story, that he'd read about the glass in the *Daily Mail* and hadn't thought for a minute that it was right there in my house.

Schramm chuckles. "Now that, Mr. Brady, is truly an incredible story. A gold-plated Coca-Cola glass, only one like it in the world? A valuable thing like that tossed into a box of junk that you just happen to buy at an auction? I guess I'd have to say, that's hard to swallow."

The two stories spin around in my head—the one I've lived through and the one that Schramm is telling me—and there's just enough fact in both of them to make me unsure of everything I know in my heart to be true.

I remember, then, the maps of downtown Chicago that Cal showed me. He had them in a manila envelope in the guest room at my house. He showed them to me and then put them in the bureau drawer. When he left the house on New Year's Eve to look for Stump, he didn't know that the message would come from Mora Grove—the one I'd deliver to him—and he'd have to run. The maps would still be in that bureau.

"He showed me a map," I tell Schramm. "A stack of maps. They showed the Sears Tower and the streets around it and the route Mink was going to take to the getaway car." Suddenly I feel like Dorothy awaking from her dream of Oz, trying to tell everyone where she'd gone and the astounding things she'd seen and done. "Cal left those maps in the bureau in my guest room."

"Mr. Brady, we've gone through your house from top to bottom, looked through every nook and cranny, just like we have your brother's truck. We haven't found anything to give any substance at all to the story he's telling."

"Are you saying I never saw those maps?"

"I'm saying we haven't seen them. That's what I'm saying, Mr. Brady."

"But that man," I say. "Hendrik. He mailed a box to Herbert Zwilling, and Cal signed for it. There's a receipt. It may be at Nancy Finn's house."

"Hendrik was a finder, too," Schramm says. "Whatever he mailed to Zwilling was a collectible. Your brother's signature on that receipt wouldn't mean a thing. In fact, the reason he had Nancy Hines's address—Nancy Finn, I guess you know her as— was because when Hendrik died, he had an item Zwilling wanted, but before he could lay hands on it, Nancy packed everything up and moved away from Michigan. It took Mora Grove a few years to track her down. She and your brother meant to get that item and make a profit on it."

I remember the brass button Nancy had on her choker at the New Year's Eve party, the one that Arthur said might be a relic from the *Titanic*. Could that be the item Schramm's talking about? Had Hendrik hidden it away and never told Nancy a thing about it?

"I know what I know," I say, but my voice is quieter now, shaken by what I'm starting to realize. There are people in this country who get to say what the truth is, and more often than not, those people aren't us, the ones who have to live with it.

"People think they know things all the time," Schramm says. "I'm here to tell you the facts, and the facts add up to this." He stands up so he towers over me. "Your brother and Herbert Zwilling were involved in a business proposition that went sour, and Mr. Zwilling happened to be a dangerous man. Apparently, your brother knew that. He had a Ruger Single Six waiting for him when he came."

Schramm stands where he is for a good while, making sure, I know, that I get it, that I understand there will be no more discussion.

"I bought that Coca-Cola glass in a box at an auction," I can't resist saying again.

"Mr. Brady, you don't impress me as a stupid man. I think you understand what I'm saying."

Then it hits me, the larger, uglier truth none of us is supposed to know. "It goes all the way to you, doesn't it? Ruby Ridge, Waco, Oklahoma City, the Sears Tower."

Schramm laughs. "Me? Who am I?"

"You're the government," I say. "Cal said there were people from the government involved."

Schramm puts his hands on the arms of my chair and leans close to me. His coat gapes open wide enough for me to see the snub-nose in his shoulder holster. "Now what in the world do you think the government would have to gain by covering over a terrorist plot?"

"I don't know," I say, and my voice is shaking because really I don't know at all.

"This is America," Schramm says. "People can say what they want, but there's a difference between saying something and making it true. Facts, Mr. Brady. That's what counts."

"Facts can disappear."

He winks at me. "Not the ones that matter. We make sure of that."

Finally, he walks over to a bamboo table where Vera has a bonsai tree. She's posed a miniature boy beneath it and a collie dog. The boy has a fishing pole in his right hand. His left is on the collie's head. A Lassie dog, sitting by his side. Schramm leans over to study those figures. "The detail is amazing, isn't it?" He turns back to me. Again, he winks. "Mr. Brady, you'd almost swear it was real, wouldn't you?"

Like that, I understand, as Schramm said, that I can say anything I want, but it's him, and the others like him, who have the facts that count.

"What's going to happen to Cal?" I ask.

In Indiana, Schramm says, you can shoot a man if you're convinced that he's about to kill you, and not have to answer for it. Self-defense. You can kill a man and go back to your life.

"So you've released him? Then where is he?"

"Why, Mr. Brady, I really can't say."

20

JUST LIKE THAT, CAL DISAPPEARS. PUT SOMEWHERE, I HAVE no doubt, by people who don't want him to talk. Like he said, when he was telling me about Mink and the Michigan Militia, someone might find him and put him where he'd never be able to say another word. "They show up one day and tap you on the shoulder," he told me. "Then it's too late. Then you're gone."

So it is. Now that the investigators are finished with my house, I have things to see to. The fact is people aren't murdered in houses without leaving blood and whatnot to clean from floors and walls. I know, because when I owned my custodial service, I sometimes did this work. Now, though, I can't face it. I hire a company here in town. I give Duncan a key to my house and ask him to please make sure everything is taken care of.

The days go by, and as they do, I wish I could say it starts to feel more and more as if none of this ever happened: Cal never came, never told me his stories about Leonard Mink, never put me in the path of Herbert Zwilling; and Arthur didn't die. I wish it could be so, but, of course, it's not like that at all. I wake each day, and in a matter of seconds, the truth washes over me and leaves me sinking into grief.

Grief over the deaths of good people, Dewey Finn included. Heartache for the way our lives can divide into before and after. Here's Maddie, so young and so much now to get beyond. She's a tough girl, though. I've known that from the moment the butcher knife slipped from her sleeve and stuck its point into the deck of Stump's ship. A tough girl, yes, but with a soft heart.

One evening, Vera has a headache. She's washing dishes, and Maddie and I are drying them and putting them away.

"Oh, someone just stuck a pin in my voodoo doll." Vera lets a plate slip back into the sudsy water, and she puts a hand to her head. "Jesus, Mary, and Joseph," she says, the strongest oath I've ever heard her utter.

I think about Bess and how she said to Arthur, "My head hurts," and then fell to the floor already gone. "Do you need to go to the hospital?" I ask. "Do you need to go to the emergency room?"

"Sam, it's just a headache," she says. "Really, ducky, not everything leads to disaster. I'll be fine. I just need . . ."

"Here you are," Maddie says, and in a snap she's produced aspirin and a glass of water.

"Thank you, dear," says Vera. "You're an angel."

Throughout the evening, Maddie fusses over her, bringing her cups of feverfew tea and warm washcloths to lay across her forehead. She dims the lights and puts on Vera's favorite CD, a soothing collection of harp music. We sit in the dark by the light of the fire and listen to "Down by the Sally Gardens" and "Scarborough Fair," and "All in a Garden Green."

Outside, snow is falling—I can see it slanting down through the glow of the gaslights—but inside we're cozy, Vera and Maddie snuggled together on the fainting couch by the fire. I'm content—downright thankful, I guess you'd say—to be here on this snowy night when, as Vera said, not everything turns to disaster. By bedtime, her headache is gone, and the three of us bid one another good night and go off to bed.

I know, as I get under the covers and Stump settles himself beside me, that it isn't fair for me to keep taking advantage of Vera's graciousness. Some morning, I'll have to get up and face the facts. I have a home in Orchard Farms, a home that has now been made spic and span and waits for Stump and me to come back to it. But for now, as I drift off to sleep, I'm quite happy to be here, snug and warm while the snow falls and the night deepens, to think of the way, only moments before, we were all comfortable by the fire—Vera and Maddie and me, and yes, even Stump, dozing near the hearth—we were all content in this house filled with love.

IN THE MORNING, THE SUN IS SHINING, AND THE SNOW IN Vera's backyard sparkles. A cardinal, his splash of red so brilliant against all that white, flies up to perch on a cedar tree bough, laced with snow.

My mother always said when you saw a cardinal it meant company was coming, and sure enough when I make my way down to breakfast, I find Vera on the sun porch, chatting with Duncan.

He's brought me my house key, and now there's no reason that I can't go home. "Mr. Brady," he says, "everything is shipshape."

I thank him. "Duncan," I say, "you're a good man." I believe this, no matter that I've always felt uncomfortable around him because he's on the trail of what really happened to Dewey. I stand here thinking that Dewey would have grown to be like this—dependable and eager to please. He would have been there, throughout my life, whenever I happened to need him. Of course, I'm romanticizing. Who knows the directions our lives might have gone had he lived? After all, more than anything, he wanted out of Rat Town. He might have gone so far he would have forgotten me. Or maybe—in my private dreams I like to think this would have been the truth—I would have gone with him, and we would have been, like Arthur and Bess, like Vera and her husband, lovers and companions until one of us left this world.

This, I realize, is what I want most of all for Maddie: a future filled with love and marriage and a home where she and her family feel safe.

She comes out onto the sun porch, munching on a piece of toast, her school bag hanging from her shoulder.

Duncan blushes, and at first I think it's because I've embarrassed him by calling attention to his goodness. Then I notice the way he's looking at Maddie, and I understand in a flash that he has a crush on her. It doesn't alarm me—nor would it Vera, I imagine, because Duncan, only three years older than Maddie, is one of those sweet boys, so rare these days, who doesn't think he's the center of the universe, would rather give the spotlight to ordinary folks and their uncommon talents or hobbies. In fact, he has just enough uncertainty about himself to make him endearing and the sort who would never take advantage of people.

"When I saw it snowing last night," Maddie says, "I thought for sure they'd cancel school. Now I'm going to be late for my first class. Vera, can you please drive me?"

Vera is still in her robe. "Why, honey, I haven't even combed my hair or put on my face."

Duncan comes to the rescue. "My car's right outside," he says.

Maddie hesitates, waiting to see whether Vera or I have any objection.

"Shake a leg, sugar," Vera says. "Never keep a gentleman waiting."

I can see how good she is for Maddie, giving her a mother's love, and through it, a way of becoming the girl she was—her heart and spirit returned—before the world began to beat on her.

Once upon a time, I was the boy who sat on the railroad trestle singing songs with Dewey Finn. I loved him, but I didn't have the words for what I felt. Or maybe I had them but I couldn't let them out because I didn't know who I was. But he knew. He knew all along. He risked that kiss in the alley, and to him it was the most natural thing in the world. *Sammy, sweetheart,* he said, and for just an instant, before I let my heart turn black and shrivel, the purest light of my essence flickered and flamed. I was *that* boy, the one in the alley who wanted to kiss Dewey back—just that brief moment, and then that boy was gone.

"Giddy up," Maddie says, and with that, she and Duncan are on their way.

AFTER BREAKFAST, I DECIDE I CAN'T PUT IT OFF ANY LONGER. I whistle for Stump and help him up into the cab of my Jeep. I ask him if he's ready, and he gives a little snort and sits up straight, looking out the windshield, as if he knows exactly where we're going, is a little impatient, really, put off just a tad that it's taken us so long to go home.

In Orchard Farms, the snow plows have been down the streets, but still I creep along, letting the place come back to me gradually, taking inventory with the new eyes absence has given

me of the sights I once took for granted or barely noticed: the
Arbor Park Grade School, snowflakes cut from paper, taped to the
windows; the stone goose still dressed in a Santa suit on the front
porch of a house; the brightly colored whirligigs twisting from the
bare trees in a yard; the brick wishing well in another; the white
squirrels scurrying over power lines, across roofs, over limbs; the
ears of corn, some gnawed down to the red cobs, left on spikes
nailed to trees for the squirrels to feed on. A man on the corner of
my street, a man my age whose name I've never known, is shovel-
ing his walks, and he waves at me as I drive by, as if we've been
friendly and he's welcoming me back to the neighborhood. For an
instant, I let myself wonder what it would be like to knock on his
door someday and say hello.

My driveway is filled with snow, so I park along the street.
Stump gets one look at his ship—yes, it's here just as we left it—
and scrabbles around the front seat, eager for me to open the door
and let him out.

But for a moment, I can't do it, overwhelmed, as I am, by the
memory of Arthur using his snowblower to clear my drive, coming
in afterward for a cup of coffee. Then, of course, it all comes back
to me: the nights we spent watching old movies on TV, the hours
we worked together building Stump's ship, the andouille jambalaya he brought to share with me that autumn evening when neither of us knew what lay ahead.

The one thing I'm learning—of course, it's silly that I never
fully appreciated this until now since it's something that's always
been true—is that time keeps moving. Like I said, this isn't rocket
science, but sometimes it takes the world to shake for us to feel the
undeniable fact of that rattle around in our bones. A new day
comes, and no matter what your life has brought, you try to keep
up with the hours unfolding before you. If you can manage to

keep your spirit away from the inclination to give up, you eventually lift a foot, you take a step, you go on, as I do now, opening my Jeep door, and swinging my foot down to the ground. I let Stump out, and together we walk through the gate into our side yard.

Stump goes directly to his ship. I make sure the gate is closed behind me, and then I face the house, which looks for all the world exactly like the house I left with Maddie and Herbert Zwilling on a night that sometimes seems as if it happened to someone else and at other times seems so fresh I swear it's happening again, and, for the life of me, I can't stop it.

I take a glance behind me at Arthur's house, and the first thing I note is that there's no smoke spiraling from the chimney, no fire in the Franklin stove. All the drapes are closed, and again I have to face the fact that Arthur is gone.

A boy—late for school, I assume—comes running down the sidewalk, long tail of his sock hat flying out behind him. He lifts a hand to greet me. "Hey, Enis McMeanus," he says and then speeds on by, leaving me to recognize him as the boy who first came to see Stump's house and told the joke about the pirate, the boy who lost his scarf on the day after Christmas.

He races on down the sidewalk now, and I feel my heart stretch out to him because he's reminded me, with that silly name, that good, decent living goes on despite the stir of evil that's always with us.

My house smells of cleaning solution, a hint of bleach and ammonia beneath a stronger scent of pine. I stand in the middle of my kitchen, where I watched Herbert Zwilling put a bullet into Arthur's head, and it comes to me that if someone walked in here now, someone who didn't know the truth, there'd be nothing to tip them off, no sign at all of the horrible thing that happened here. But for Maddie and me, that night with Herbert Zwilling is something we'll never escape. It visits me now in my dreams, and the only relief I take from this—selfishly take, I admit—comes from knowing that no matter where Maddie ends up living, no matter where she goes in this world, she and I will always be bound by what we watched here.

In the guest bedroom, I go to the bureau and open the drawers, but the only things I find are the spare sheets and pillowcases I've always stored in them. I don't find the manila envelope of maps that Cal showed me. In fact, I don't find any sign of Cal at all, not in the bureau drawers, or in the closet, or on the nightstand. When he ran with Stump on New Year's Eve, he left behind toiletries, clothes, CDs, but there's none of it here now, Schramm and the other agents having made away with every trace. The only thing to remind me of the days Cal spent here is the lamp beside the bed, the one with the explorers' routes curving across the oceans, that and the sheets still folded and tucked (I lift up the bedspread to check) in those hospital corners my mother taught the two of us when we were boys.

I go into my own room, and here, folded neatly on top of my dresser, is the flannel shirt Cal bought me for Christmas, the shirt Maddie wore one morning when she was cold. I pick it up and press it to my face, and her scent is still there, just the faintest scent of baby powder and vanilla. I'm not ashamed to tell you this, how I stand here, comforted by that smell and the soft flannel and the fact that the sun is streaming through my window, and in the side yard Stump is curling up on the deck of his ship.

I go out into the yard, and I stand in the brilliant sunlight, trying to convince myself that all we need is a spirit to take hold of us, something to lift us and carry us through the rest of our days. Call it Enis McMeanus. Call it this dog, Stump, this sailing, Captain Stump, glad to again be the commander of his ship. Call it

Maddie. Call it Vera. Call it Duncan Hines. Call it the good lives of good people. Count the ways, as I intend to do from now on, that I deserve to be among their number.

The man from the house on the corner is coming down the sidewalk. He has a round, friendly face, and when he smiles at me, though I don't know a thing about him, I fall in love with the lines around his eyes.

"You've been gone," he says. "You and your dog."

I never knew this man had taken any notice of me at all.

"Yes," I tell him, "but now we're back."

MARCH AND ITS TANTALIZING WARM DAYS TURN SUDDENLY to cold and snow blankets the daffodils before the month goes out like a lamb. Then one morning in April—the grass is a green so brilliant it's impossible to remember from year to year—I hear Stump barking, and I go to the window to see what's caught his fancy.

It's Duncan, just now coming through the gate. I wait to see that he closes the gate behind him. He latches it and gives it a shake to make sure it's secure. Then he squats down and claps his hands, and Stump waddles over to him for a good rub and belly scratch.

I step out into the yard to see why Duncan's come to visit. He hears the screen door shut, and he rises out of his crouch and gives me the news.

"They found a truck like your brother's." He says it to me plain, no hint of pleasure or regret in his voice, just a newsman stating a fact. The state police found a Ford Explorer abandoned along a river road down by Grayville, no more than thirty-five miles from here. "It was burned out," he says. "There were no plates on it, but they traced the VIN. You know, the vehicle identification number stamped into that metal plate on the dash?"

I listen to him. Then I ask the question I have to ask. "Was he in it? Cal? Was he in the truck?"

Duncan hands me this morning's *Evansville Courier* folded to a small item: BODY FOUND IN CAR NEAR GRAYVILLE. "Like I said, no license plates. Just that VIN, and they traced it and found out it was registered in Ohio. Registered to Calvin Brady."

At first, I can't find room inside me for the fact that Cal's dead. "So it's him?" I ask Duncan. "Not someone else? They're sure."

"Dental records, Mr. Brady."

"No one's come to tell me," I say. "The police haven't come."

If that hasn't happened, I try to reason, then maybe I can pretend awhile longer that Cal's still alive. Then it starts to sink in, and I can't deny the fact that someone set fire to that Explorer with Cal still in it—either folks connected with the Michigan Militia or the FBI, or even Cal himself, no longer able to live with his guilt.

"That's what I'm doing." Duncan says this as kindly as he can. "I'm telling it to you right now."

And I can't stop myself. His voice is so gentle, and now that Cal's gone the secret is mine and only mine, and I have to admit I'm not strong enough to carry it any longer. I tell Duncan everything he's been trying to learn. I tell him the story of the tracks and what really went on there.

IT WAS APRIL AND THE RIVER WAS RISING, AND I SAW DEWEY heading toward the railroad trestle. He was taking the long way around because of the floodwaters. He had to make his way out of Rat Town to Christy and then down the B and O tracks that cut past the grain elevator. Since the night he'd kissed me and called me his sweetheart, I'd kept him out of my life. Then I called him a queer and Arthur and those other boys heard me, and I let the guilt eat away at me until I couldn't stand it anymore. So when I saw Dewey that night—that April night—I knew where he was going, and I knew what I had to do.

I caught up with him at the trestle. "Dewey," I said, and he turned around and waited.

He was standoffish at first, hurt and pouting. He had his hands in the pockets of his dungarees, and he kept stubbing at the rocks in the rail bed with the toe of his Keds.

"Thought you didn't want anything to do with a queer," he said.

The floodwaters stretched out across the fields. I picked up a rock and slung it off the trestle and watched it plunk down into that water. The ripples spread out. Then there wasn't any noise save the sound of a crow calling overhead, and I had to make myself look at Dewey, and I told him I was sorry. Sorry for saying what I did in front of the pool hall, sorry for whatever misery I'd caused him.

He had on that blue and yellow striped shirt. It was tucked into his dungarees, and he was wearing that concho belt, the one with the treasure chest buckle that locked. He took his hands out of his pockets and patted his unruly red hair as if with a touch he could flatten it down and make himself more acceptable. The gesture shot straight to my heart, so shy and beautiful it made him, the way he'd been the night he took my hand without saying a word and we walked down the dark alley.

Now, he was hooking his thumbs into his belt and rocking up on the balls of his feet as if he had all the confidence in the world. "Sammy," he said. "You love me, don't you?"

I was balanced on a rail, and through my sneakers, I could feel a vibration in the arches of my feet. Off in the distance, a train whistle sounded, and I knew it was the National Limited coming and soon it would swing through the big curve to our west, and Dewey and I would have to get off the tracks.

"Aw, don't talk like that," I said. "Jesus, Dewey."

He gave me that grin, the one that always got me, made me feel like I always wanted to be near it. Then he slipped a finger between his dungarees and his belt, unzipping that leather pouch where he kept the key that unlocked his treasure chest buckle. He held the key out to me. "Key to my heart, Sammy," he said, joking, and I took it. I even sang a little of that Doris Day song, "If I Give My Heart to You," and Dewey joined in on the tune's bridge, that part about always being as you are with me tonight, and for a moment it was like it used to be those evenings when we sat on the trestle and sang together.

Then Dewey took my hand, and he leaned his face in close to mine, and he closed his eyes, waiting, I knew, for me to kiss him.

That's when I heard a noise off in the woods, a snap of a twig, and when I looked, I saw a flash of color, a blaze of red, and I recognized Arthur Pope, as he ducked farther into the brush and headed back toward town, removed forever from what was about to happen.

Then I heard footsteps on the gravel roadbed behind me. I turned around and saw Cal coming down the tracks. I saw him, and everything I thought I'd got beyond, every fear of being who I really was, went scattering out into the air.

I shoved Dewey in the chest. He stumbled backwards a little ways along the rail bed. Then his heels caught the lifted edge of a tie, and he fell, twisting so he ended up lying along one of the rails, his arm slung over it, his head resting on a tie. He was stunned. I could see that, but I kept waiting for him to get to his feet. Then he said, "I'm stuck."

On the inside of the rail, two spikes went down through an

iron cleat into the wooden tie. The heads of the spikes weren't flush against the cleat. They stood up just enough for a belt loop on Dewey's dungarees to fit over one, which wouldn't have been a problem if not for the fact that somehow, when his body twisted, one of the belt's conchos—those slim, round disks—had tilted up and hooked itself between the belt loop and the spike head, essentially acting like a button, one on a shirt turned inside out, nearly impossible to undo. The truth was Dewey was held fast to that railroad spike, and just then I heard the engine of the National Limited—heard it before I ever saw it in the curve.

"The key," Dewey said, and I realized I was still holding the key to the treasure chest buckle and that he wanted to unlock it and slip the belt out of as many loops as he could, unfasten his dungarees and wriggle out of them, all before the National Limited's engine was upon him.

He reached out his hand to me, and I took a step forward, meaning to give him the key.

Then I heard Cal call my name. He was close enough now to grab me by the arm. "Leave him," he said.

I remember that I hesitated for just a fraction of a second, not enough time to mean anything at all, but it does to me now, the memory of that split second when I resisted, when I could have broken free from Cal. Then, to my surprise—and this is the thing that haunts me—I let him drag me down the embankment to the woods below.

The last image I have of Dewey is his face, eyes wide open with fear, as he reached out to me. "Sammy," he said. "Don't leave me. Sammy, please."

By then, Cal and I were running down the embankment. I heard Dewey's voice one more time. "Sammy." Then there was only the noise of the National Limited, and any other sound got swallowed up in its roar—did Dewey, so desperate with fear, summon the strength to tear his belt in two, or did the force of the accident rend it?—and then the squealing of the wheels over the rails as the engineer tried to stop.

In the woods, hidden from the view of anyone on that train, I pounded my fists into Cal's chest, and he let me do that, let me beat against him because there was nothing else I could do with the rage I felt.

"You left him there," I said to Cal.

"You're the one who pushed him," Cal said, and I knew it was true. I'd pushed Dewey, and he'd fallen, and then the train was coming and there was nothing I could do—nothing I'd ever be able to do—to make that not happen.

Finally, Cal grabbed me by my wrists, and he shook me. "We can't tell," he said. "We can't ever tell."

The ground was starting to puddle with floodwater. I tucked the key to Dewey's belt buckle into my pocket, and Cal and I made our way back into town, where we waited for the news to come.

I TELL DUNCAN ALL OF THIS, THE WHOLE STORY, AND HE stands in my yard, his face going slack with disbelief.

What's more, I tell him the most important thing, the thing I've carried with me ever after, the thing I never even said to Cal. I tell Duncan I'm not sure whether I didn't try to help Dewey because there wasn't enough time or because I didn't want to, because, in my youth-fed, ignorant way of thinking, for just the briefest moment I believed that I could walk away from that trestle, saved. I didn't know, when I let Cal drag me away from Dewey, that even as we ran down the embankment, locked together with our secret, we were already starting to run away from each other, two brothers coming apart.

"You," says Duncan, and then he can't find any other words, stunned as he is, choked with what I know is disgust, poleaxed by exactly how ugly this life can be. "I can hardly believe it. How could you do it? How could you leave him there to die?"

That's when I reach into my trousers pocket and take out my coin purse. I squeeze it open and take out the key I've kept all these years. I let it lie on my open palm.

Duncan understands immediately what I'm showing him. He reaches out his hand, his fingers trembling, and I let him take the key from me, let him hold it, such a dainty key, but the thing that now makes Dewey's death and my account of it real to him.

"You," he says again.

"Yes," I tell him. "Me."

He closes his fingers, and the key disappears into his fist. "You know, I'll have to tell this to my grandmother," he says.

I close my eyes, imagining what Nancy will think when she finally learns the truth. "I'll tell her myself," I say.

When I open my eyes, I see that Duncan has unclenched his fist and here on his palm is the key. He expects me to take it, and it's clear he wants me to always have it to remind me, as it has all these years, of what went on that night at the tracks, to remind me of how I failed Dewey, to remind me that I loved him and yet that love wasn't enough because I closed off what my heart was telling me.

So I take the key, and that's how it ends, this long story between my family and Dewey Finn's, ends on this day when I know my brother is gone from me forever, this brilliant day in April, no rain in sight like there was all those years ago when Rat Town was flooding and Dewey was still alive. No, it's sunny now. It's springtime, and it's sunny, and Stump is rolling over on the grass, letting the sun shine down on his belly.

If I want to I can pretend there's nothing uncommon about the day at all. Here's the man who lives on the corner. He's out for a walk, and he waves and says hello. Here's a group of boys coming home from school, their bright voices chattering. One of them—the one I know as Enis McMeanus—is telling his pirate joke. "Arrgh," he says, "and it's driving me nuts." The boys burst out laughing and go running down the sidewalk.

A car comes down the street, and it's Vera's. Maddie's in the passenger seat, and as Vera pulls the car to the curb, Maddie leans out the window and calls to Duncan, "We're going shopping for a prom dress." She holds her arms up in the air, and tips back her head. "Whoo-hoo!"

I'll have to tell Vera and Maddie that Cal is dead, and once I start I know I'll tell them the whole story of Dewey and me. I'll have to if I want to have any chance of thinking well of myself as I head into the last years of my life. I'll have to tell that story even though it may very well cost me what I've come to need most, the love of good people like Maddie and Vera.

I don't know how to explain it, but now that it's done—now that Duncan knows everything there is to know, from that kiss Dewey gave me in the alley, to the evening I left him there at the tracks, to the moment along that river road when the flames filled Cal's Explorer—I feel the way I often do at the end of a story, even those old shoot-'em-ups Arthur and I used to watch on television. I feel like I'm a different man from the one I was when the story began. A little wiser, a little worn out with carrying the lives people live, but glad for them, too, and eager to see what might be around the corner in the here and now. *Just a made-up story,*

Arthur sometimes said after a show was over, and he was getting ready to go home, *not a word of it true.*

That's the way it seems sometimes, like this world we're moving through is something invented. Good Lord, surely people don't do the things we do in the real world, the one God intended.

Stump has gone up on the deck of his ship. He sits in the bow, a dignified captain staring out at the course ahead of him.

Times like these, I try harder than ever to believe there's a kinder world going on somewhere else beyond this one, and, if there really is, we'll all find it one day. We'll cross over. Maybe we do it a little bit at a time and we don't even know it, times like when Vera rubbed my back at the Seasoned Chefs, or when Cal and Maddie danced to "Blue Suede Shoes," or the evenings Dewey and I sat on the railroad trestle and sang. Maybe that's what the dead would tell us if they could: from time to time we touch that other world, their world, where no one betrays friends or brothers, and there's no one to hate, not even yourself, and nothing to regret, and no reason to live in shame. We touch it, this paradise. A kiss in an alley, a chili con carne cooked with a little zest that's very Vera, the pleasure of seeing Stump sitting now in the sun.

"It's too much," Duncan says, and he says it like all his breath has left him.

I know he's talking about the fact that he can stand here on this glorious April day, close to being destroyed by the fact that I could do the ugly thing I did, and despite that, here's this girl who looks at Duncan now as if he's the most wonderful thing in the world. In a few weeks, he'll take her to the prom, and I know she'll feel lucky to have survived all she has and to have the life she has now. Truth be told, I feel the same. Here's Stump on the deck of his ship. Here's Vera and Duncan and Maddie.

"Say something to her," I whisper to him, afraid that if he doesn't, he'll lose himself, as I did for years and years.

He calls out to her in a voice loud enough to carry to my neighbor, still making his way west on the sidewalk, and to the Enis McMeanus boys gathered now to the east. He says it, not caring who hears. "I love you, Maddie."

The Enis McMeanus boys giggle. They push at each other, and some of them say, "I love you, Maddie," and then make kissing noises with their mouths on their arms.

My neighbor calls out, "Tell her again, son. I'm not sure she heard you."

Oh, but she has. Maddie puts her hand to her lips and throws Duncan a kiss.

"Catch it," I tell him.

It's nothing I can trust to last—they're just kids, and heaven knows what they feel for each other might change tomorrow—but for now it's enough. In fact, it's exactly what I need: to stand as witness, to watch Duncan snatch at the air, close his hand into a fist, and then press it to his heart.

Please don't misunderstand. I claim no pardon for my wrong turns and tumbles, but considering all that's gone on and all that's yet to come, I'm content to feel the warmth of this love beginning, to call it the best thing that could have happened next in the story of my life.

Then my feet move over the grass, to the gate, and out to the street where Vera and Maddie wait to see why I'm coming out to join them. I realize that everything that's happened since Cal came back to Mt. Gilead has been leading me to this point where I no longer have him to hide behind. He can't save me now. Really, he never could. The story is mine, and mine alone to tell. It has been all along.

I'm not sure how I'll start, but once I do I know I'll tell it all. *Once there was a boy named Dewey.* I'll tell Vera and Maddie everything. Then when the last word falls away, I'll keep quiet, knowing the next words will be theirs, one after another until so many pile up we won't be able to make our way back over the trail of them to where we began, and then everything will change for better or worse. I'll wait, my heart in my throat, scared to death, unable to stop what's coming, ready to give myself over, at last, to whatever bears down on someone—a man like me—from the other side of the darkest truth he can tell.

Acknowledgments

I OWE A GREAT DEAL TO SALLY KIM AND PHYLLIS WENDER, who so often saw the possibilities that I didn't. A portion of this book appeared under the title "Sea Dogs" in *Glimmer Train Stories*, and I'm grateful to the editors, Linda Swanson-Davies and Susan Burmeister-Brown, for their interest in my work. Thanks to The Ohio State University, The Ohio Arts Council, and the Greater Columbus Arts Council for their support during the writing of this book, and, as always, my immense gratitude to my wife, Deb, who keeps me afloat.

About the Author

LEE MARTIN is the author of the Pulitzer Prize finalist *The Bright Forever*; a novel, *Quakertown*; a story collection, *The Least You Need to Know*; and two memoirs, *From Our House* and *Turning Bones*. He has won a fellowship from the National Endowment for the Arts, the Mary McCarthy Prize in Short Fiction, a Lawrence Foundation Award, and the Glenna Luschei Prize. He lives in Columbus, Ohio, where he directs the creative writing program at The Ohio State University.

Note on Type

This book was set in Bauer Bodoni, originally designed by Heinrich Jost and released by the Bauer Type Foundry in 1926. The typeface is based on the "modern style" Bodoni typefaces created by Giambattista Bodoni in the late eighteenth century.